YORK
STREET

Other Published Books by Jan Walters

Believe (August 2013)

YORK
STREET

A GHOST AND A COP SERIES

JAN WALTERS

YORK STREET

A Ghost and a Cop Series

iUniverse books may be ordered through booksellers or by contacting:

iUniverse
1663 Liberty Drive
Bloomington, IN 47403
www.iuniverse.com
1-800-Authors (1-800-288-4677)

Certain stock imagery © Thinkstock.

ISBN: 978-1-4917-4302-7 (sc)
ISBN: 978-1-4917-4303-4 (e)

Library of Congress Control Number: 2014915072

Print information available on the last page.

iUniverse rev. date: 06/03/2016

The Ghost and a Cop series is my way of honoring the men and women who proudly serve on the Des Moines Police Department (DMPD) and other law-enforcement agencies. Each of them is a hero.

ACKNOWLEDGMENTS

Four generations of men in my family have served on the DMPD, dating back to the 1890s. I grew up listening to my grandmother telling me wonderful stories of the DMPD and the crazy cases they would occasionally encounter. So, with a little fact and a lot of fiction, I've created this series.

I couldn't have created the characters in the story without the fab four (Bill Nye, Jerry Viers, Steve Walters Sr., and Steve Walters Jr.) from the Sunday breakfast club at Crouse Café in Indianola, IA. All these men have served on or are currently serving on the DMPD.

I want to thank Portraits by Susannah in Indianola Iowa for the wonderful model shots that were used in the book cover. They all turned out wonderful!

As a lifetime Des Moines resident, I have taken liberties with various locations in Des Moines and the surrounding area for the purpose of the story.

Any minute now I'm expectin' all hell to break loose
People are crazy and times are strange
I'm locked in tight, I'm outta range

—Bob Dylan, "Things Have Changed"

PROLOGUE

1933

Des Moines detective Michael O'Shea parked the unmarked car in front of the darkened Cavanaugh mansion. He hated working double shifts, but duty sometimes called.

A quick glance at his pocket watch revealed that it was only 2:00 a.m. When he had checked in on the call box, dispatch asked if he could back up a patrol car at this address on York Street. Supposedly one of the neighbors had spotted someone breaking in at the Cavanaugh mansion.

He hated burglary calls, especially at the homes of those as rich and political as Henry Cavanaugh. The man controlled the city's machinations with an iron fist. Even Michael had heard the rumors that the man might run for governor in two years. Pity the idiot who had the balls to break into the Cavanaugh home.

Michael groaned inwardly at the thought of the paperwork it would take to satisfy Cavanaugh. One mistake and his sergeant would be all over him. With a new baby on the way, Michael needed to play it straight. He had been suspended twice as it was.

Using his hand, he wiped the moisture from the inside of the car window and stared at the unlit house. Twisting his head, he glanced down the street. Where was the backup? Someone needed to get in there and check things out.

From the car, he stared at the house. Like many homes built at the turn of the century, the mansion was set back far from the street. Ancient bur oak trees lined the winding driveway. The twisted branches draped low across the driveway, giving the impression of willowy fingers reaching out for solace. It gave him the creeps.

The cool night air seeped into the parked car. With a sigh, he reached for his tweed jacket and quickly slipped it on before opening the car door and stepping outside. Instinctively, he patted his shoulder holster, ensuring his gun was in place. He reached in and grabbed his black fedora, angling it low and tucking his sandy brown hair under the brim. The hat was a gift from his wife. She had wanted to buy him a trilby, but he liked the wider brim on the fedora better. Even though it was a little large, he liked wearing it low on his brow. Besides, his wife thought it made him look sexy.

Michael leaned against the car, watching the house. *Damn it! Wait till I get my hands on the patrolman who was supposed to be here.* Rather than returning to the call box and wasting more time, he decided to check it out on his own. Opening the back door of the car, he grabbed his "bullet," a copper Winchester flashlight. Its rounded end looked similar to the ammunition made by Winchester.

A full autumn moon filled the sky, providing light for him to quickly make his way past the yard and garden without tripping on the various statues placed about the garden. Ducking behind a large stone angel, Michael looked down the street. Not a light was on in any of the neighbors' homes. So who called the station? He hoped his backup would hurry up and get here. He was ready to check things out.

Michael pulled the collar of his jacket up around his neck. The cool wind sent shivers down his back. Removing his gun from the holster, Michael peered toward the side of the house. No activity.

A brisk breeze rustled a pile of dead leaves at his feet, causing them to flutter through the air. Turning his head, he met the angel's fearless-looking gaze and smiled.

Refocusing his thoughts, he darted toward the edge of the driveway. The golden glow of a pair of lanterns near the street cast faint shadows on the damp brick driveway. He stayed in the shadows until he reached the side of the porch. With adrenaline flowing, his breathing sounded harsh even to his ears.

Suddenly, something brushed against his back. He nearly dropped the Colt .38 revolver in his hand. He whipped around, stopped, and let out a deep breath. It was only a bush. *Mother Mary!* His heart pounded in his chest. Using the back of his hand, he wiped the beads of sweat off his brow.

High in the tree above, a lone owl called out. Glancing upward, Michael hissed, "Don't distract me. Damn owl."

Yellow eyes narrowed and glared back at him as he inched across the sweeping porch. His foot bumped into a potted fern. He held his breath as the plant tottered from side to side before righting itself.

Shielding his eyes with his hands, he peered through a window. He saw what looked like a large drawing room by the way the furniture was positioned. He couldn't see anyone. He wished he could look through the front door window, but the oak door had a large, oval-shaped mosaic glass panel consisting of mostly white opalescent glass. Louis Comfort Tiffany had designed the panel himself. He recalled reading a big article in the newspaper the year before about how prestigious it was for Cavanaugh to have Tiffany himself design the window. Michael knew it had cost a pretty penny.

Standing to the side of the front door, he gripped the brass knob and slowly turned it. As he suspected, the door was locked. He walked over to the edge of the porch, leaned over, and checked to see if any windows on the side of the house had been broken. Everything looked fine from the front of the house. He decided to go around back and check things out there.

As he turned to go down the steps, a loud crash from inside the house jarred his senses.

"Son of a bitch," Michael said. He turned back toward the window and caught a glimpse of something moving. Someone was staring at him from inside the house.

Pointing his gun at the figure, he yelled, "Police! Come out with your hands up."

The person stood there watching him, not moving. Sliding his flashlight out of a pocket, he stepped closer to the glass. As Michael shined the light on the man before him, he frowned. Something dark covered the front of the man. Michael recoiled as the man suddenly raised his hand, touching the glass pane separating them. What was the guy doing? Michael winced as the man's fingers lazily scraped down the glass, leaving behind something wet that dripped down the window. Focusing the light on the streaks, Michael stared in disbelief. *Oh shit! Is that blood?*

A crazed cackling sound came from the other side of the glass, making the hair on the back of his head stand on end. What kind of person would make such a horrific sound?

A hiss from behind him caused Michael to twirl toward the sound. When he realized it was only a cat, he whipped back to the window. The man had disappeared. *Where did he go?* After rushing back to the door, Michael hesitated. For the first time in his life, he was afraid. What was making him feel uneasy tonight?

Screw it! Enough bullshit. He would take care of business, and that would be the end of it.

After several kicks, the heavy door gave way. A canyon of darkness waited before him. He crouched down and ran into the room, stopping with his back against the wall. Sweat ran down between his shoulder blades.

Using his flashlight to scan the immediate area, he saw a faint light shining from under a closed door at the far end of the hallway. His first priority was to secure the first floor. Moving silently from room to room, he found nothing out of place. More importantly, he saw no intruder.

There was one more room to check—the one with the light under the door. Why was the light on only in that room? Was the intruder trying to draw him in?

He tightly gripped his gun as he prepared to enter the room. With an indrawn breath, Michael threw open the door, causing it to slam into the wall behind it. If anyone had been hiding behind the door, he would have been knocked in the head.

Ducking low, he rolled to a defensive position. A desk lamp provided a soft glow to the room. He jerked open a closet door and shined his flashlight in the shadows to make sure it was empty.

As he peered about the room, it became obvious to him that a struggle had taken place. Toppled furniture littered the room. Broken glass covered a floral rug. With his flashlight in hand, he slowly turned about the room. Something odd caught his eye. A section of the far wall appeared to be cracked. He walked across the room and ran his hand down the wall. He knelt near the floor, following the slight edge. The crack ran from the floor to the ceiling. On closer inspection, he discovered that a door was built into the wall. A hidden room! He had almost missed it. Near the fireplace, he saw a bronze handle on the wall. He thought it could be a lever to open the damper in the fireplace—or it could be the way into the room.

He quietly crossed the room and turned the handle. A slight whirring sound greeted his ears. He looked back over his shoulder. The concealed door began to inch open, revealing another room.

Crossing the room, he stayed out of sight until the door was completely open. With his flashlight in hand, he ducked and scrambled into the dark chamber. His fingers began to cramp from the tight grip on the gun. He quickly swept the flashlight around the room, searching for the intruder. He realized that he needed more light to search further. Using his flashlight, he spotted a light switch on the wall and flipped it on. He then shut off his flashlight and shoved it back into his pocket. Absently, he noticed the dark wood floors and massive mahogany bookcases lining the room. Leather-bound books adorned the shelves. A large walnut desk dominated the center of the room. Papers were scattered across the floor.

As he walked around the desk, he stared at the floor. There was a small pool of blood. Whose blood was it? Cavanaugh's?

Michael leaned against the desk and pushed his hat up off his brow. He had thought that this was a simple break-in. It now looked as if it was much more. If something happened to Cavanaugh, it could shake up the entire state.

His gaze darted about the room. Where was the man he had seen in the window? Could he have attacked Cavanaugh? Cavanaugh was a brute of a man. Michael had seen Cavanaugh at city events and knew the man was built like a gorilla. The man he had seen in the window was much smaller. Cavanaugh could have easily crushed him.

He shook his head in frustration. He wished he knew where the Cavanaughs were. If they were home, they'd have heard him kick in the front door. That meant they were either not home or injured.

By now the patrolman should have been there. The rest of the house needed to be searched. There were two more levels to search, as well as the basement. Time was of the essence. He needed help.

Standing by the desk, Michael straightened himself. His decision was made. He would go get help. With one more look around the room, he fixated his gaze on the drapes on the far wall. The tips of a pair of men's shoes were peeking out from underneath the heavy fabric. The pounding of his heart underscored his mistake. *Damn it to hell!* How had he missed that?

He tiptoed to the window and stood to the side. In a single movement, he whipped aside the fabric and raised his gun at man leaning next to the window.

Before his brain registered that he was looking at a dead man with a bloody organ tied to his hands, the body tipped forward and hit the floor.

Michael jumped back. His heart pounded hard enough that he was sure it was going to jump out of his chest any minute. Adrenaline flooded his body. He clenched his jaw so tightly that it made his teeth hurt.

Using his foot, he rolled the man over onto his back. Michael stared down at the man's face. It was Cavanaugh! His gaze traveled down Cavanaugh's body, stopping suddenly. Cavanaugh's chest cavity had been cut and cracked opened. Michael had seen enough autopsies to know that someone with skilled precision and plenty of time had done this.

Michael stepped back. His stomach twisted as acid rose up in his throat. He sucked in deep breaths of air.

"Damn," he whispered. Cavanaugh's heart lay next to the body. "Who in the hell would cut out a man's heart?"

His thoughts were jumbled together. He bit his lip in consternation. He had to think clearly. He needed to call the station and get help. He remembered seeing a telephone in the hallway. After glancing in both directions and reentering the hallway, Michael crouched down and ran to the telephone. He clicked the receiver several times without getting an operator before he saw the cut cord. His shoulders drooped. Now he had no choice but to go down the street to the call box, but by the time he got back to the house, the murderer would be long gone.

With no time to waste, Michael ran to the doorway. A shrill scream echoed from the basement before he was out of the house.

"Mother Mary and Joseph! Who was that?" Instantly, he knew it had to be Mrs. Cavanaugh.

He raced down the hallway, throwing open several doors before locating the basement stairs. Turning on the lights near the door, he prayed he wasn't too late.

He stormed down the stairs, vaguely aware of the damp, musty air filling his nostrils. The next thing he knew, he was in a heap on the floor, his body contorted in an unnatural position. Pain in his leg tore through him. *What happened?* He looked about the room. *Is the murderer down here?*

The room swam before him. He squeezed his eyes shut to stop it from spinning. From the way it was bent, Michael knew his leg was broken. His face had slammed into the concrete when he fell, and blood flowed from his head. He struggled to remain conscious. He reached out for his gun. *Where is it?*

Finally he saw his gun near a pile of crates across the room. He knew that, somehow, he had to get the gun. He thought that if he could straighten his leg enough, he could drag his body across the floor. He rose up on his elbows. When he touched his leg, tremors gripped his entire body. He wanted to scream. Instead he took several deep breaths, waiting until the pain diminished enough to move.

With every inch he advanced, the pain threatened to take him out. Unable to stop the tears, he ignored his agony. The only thing that mattered at this point was to get his gun. Only a couple more feet.

His arms shook from pulling his body across the floor. Unable to make his body move, he was forced to stop. Once he had the gun, he'd feel safer, more in control.

He turned his head, squinting toward the stairs. A thin wire was stretched across one of the steps.

"Son of a bitch," he growled, wondering if it was some kind of trap.

He shook his head. No, it couldn't be. No one knew that he was going to be here tonight. Was it because he was a cop? He didn't think so. There had been a string of burglaries in this neighborhood for the past few months. Many wealthy men like Cavanaugh called this section of town home.

He turned back, feeling additional pressure to get his hands on the gun. A gasp escaped his lips; he couldn't believe what he saw. Partially hidden behind a pile of crates lay a woman.

Without thinking, he started to rise to go help her. Instead his body collapsed back on the floor.

"Argh! Damn, damn, damn!"

He clutched his arms together, trying not to touch his leg. One touch would make him scream in agony. He pressed his fists against his head and rocked it back and forth.

He fought to push back the pain. He turned back to face her and saw a deep neck cut and a pool of blood. The vacant glare of her eyes signaled death. From pictures in the newspaper, he knew it was Mrs. Cavanaugh.

A sob rose up in his throat before he choked it back. Now was not the time to be overcome with emotion. One look at her face and he knew she had suffered before she died. The terror in her eyes was a sight he wouldn't forget. He needed to keep his head straight. Besides, the department knew the location of his trip, and the street cop would be here any time. By now, he should have called in. Dispatch would send someone to check out the house. He just needed to get the gun, and he could hold on until help arrived.

Mustering a reserve of strength, he inched toward the gun. At last, he was within arm's reach of the weapon. He stretched out his arm until his muscles ached. All his energy was focused in that one arm; one hand.

Suddenly a foot came from nowhere and kicked the gun to the other side of the room.

Damn! He tried to roll into a defensive position, but his leg hampered his movements.

A man's boot stomped down on his hand. The bones cracked before the pain registered in his brain. Before he could recover, a foot kicked the air out of his body. He writhed in agony as kick after kick pummeled him.

The physical attack abruptly stopped. Eyes closed, Michael started to gag. As he turned his head, a flow of blood trickled from the corner of his mouth. His muscles twitched from the unrelenting pain. A hissing sound drew his attention. His eyes flew open when foul air cloaked his face.

A man knelt before him. Michael saw a white shirt stained with blood. Wispy brown hair fell over the man's narrow brow. His thin lips had a cruel slant. But it was the glowing red eyes that captured Michael's full attention. What was this thing?

"Well, well. The mighty Mike O'Shea flat on his ass. You and your high morals. You should have heeded the warnings that Sergeant Wilkins gave you."

Spitting a loose tooth across the floor, Michael forced a grin. "Wilkins is an asshole."

The man shook his head, his eyes glowing even brighter. "Tsk, tsk. Always the smart mouth, aren't you? You should have minded your own business. But no, you had to poke and pry into things that didn't concern you."

"Did you know that I was an eagle scout?"

The man chuckled. "O'Shea, I know everything about you. Even when you take a piss."

Michael bit back a groan as blood filled his mouth. Turning his head, he spit as hard as he could. Droplets of blood covered the man's face.

The man's tongue darted out, licking the blood off his lips. His head tilted to the side, as if he were studying Michael.

"My master doesn't like you, O'Shea, but I do admit admiring your conviction and stamina."

Barely able to keep his eyes open, Michael rasped, "Master? Who are you?" He jolted when a knife came into view.

Burning heat ripped his insides. The blade plunged again and again into his body. Michael's eyes drifted closed. Incoherent guttural sounds and wild laughter filled his ears. It was the same laughter he had heard earlier.

His body was numb, no longer feeling the pain being thrust upon him.

Michael silently prayed, "Forgive me. I've tried to do right. You know I have. But it can't be my time."

Visions of his wife and children flashed through his mind. He knew he'd never see them again. He'd never see his unborn child that was due in two weeks. Never hold it in his arms. This wasn't right. He didn't even have the energy to cry out.

The sounds around him faded away. A heavy weariness consumed his soul. Each breath was a painful reminder of what he was leaving behind.

Then there was nothing.

CHAPTER ONE

TWENTY-FIRST CENTURY

B rett O'Shea's biceps bulged as he gripped the prisoner's wrists and quickly slipped the cuffs into place. The man beneath his knee struggled to roll onto his back. Only cops could count on being spit at, cursed at, or hit all in a day's work. Hell, on a good day he was even shot at.

Brett jerked the prisoner to his feet, shoving him toward the paddy wagon. *Why don't these idiots ever learn? You run, you pay! It's that simple.* What did they expect to happen when they busted up a bar and a cop had to tackle them? The guy he arrested was huge. If Brett hadn't worked out all the time, he wouldn't have been able to overpower the guy.

Brett rubbed his knee. Sliding on the pavement to tackle this guy wasn't something he had wanted to do, but no dirtbag was going to outrun him. Shit, the guy was only twenty-eight. With two years on him, Brett had easily overtaken him.

The prisoner's groan drew Brett's attention. Blood trickled from a jagged cut on his brow. Brett cursed as a drop of blood fell on his shoe. "Man, see what you did? Now my shoes need polished." Brett's nose wrinkled as the scent of stale body odor filled the air.

The prisoner squinted, staring at his name tag. "Hey Officer O'Shea, you're Irish, aren't you? Me too!"

Brett held up the man's license, reading it aloud, "Robert Cataldo. That doesn't sound very Irish to me." Several people in the gathering crowd began laughing.

The prisoner grinned, revealing a missing front tooth. "On my mom's side of the family. We even go to the St. Paddy's parade. C'mon. Can't you cut me some slack? I can't do any more jail time. My old lady said she'd kick my ass out the next time I got arrested."

Barely sparing the man a glance, Brett got him loaded in the wagon that would take the prisoner to the hospital before going to jail. "Maybe you should have thought about that before deciding to get drunk, tear up a bar, and resist arrest."

"Oh hell. It's not my fault. My old woman drives me crazy." Swaying in a drunken stupor, the prisoner muttered, "Don't women ever drive you crazy?" The man kept talking, spittle flying in the air. "What's the matter with you? Didn't you ever make a mistake?"

Brett slammed the heavy door shut, smiling at the surprised look on the man's face.

"Hey! I'm speaking to you, Officer. Oh, oh. I feel sic—"

Brett winced as the sound of vomiting came from inside the wagon. He pounded on the side of the van, letting the other officer know that the prisoner was ready to go.

"Have a nice trip," Brett called.

As Brett turned toward his squad car, he noticed that a crowd from the bar had flowed outside to watch the action. A couple of the man's friends glared at him.

One of them called out, "Did you have to arrest him? He was just having some fun."

Brett bent down and picked up his hat off the ground. He brushed it off and paused to put it back on, centering the brim. He then turned on his heel and walked toward the burly man who had called out. A sudden silence filled the air. Inches from the man's face, Brett assessed the heckler, who was several inches shorter than his six-foot-two frame.

"Perhaps you would like to reimburse the owner for the damage you and your friend caused?" Brett replied in a quiet voice.

The man's friends faded back into the crowd. Licking his dry lips, the man glanced down at his feet. "No, sir. I mean Officer."

Brett felt the muscles in his jaw clench. *Does anyone take responsibility anymore?* "Are you sure?" he asked.

Eyes downcast, the man stepped back. "Yes, sir."

Brett glanced at the crowd. "Okay. Everyone is happy. Now go back inside or go home. If I come back here tonight, I'll bring several paddy wagons and take you all to jail."

Brett forced back a smile as the crowd bitched about his request, but they dispersed quickly. He turned and headed back to his car. He had little tolerance for irresponsible people. When he had started in the force eight years prior, he had felt sorry for people like Bobby. But when you keep arresting the same people over and over for the same thing, any empathy quickly fades. He was taught responsibility at an early age by his father, John O'Shea, who had been a cop before he died three years before from a heart attack. All the men in Brett's family were cops.

He set his hat on the seat and started the engine. After radioing in that he was back in service, he drove down the empty streets. It was dead. The bar trip had been his first one of the night. Not that he was complaining; sometimes he liked it slow. It gave him time to stop in the stores and shops to do a little PR work.

Tonight his mind wasn't on work. His favorite person, Grandma Maybelle, was dying and had requested to see him. As a child, he took every opportunity to stay with her. She had entertained him with stories of her father, Michael O'Shea, who had been a police detective.

He glanced at the clock. He wanted to see her and make her laugh for a few minutes. She was a sweetheart. According to his mom, Sandy, she had been talking strangely lately, seeing relatives that she had known as a child.

Brett pulled up to his grandmother's house. Seeing her bedroom light was on, he shut off the car. He needed to write up a report on the bar incident, so he decided to stop and visit her while making his report. Using his key, he let himself in. The smell of recently baked cookies filled the air. It was late, but his mom and grandmother would frequently watch old movies in the middle of the night. Of course, his mom would whip up a batch of cookies to snack on while they watched TV.

13

He set his papers on the worn oak table in the kitchen. Turning toward the living room, he saw his mom sleeping on the sofa. Dark circles shadowed her eyes. She'd been taking care of Maybelle, her mother-in-law, for the past month, as well as her own house. Brett felt a pang of guilt for not helping more. Gray strands were mixed with his mom's dark brown hair. When had that happened?

Brett bent over the sofa to give his mom a kiss on the cheek. "How's grandma doing?"

Sandy's eyes flew open. "Good lord. You scared me. Aren't you working?"

"I am, but I wanted to visit Grandma. Besides, I've got some paperwork to do."

A faint voice echoed down the hall. "Is that my favorite grandson? Don't you two start whispering about me. I'm not dead yet, so I suggest you get yourselves in here."

Brett smiled at his mother. "She hasn't mellowed yet, I see."

"You know Grandma. She'll go kicking right up to the end."

As they entered the bedroom, he saw her frail body surrounded by at least ten lavender pillows. The dimly lit room smelled like fragrant bouquets of lilacs, her favorite flower. Just breathing in the scent brought back memories of his childhood.

Brett pressed a kiss to his grandmother's wrinkled forehead. "How's my favorite lady doing?"

Hazel eyes twinkled with amusement. "I'll be up before you know it. It's about time you stopped by. Do you have to work so much?"

Brett laughed. "Did you tell Dad the same thing?" When she shook her head, he patted her chilled hands. "Maybe you can tell the bad guys to stop breaking the law so I can spend more time here. Now, quit stalling, and tell me how you're doing."

Maybelle struggled to sit up. Brett hooked his arm around her to pull her forward.

Looking toward his mom, Maybelle asked, "Would you mind leaving us alone for a while? I want to have a serious talk with my grandson."

At Brett's nod, Sandy walked to the door. "Sure, I'll be in the kitchen if you need anything."

As footsteps faded down the hall, Maybelle patted the empty space beside her. "Come and sit down. It's been a while since you spent the night with your old grandma. I bet you have a girlfriend."

Her bent fingers clenched his hands. She had lost more weight. He didn't know how she could keep going.

His throat tightened. "Not yet. I can't find anyone as good as you. Speaking of spending the night, do you remember all those stories you used to tell me about your dad, the infamous Mike O'Shea?"

His grandma's eyes twinkled at him. "Yes, I do. He was such a prankster. I wish I had actually known him. Your dad was a lot like him."

"It's horrible that your father died a week before you were born."

His grandmother tightened her grip on his hand. Her eyes flashed with anger. Brett had seen that look many times as a child. "Died! He was murdered. Thankfully, the other detectives took me under their wing as soon as I could walk. I was always sneaking down to the station. You wouldn't believe the stories those men told me about your great-grandfather. He was such a rascal!" Peering into his face, Maybelle asked, "You always seem so serious. Are you happy?"

"Of course I am. I think the O'Shea gene for breaking the rules skipped my generation. You know that I'm interested in applying for a detective job."

"Oh dear. That would be wonderful. You'll be just like my father. I'm sure they'll promote you."

Brett would never tell his grandma that he would never act like her father. Mike had been suspended twice that he knew of. He couldn't imagine stuffing a drunk into a sergeant's car overnight or loading a drunk on a train to Chicago like Mike had done. Mike was still a legend at the station. All the old-timers would ask if various stories were true. Brett followed the rules. His ancestors didn't.

Maybelle's eyes drifted closed. Brett wondered if she had gone to sleep. As he slipped his hand from hers, her eyes flew open. He leaned over, tucking a loose strand behind her ear.

Clearing her throat, she peered up at him. "I have something I would like to discuss with you."

He turned aside, quickly wiping away a tear. "Are you sure Mom shouldn't be in here?" he asked gruffly.

His grandmother surprised him by pinching his arm. "Ouch! What was that for?"

"Listen to me. It's about your great-grandfather. After I'm gone, you have to fulfill the promise."

Brett stared at his grandmother. Poor Grandma. Her mind was going. "I don't understand what you are talking about?"

"Solving your great-grandfather's murder, of course."

Brett bit back a laugh. They had discussed this issue before. He gave her kudos for not giving up.

"Grandma, you know the case has been closed for decades. I'm not even a detective yet. I have no training in investigating murders."

Bony fingers gripped his forearm.

"I don't want to hear excuses!" Maybelle's pulse beat wildly in her neck. "Your great-grandfather has specifically asked me to talk to you. He says you're the only one who can help."

Brett shook his head. Had her mind snapped? Maybe the painkillers had taken a toll. Gently kissing her hands, Brett attempted to pacify her. "You're confused. You were probably dreaming."

Maybelle jerked forward, sitting straight up. "I still have a few marbles rattling around upstairs. I know the difference between reality and a dream."

Brett smiled. "Hang on, Grandma. Think about what you're saying. Your father died in 1933. There is no way you can speak to him." The glimmer in his grandmother's eyes glowed even brighter. Where in the heck was his mother when he needed her?

"I know when he died. He reminds me all the time about how long it's been. He is getting tired of being held to earth. He wants to move on. According to him, being a specter isn't what it's cracked up to be."

Nervous laughter escaped from Brett as he stood. "Grandma," he sternly stated, "there are no such things as ghosts, spooks, or goblins. We need to adjust your pain medicine. You're imagining this. Who knows what you saw, but I know it wasn't your father!"

"Hmmph! Just because you have a college education doesn't mean you know everything, Mr. Smartypants. I see you're going to be hardheaded about this. I told Father that you wouldn't believe me.

I had better warn you that he is quite determined that you help him. He always liked to create a ruckus."

Clenching his teeth, Brett blew out a big breath. "I'll get Mom. Maybe she can convince you."

Maybelle jabbed a finger at her grandson. "Listen here, young man, I'm telling you the truth. Father wants you to solve his murder. You're his only descendent on the force. Therefore, you're the only one who can help him. If you don't help him, his spirit will never rest."

His chest muscles tightened. He couldn't breathe. He threw open the door and rushed down the hallway, the scent of lilacs following in his wake. Photographs of the infamous Mike O'Shea lined the walls. Every story about his great-grandfather came back to him. It was as if the eyes in the photographs followed his movements.

When Brett stormed into the kitchen, Sandy jumped to her feet. "What happened? You look as pale as a ghost."

Brett groaned. "Don't even say that word. I think Grandma is hallucinating."

His mom looked puzzled. "What word? What are you talking about?"

"Oh nothing much, except Grandma has been talking with her father's spirit. It seems that I'm supposed to help solve his murder." Brett ran a hand through his short hair, making it stand on end.

His mom took one look at him, and her laughter rang out. "I'm sorry. It's just that you look so frazzled. Don't worry about it. She's confused, and her memory plays tricks on her. Confusion is just part of the growing-old process."

"But you should have heard her. She really believes that her dad talks to her."

Sandy patted his broad shoulders. "Don't worry; I'll talk to her."

Somewhat mollified, Brett gave his mom a kiss and grabbed his papers. "I have to go. Call me if Grandma gets any worse. I'll see you tomorrow."

For the remainder of his shift, he stopped several speeders and wrote a record number of tickets. What were people doing out at 3:00 a.m. anyway? If they weren't going to or coming from work, then they probably deserved a ticket. Even though he kept busy, thoughts of his grandmother were not far off. He'd never seen her like this. With modern medicine, you'd think there was something that would help her.

Rather than shooting the bull with his coworkers after work, Brett hurried home. He was tired—so tired that his brain ached. All he needed was a few hours of sleep to block out the doubts and worries that had plagued him all evening. He crawled into bed, pulling the cover over his head. He was even too weary to get up and close the curtains.

Sleep came quickly. Dream after dream filtered through Brett's subconscious. His body rolled across the bed. An encompassing shroud of fear filled his senses. Brett jerked awake. A sheen of sweat covered his bare chest. His feet hit the floor with a thud. Dazed, he sat on edge of the bed, his body shivering in the cold air that swirled about the room. His pulse raced as he relived the dream. The image of his great-grandfather was fresh in his mind. The same image in the picture that sat on his grandmother's dresser. The picture of Mike O'Shea in his dress blues being awarded a medal for bravery. He had thwarted a robbery and caught the suspects single-handedly.

Brett's eyes squeezed shut as he vigorously rubbed the sleep from the corners. The only reason he had dreamt of Mike O'Shea was the crazy ravings of his grandmother. Yet the strange dream lingered in his mind. It was like he had been there watching the ceremony in person. *God!* He was becoming as batty as his grandmother.

He darted to the bathroom, where he splashed cold water on his face. He stared in the mirror. Beads of water trickled down sculptured cheekbones. His lips narrowed. He had to get his life back under control. Interviews for the detective position were scheduled for the following month. He couldn't afford wild fantasies or hocus pocus to disrupt his plan.

His pulse finally slowed to a normal rate. His breathing became slow and deep. Feeling in charge of himself again, he returned to bed. Yes, everything would be fine. He wouldn't waste any more energy even thinking about Grandma's conversations with the spirits. Sighing, he stretched out, allowing sleep to claim him once again.

A shadow rose from a sleek black recliner in the corner. Drifting near the bed, the shadow stood, observing the sleeping man. Stuffing a pipe into a pocket, the shadow smiled. Dawn peeked through the window. The shadow glanced up and nodded. Seconds later, only the faint scent of tobacco remained.

CHAPTER TWO

The cemetery road was lined with car after car. Dozens of people came up to Brett, offering their condolences. Grandma would have enjoyed this day. It was a warm October day. The sun filtered through the trees. The fall leaves were at their pinnacle with bold autumn colors. She loved the crisp autumn weather and the crunching sound of leaves when she stepped on them.

He had only seen his grandmother once since that night she tried to convince him to solve her father's murder. Even though the family had known she was dying, it still came as a shock. No one could ever prepare for something so final.

Brett looked up from the grave as his mother slipped her arm through his.

"How are you doing? You and your grandmother were always so close. You were always her favorite." Sandy's smile faltered.

Brett wrapped his arms around her. "Don't worry about me. I'm more concerned about how you're doing. You've been trying to do everything yourself the last couple of days. How about slowing down and letting me help?"

Sandy brushed away a tear. "Your grandma was so organized that even her burial was planned. She made me a list of what to do and who to contact when she died."

"If she was that rational about her funeral, how come she was acting delusional a couple of weeks ago? I can't believe she thought that she had conversations with her father."

"We'll never know what she saw. C'mon, we better get home before the visitors start arriving."

"I'll be right behind you." As his mother walked away, Brett turned once more to the casket. For a second, he almost wished his grandmother had talked to her father. That would mean that death wasn't final and that he might see or visit with her again.

Shaking his head as if to clear it, Brett drew a deep breath. *Don't go there*, he told himself. Abruptly, he turned to follow the crowd mourners. There was no use even speculating on something crazy like that. Dead was dead!

The reading of the will was held the day after the funeral. As expected, Brett's mother, being the wife of the only son, inherited the bulk of the estate.

A cardboard box was brought out. Duct tape sealed the tattered container. The executor placed it before Brett.

"What's this?" Brett looked toward his mother, who shrugged. Tearing through the gray tape, Brett gaped at the contents. "Oh my god!"

"What is it?" Sandy asked.

In awe, Brett pulled out a .38 caliber handgun. The leather holster was cracked with age. Pieces of the leather fluttered to the ground as Brett studied it. A tarnished detective's badge lay beneath the gun.

Sandy smiled. "They're your great-grandfather's. She knew you would cherish them as much as she did."

Gingerly, Brett placed the gun back in the box. "I can't believe she gave them to me. I thought you would get them." Opening the gun's chamber, he wondered if this was the gun Mike O'Shea had been using when he was killed? With a click, he closed the chamber. If only this gun could talk.

Sandy's eyes glistened with unshed tears. "I knew you would want them. Besides, what would I do with them? I don't even know how to properly clean a gun, and this one looks like it needs a good cleaning."

Brett kissed his mother's cheek. "Thank you, Mom."

Sandy reached over to hug Brett and gave him a little shake. "Now, I don't want you worrying about the job interview. You're a great patrolman, and besides, they know the family history."

Brett shook his head. "I don't know. Ever since they brought in Chief Ellison from the outside, morale has gone down the toilet. You wouldn't believe all the brass that he has moved around. Rumor has it that he doesn't like to promote from within."

"Well, he isn't the one interviewing you and if he was, he'd be an idiot not to promote you to detective."

He tightly embraced her. "Yeah. Too bad you're not the chief." They laughed together, and he gave her a quick kiss. "Call me if you need anything, Mom." He collected his new gun and went to home to crash for a few hours.

Later that afternoon, Brett decided to head to the gym. He wanted to burn off the tension from the last few days. Funerals were exhausting. And regardless of making light of the interview, Brett knew he had to watch himself. You never knew who might be your commander one day.

Two hours later, his workout routine completed, he rushed home to change into his uniform. After showering and grabbing a quick bite to eat, he dashed out again to head to work.

His heels skidded on the polished marble floor as he slid into a seat for roll call. He grimaced as he caught Sergeant Taylor's heated gaze. Taylor was about forty years old and as thin as a rail. His stringy brown hair was combed to the side, matted down by some goop he put on it. He reminded Brett of Barney Fife, from the old Andy Griffith Show that he watched on Nick at Nite. But Barney was harmless. Taylor wasn't. Taylor would stab others in the back if it benefited him.

Taylor continued to frown at him. "Cutting it close, O'Shea."

"Drop it, Taylor. Give the guy a break. His grandmother just died." Captain Miller stood in the back of the room, his arms folded across his broad chest.

Sergeant Taylor stared back at his commander as if challenging him. It was several minutes before Taylor glanced away.

"Okay, guys. We have a rash of burglaries on the east side. I want you to keep your eyes open and check out any suspicious vehicles or people loitering near houses tonight. Especially check out the new housing developments. It seems that the wealthier neighborhoods are being targeted. Stay safe. Don't forget to write some tickets tonight. Any questions."

A few men shook their heads. Most just ignored the sergeant. They quickly filed out of the room and headed to the lot where the squad cars were parked.

Behind the wheel of the black-and-white, Brett headed toward the east side of Des Moines. He hated Friday nights. Every high school kid was out looking for a good time or heading toward a football game, which translated into drunk high school kids, car accidents, and general mayhem.

A green Mustang zipped by, heading in the opposite direction. "Here we go," Brett muttered.

Whipping the car around, he went after the Mustang. As he neared the flashy car, he flipped on the lights and sirens. The car had dark tinted windows. Brett hated tinted windows; they made it impossible to know who or what was inside.

Gradually, the Mustang slowed and pulled into a parking lot. Brett pulled in behind it, his car engine still running. He ran the plates before getting out of the car. Music blared from inside the Mustang. When the license came back clean, he got out and cautiously approached the car. Standing off to the side, he rapped on the window.

"Roll it down." His hand rested on his Glock 21. The .45 caliber pistol was an icon among law enforcement agencies. With a magazine capacity of thirteen rounds, the weapon had a rapid-fire ability that could be the difference between life and death.

The driver's-side window eased down. The driver, in his early twenties with spiked blonde hair, leaned his head out the window.

"What's up, Officer?" he asked, holding out a hand for a high five.

Brett wanted to groan. Peering into the backseat, Brett glared at two other young men who were snickering. "Turn off the music. I need your license and proof of insurance."

The driver opened his mouth as if to say something but stopped.

Brett looked up from examining the license. "You're from the north side. Where are you fellows headed?"

The man behind the driver leaned forward with a challenging look in his eyes. "Hey man. It's a free country. We can drive where we want, and there's nothing you can do about it."

The driver reached back and punched his buddy in the leg. The driver then glanced up at Brett, who smiled back. It was his "you're so screwed" smile.

Brett opened the car door. "Why don't you all step outside."

"Man, now you done it," said the driver. "We're gonna be late for the party."

Brett ignored the disrespectful glances and muttered comments as he took all their licenses and returned to the squad car. After letting them sweat for twenty minutes, he walked back to their car. "You guys are lucky. I should write you up for speeding, but I'm feeling generous tonight. I'm going to give you a little advice. Go home. You keep driving around, I'm sure you'll find trouble."

The mouthy guy stepped forward but was quickly pulled back by the driver. "Uh, okay. Whatever you say."

The driver was smart enough to keep his mouth shut.

Brett smiled as he watched the Mustang inch out of the parking lot. *Punks!* He should have given them a ticket. Taylor would probably get on his ass, but what the hell. It was one of those nights when he just didn't give a shit. Brett tossed his hat on the seat and picked up his tablet.

As he finished an accident report, a call came over the radio. Another break-in had been called in. Brett knew there had been a rash of burglaries in his east-side territory. It seemed like the violence escalated with each incident. There were never any witnesses, which hindered solving the case. What appeared to start out as simple break-ins grew into something more serious. At the last house, the attacker had knocked out the homeowner with some type of club. The man was lucky to have survived.

Brett would give anything to be able to work with the detectives. He hoped to get the promotion; then he'd have an opportunity to go after these guys.

Brett finished his shift with a sigh and turned to return to the station. He failed to meet his personal quota, the two-to-five rule. Two to jail and five tickets each shift. He had only taken one person to jail tonight. Taylor would probably get on his ass if he knew that Brett had made up his own quota. Cops weren't supposed to have quotas.

As fate would have it, he saw a car stopped along the curb, the engine still running. Brett slowed down, catching sight of a figure near a tree.

"Bingo!" Brett said.

The man quickly zipped his trousers and walked back to his car.

Brett smiled. Damn, life was good! Brett got out of the car and walked toward the middle-aged man who stood in front of him. He didn't look drunk, but it was hard to know sometimes. Before Brett could say a word, the man started babbling.

"Hey, Officer. You scared me with that spotlight of yours. If you are okay, I think I'll be heading home now." The man took a step toward his car.

Brett moved in front of the man. "What's the hurry?"

"I'm on my way home from work. I guess I drank more than I thought tonight. Water! I mean water."

"Really? Water? Do you know it's against the law to expose yourself and urinate in a public place?"

Smirking, the man shrank back from Brett's glare. "I was just taking a leak. It's not that big of deal. It's not like I was streaking down the street or window peeping."

Brett whipped out the handcuffs and slipped them on the stunned man. "Okay, smart-ass. I'll have you know that you've violated city ordinance 42-348(11) for public urination and earned yourself a trip to jail."

Brett informed the man of his rights and helped him into the backseat of the squad car. He glanced into the rearview mirror and saw the prisoner's mouth hanging open. He choked back the laughter that threatened to erupt. Apparently, the man hadn't heard of the city ordinance.

The prisoner ranted all the way to the jail. Brett had to drag him out of the backseat.

When the jailer booked the prisoner, he looked up at Brett. "Public urination? Not again! How many does this make now? Five or six?" The nearby prisoners, who heard the jailer, swung toward Brett.

"Six so far this year," said Brett. "What the hell is wrong with people?" He ignored the jeers of the prisoners as he left the booking area. He was ready to clock out and head home.

Brett set his gun belt on the dresser and flipped on the television. After tossing his uniform on the floor, he slid into a pair of sweats. The early morning news carried the story of the break-in last night. The homeowner remained in serious condition at the hospital. When the reporter mentioned Michael O'Shea, he paused and turned up the volume.

It was again the anniversary of Michael's death. The TV station usually did a story every few years. Brett assumed it was because it was the only unsolved murder case involving a police officer. The screen flashed old photographs of the 1933 murder scene. Brett stared transfixed at the black-and-white picture. His great-grandfather's body lay in a pool of blood. He had never seen that picture before. It looked gruesome. His great-grandfather had died a painful, tortuous death.

Brett flopped on the bed, his eyes squeezed closed, trying to shut out the picture of death that lingered in his mind. Brett had thought he knew every detail of his relative's death, until now. Seeing the pictures on the screen made his death more personal; made it all too real. Brett's throat tightened, and he abruptly turned off the television. He didn't want to hear any more.

His senses were attuned to every noise that filtered throughout the house. Brett grabbed a pillow and pressed it over his face. He took a deep breath and exhaled slowly. He repeated the process several times. Slowly, his mind and body became numb to his surroundings. He gave in to the exhaustion and fell asleep.

He had no idea how long he had been asleep, but something

caused him to wake. Through a sleep-induced fog, Brett squinted toward the far corner of the room. Shadows danced on the walls from the moonlight filtering through the window. Rubbing his eyes, he glanced back at the wall. A tall shadow leaned against the wall with folded arms and a crooked smile.

CHAPTER THREE

In a series of fluid movements, Brett lunged across the room, grabbed his gun, and rolled to the floor in a defensive position, ready to fire at the slightest provocation.

Loud, resounding laughter ricocheted off the walls. The half-hidden figure slapped his knee in merriment.

What the hell was going on? Brett slowly rose, keeping his gun trained on the shadowy figure. The hat the man wore made it difficult to see his face. "Who are you? What do you want?"

Brett watched the man's smile fade when he realized the gun was pointed in his direction.

Tugging the hat lower, the man warned, "You'd best not be waving that weapon around, sonny, unless you plan on using it."

After flicking on the ceiling light, Brett studied the intruder. He gauged him to be about thirty years old and in good physical shape by the looks of his broad shoulders and muscular build that stressed the seams of his old-fashioned tweed jacket. Brett guessed the man to be just over six feet tall, slightly shorter than he was. The man's hat looked like something out of a gangster movie.

"I'm giving the orders, not you. Why did you break into my house?"

"Don't be getting your knickers all in a twist, sonny. I'll tell you what you need to know and no more."

Brett gritted his teeth. "Don't call me sonny! I'm going to throw your ass in jail."

The man shook his head, sighing. "You need more time to understand, but time is something we don't have much of."

Brett scowled. "I have no idea what you're smoking, buddy, but you are still going to jail."

Shifting his weight to the other foot, the man studied his fingertips, seeming to have not a care in the world. "You are more difficult than I imagined."

Brett's hand tightened on the gun. He reached for the handcuffs on his dresser. Tossing them to the man, he ordered, "Do you want to see difficult? Put the cuffs on. Maybe a little time behind bars will give you an attitude adjustment." Brett leaned over, picked up his cell phone, and pointed toward the bed.

"Sit there where I can watch you."

He pressed 911 several times, but nothing happened.

Al sat on the edge of the bed, staring at every item contained in the room. He was amazed by all the technical advances that had been made since his time. When that was, he wasn't sure. He knew his name and that he had been sent to help Brett. Other than those two things, his memory was pretty much blank. Though, there were times when things from his past would suddenly be revealed. He knew he liked beer and smoking a pipe.

He watched Brett pace in front of the bed. From the look of things, it appeared that Brett didn't want his help. Brett looked as if he were going to explode if his face turned any redder. Brett kept glaring at him. He choked back laughter as Brett started cursing.

"First things first. My name is Al. There is no use getting mad. That gun of yours is not going to work. Just give it to me so you don't get hurt."

Brett quirked his brow. "Al, I'm not giving you my gun." He blinked several times before looking back at Al.

"Sit down. You make me nervous pacing about like that. I was sent to help you."

Leaning against the dresser, Brett smirked. "Why would you think

I need your help?" He straightened. "Wait a minute. Who sent you? And take off that damn hat! I want to see your face."

"There you go again, getting your feathers all ruffled up like an ornery rooster. I've got my orders. The hat stays."

Brett's body shuddered. "Have you forgotten that I have a gun trained on you?"

Unappreciative of Brett's sarcasm, Al clenched his fists. "You seem to have forgotten what I just told you. The gun doesn't work." Al leaned forward on the bed, resting his elbows on his leg. "You're really pissing me off, sonny."

"Well, same here. Maybe you think you're Superman and bullets won't hurt you. If I had to guess, you're just some loser down on his luck who likes to wear old clothes and ugly hats. Dude, you picked the wrong house to break in to."

Al started counting to ten, holding his head in his hands. Once he reached the number ten, he exploded, "Saints alive! Your babbling is giving me a headache, and I can't even get a headache!"

Brett glared down at him. "Al, who the hell are you?"

Al rose to his feet, causing Brett to step backward. "Thick skulled, that's what you are. You young cops think you know everything. I've seen things that you can't even imagine."

Brett rubbed his eyes, his body wavering from side to side.

Al's anger faded. "Lean over and get some blood back in that head of yours. You're as white as a ghost."

Brett dropped the gun on the floor and sank to the floor. Al reached down and patted Brett on the shoulders. Brett jerked sideways, looking as if Al were going to hit him. Brett ended up cracking his head on the corner of the dresser. Al watched as he slid to the floor in a heap.

Al looked down at Brett's still body as he slipped out of the handcuffs. He was a strapping lad. Bigger than Al was. He leaned down and effortlessly picked Brett up and laid him on the bed. One of the benefits of being a ghost.

With a look upward, Al muttered, "How about a break here? While you're at it, add some divine guidance. I have a feeling I'm going to need it."

Al sat down on the edge of the bed, his gaze stopping on the wall. He stared at black rectangle hanging there. "What's that?" He stood, walked over, and touched it. Hard. On the bottom, it had Samsung written on it. What was a Samsung? What did this thing do?

He turned, hearing Brett moan.

Brett slowly came to and rolled over on his side. "Man, what a headache. I need some Tylenol." He started to get out of bed but stopped when he saw Al.

"Shit! You're real!" Brett quickly rolled away to the other side of the bed and tumbled back to the floor.

Al jumped on the bed and leaned over the edge, staring down at Brett.

"Do you always spend this much time on the floor?" He paused and bounced on the mattress. "I like this bed of yours. It's comfy." Al held up his hand when Brett opened his mouth. "Don't start ranting again. This isn't a dream. It's the real thing, sonny. I'm a ghost."

Al hesitated. Brett's face crumpled. *The poor guy.* Brett looked at Al in horror. "Hey, it's okay. I don't know your history, but the *guy up above* sent me to help you. We're supposed to work as a team to solve the mystery of Michael O'Shea's death. Do you know who that is?"

Brett nodded, not looking up at Al. "He was my great-grandfather."

"Well then, we're going to be a team. I haven't worked with anyone human before."

Brett groaned. A ghost! Why would God send him a ghost? Could things get any weirder? He wanted his life back to the way it had been. Brett could see only the lower half of the man's face, yet somehow he could sense the man's eyes staring at him. Laughing at him. He was in trouble. Big trouble!

CHAPTER FOUR

Brett shut off the lights to try to get a few hours of sleep. He didn't want to talk to Al any longer. He wasn't even sure that he believed the crazy story that Al had given him. He punched his pillow, and his eyes finally drifted closed.

Brett felt a breeze drift across his face. His eyes peeked open. Al stood by his bed, his hands on hips.

"Al, what are you doing here?" Brett rose to a half-sitting position.

"I wanted to make sure you were okay. You seemed shaken up earlier when we talked."

Brett glanced at the clock and sighed. Roughly rubbing his face, he tried to temper his annoyance. "I'm fine. Just give me some time. It was a lot to take in. Now can I go to sleep?"

Al muttered something under his breath. The next second, Al disappeared into his bedroom walls. Brett jumped out of bed and went to the place where Al had disappeared. Running his hand up and down the wall, he stared in disbelief. *How did he do that?*

Al reappeared, a moment later, walking out of the wall as if there were a hidden doorway.

"Holy crap! How did you do that?"

Al smiled. "Did you forget that I said I was a ghost? Or did you think I was pulling some bizarre parlor trick?"

Unable to respond, Brett walked over to Al and grabbed his shoulders with both hands.

"Well, do I feel real?" Laughter shook Al's body.

Brett nodded, looking back and forth from Al to the wall.

Al squeezed his shoulder. "Get some sleep. I will see you soon. We have work to do."

After Al disappeared again, Brett climbed back into bed. It took hours for him to fall asleep.

It was midafternoon before Brett woke. He quickly showered and dressed before searching the fridge for something to eat. He stood by the microwave, waiting for the timer. He wasn't that hungry but was trying to retain a resemblance of sanity. He felt that if he ignored his ghostly guest sitting at his table long enough, maybe he'd disappear.

Brett set the steaming tray of food on the table and removed the cellophane wrapper. The aroma of hot beef and potatoes filled the air.

Leaning over, Al eyed the food suspiciously. "You're not going to eat that, are you?"

"Of course. Do you want something to eat?" Brett pressed the back of one hand to his forehead in dramatic fashion. "Wait, can ghosts eat?"

Grinning from ear to ear, Al leaned back in the chair and crossed his legs. "We're relieved of the need for earthly sustenance. Although I must admit to craving a beer from time to time."

Brett sat down and began eating. "So you can't eat. What else can't you do, Al? And how do you expect 'us' to solve a cold case?"

The man pulled the collar of his tweed jacket up around his face. "I can do what needs to be done. You can count on that. I'm not sure exactly how we will solve the case, but I'm sure the big guy will keep us informed."

Brett choked on his soda. "Big guy? You're being kind of irreverent, aren't you?"

"Nah. He knows I'm just kidding around."

Brett tossed his dirty dishes in the sink and wiped his hands before turning back to Al. "Why do you need me to help you? Can't God just tell us who did it? Case solved. Besides, there have been several investigations, but no one could ever figure it out."

Al crossed his legs and leaned back in the chair. "I can't explain how I know that we will help each other. You've got to trust me in this."

Brett hooted with laughter. "Trust you? I can't even see your face. I don't know if you're a ghost, spirit, or just my imagination."

Al sighed, looking exasperated. "I thought we already covered this once. I'm as real as a ghost gets, sonny. Don't you be worrying about the technicalities. Just let me and the man upstairs handle things. Why don't you start by giving me some background on your deceased relative."

Brett grabbed the car keys and a gym bag. "I need to get out of here for a while and think. When I come back, we'll talk. I should be back in a couple of hours. Try to stay out of trouble."

Brett revved up the engine and backed out of the driveway, grateful to be alone. He needed to think about what Al had told him. How could it be possible to converse with a ghost?

He was thankful to find that the gym was nearly empty; he wasn't in the mood to talk. Once he was done on the treadmill, he walked to the free weights. While adjusting a weight bench, Brett glanced up. He blinked, not believing what he saw. Al waved back at him. The bar slipped from his hands, drawing the attention of those across the building.

Brett apologetically murmured aloud, "Sorry." He picked up his towel and covered his reddened face, wiping the sweat from his brow. Cautiously, he opened his eyes. Al stood nearby, cackling with laughter.

"That was loud enough to wake the dead." He slapped his knee, amused at his own cleverness.

Brett glanced around the gym. No one seemed to be paying them any attention. They obviously couldn't hear Al laughing like a hyena. "What are you doing here? I thought I told you to wait for me?" Brett hissed.

Al shrugged. "I got bored. Besides, we have work to do."

Brett angrily stuffed his towel and weight belt into his bag. "Tell me, can anyone else see or hear you?"

"No. Just you."

"Great! I have my own George Kirby, the ghost from the old Topper movies. Grandma loved those films."

Al folded his arms against his chest. "Your sarcasm isn't appreciated.

34

Stalking toward the doorway, Brett glanced sideways at Al. "You could disappear."

Chills ran up Brett's spine as Al melted through the plate-glass window and came out on the other side.

Brett drove home by himself. *No Al, thank God.* Tossing the keys on the counter, Brett quickly showered and changed into his uniform. He grabbed a sandwich before driving to work. He assumed that his sharp words at the gym must have pissed off Al. He had remained out of sight the rest of the day. Brett smiled as he hurried down the hall toward the roll call room, determined not to be late again.

The sergeant announced that there still were no leads in the burglary case. In fact, it had been quiet the previous two nights. The officers headed to their cars with one thought on their minds—find the man who threatened their community.

Brett looped through the major intersections of the east side. Midway through his shift, he pulled into McDonald's for dinner. Every night, it was a double cheeseburger, large fries, a drink, and apple pie. Enjoying the hot fries, Brett quickly checked messages on his cell phone. The guys were meeting for beers after work. Maybe he should go. He quickly texted his reply. He popped another fry into his mouth and remembered that he had to write up the report for his last call. He reached behind to the backseat to grab his tablet, and his hand came into contact with someone's knee. He swung around and saw Al sitting in the backseat.

"I've never seen a man eat as much as you and still look so fit. What has this world come to? Now you can drive up to a little window, and they hand you your food. Don't people ever sit down and have a normal meal anymore?"

Brett's hand flew to his chest as he choked down the food caught in his throat. "Damn! Do you have to scare me like that? I thought you agreed to stay put at my house?"

Al disappeared in a mist and reappeared in the front seat next to Brett. "No, you told me to stay at home, and I just listened. I can't spend the rest of my life here. Time is a-ticking, my boy."

"Why the rush?" Brett snapped. "It's been eighty plus years. What difference will a few days or weeks make?"

Al sucked in his cheeks. It looked as if he were biting his lips. "You've got to work with me. I don't know what difference it will make. All I know is that I feel a sense of urgency and have no idea why."

For the next half hour, silence reigned in the car. Brett wadded up the rest of his uneaten food and threw it in the backseat. He wanted to tell Al to get lost, but the words never came out.

Out of the corner of his eye, Brett saw a familiar green Mustang zoom by. Flashing a malicious grin, he turned to Al.

"Hang on!"

Al's head banged against the window as they zipped out of the parking lot. Tires squealed as the squad car raced after the sports car. They sped up the freeway ramp.

Al leaned over and stared at the speedometer. His face turned even paler than his normal pasty complexion.

"Saints preserve us! Are we going seventy-five miles an hour?"

Focused on his prey, Brett shook his head. "Nope. We're doing eighty now." A chuckle escaped him when he saw the look on his passenger's face. "I'd tell you to fasten your seatbelt, but since it wouldn't make any difference, why don't you relax and enjoy the ride?"

Buildings and cars flew by as they came closer to the green car. Al made the sign of the cross as they narrowly missed a parked car when they exited the freeway and rounded a corner.

Ahead of them, the Mustang hit the brakes, causing the rear end to swerve and slide into a telephone pole. Steam and smoke billowed from underneath the crunched hood. Brett called in to report the accident before jumping out of the squad car. He opened the man's car door and helped him from the vehicle. The young driver groaned before plopping down on the curb.

The young man looked up at Brett and moaned. "I knew it was you."

"You like pushing your luck?"

With a shrug of his shoulders, the driver wiped the dripping blood from his nose. "No, I just didn't need another ticket. Now I'm going to lose my license."

Brett whipped out his book and started writing. "Oh yeah, you're right about that. You're lucky that you slowed down before hitting that pole. You could have been killed."

The driver smirked up at Brett. "Duh. I'm not stupid."

"You'd have been smarter to use your seat belt and not try to outrun me. Your broken nose will be your souvenir."

From the corner of his eye, Brett saw Al approaching. "Get back to the car," he hissed.

The driver looked questioningly at the smashed car. "Why?"

"Not you."

Smirking, the young man asked, "Who ya talking to?"

"None of your business. Just sit there and shut up."

Al leaned over Brett's shoulder, staring at the injured man. "Shouldn't we get him some medical help?"

Scribbling his name on the ticket, Brett muttered, "We'll take him to the county hospital to be checked out. Now go sit down."

Clearly puzzled, the driver responded, "I am sitting down."

Al cocked his head as if waiting to see how Brett would answer.

Pointing to the driver, Brett grunted, "Not one more word. Get in my backseat."

With the man in the backseat, Brett waited for the tow truck to arrive before leaving for the hospital.

During the drive, Al touched and poked every button on the dashboard. "This is neat! I wish we'd had something like this when I was alive. What does this do?" Some shotgun shells dropped on the floor, rolling back and forth.

Brett angrily whispered, "Would you leave things alone? Pick those shells up before they get lost." Staring at Al, Brett quietly asked, "Do you know when you were born or lived?"

Al shrugged and glanced out the window. "I'm not sure. I've been trying to figure it out, but I can't."

Brett pulled up to the hospital and waited for his prisoner to be examined. The doctor indicated that the prisoner had a concussion and ordered him admitted for observation. Once the paperwork was completed, Brett strode back to the squad car, where he found the red lights flashing and siren sounding. He brushed through the crowd of people staring at what they thought was an empty car and quickly shut off the lights and siren. "Quit acting like a child! You're supposed to be helping me. Haven't you ever been in a squad car before?"

Al ignored Brett and let out a low whistle. "I don't know, but this car is amazing. What does this do?"

The muscle in Brett's jaw twitched. "It's called a wireless radio. It lets me communicate with dispatch."

Al continued to examine the radio until Brett grabbed it from him and slammed in back into the case. He jammed the car into drive, and they headed back to the east side.

Al's unbridled enthusiasm was getting on Brett's nerves. A call came across the radio. Some drunk had decided to beat up his wife. Brett hated these types of calls. As he pulled up to the house, the woman waited outside, one eye nearly swollen shut. "Thank God you're here. He's in there, passed out on the floor."

Brett eased past the woman. With one glance, he knew she wouldn't file charges. *Shit!* These trips were a waste of time.

The husband lay sprawled out on the floor, his deep, rumbling snores echoing through the tiny home. With his foot, Brett nudged the man. "Hey buddy, wake up. Do you hear me? I said get up."

Slowly, the man's eyes opened. Rubbing his flabby cheeks, he mumbled, "Who are you?"

"I'm the Good Humor man. Get your ass off the floor or I'll do it for you."

The drunk snarled. "Don't like ice cream. Gives me gas."

Brett sighed. Everyone was a comedian tonight. The man on the floor had to weigh three hundred pounds. There was no easy way to do this. Brett reached down and took hold of the man's wrist, quickly slapping on the cuff. The man's other arm came to life and slammed into the side of Brett's head. Shaking off the dizziness, Brett drew back his fist and ground it into the man's slack jaw.

Brett snapped on the other cuff and hauled the man to his feet. His eyes widened as he saw Al jabbing at the drunk's head. He noticed that Al's hat seemed to be glued to his head. Even while he was jumping around, his hat remained in place, concealing the upper part of his face.

From the look of Al's scrunched-up mouth, he was furious. He threw all of his energy into his movements, but it was futile. His fists flew through the air like a windmill, yet hitting nothing. Brett wondered why Al couldn't touch anyone else.

"Enough already! You've made your point. Too bad he can't feel anything."

Al scowled. "Don't be telling your elder what to do. No man is going to hit a friend of mine and walk away."

The wife anxiously watched as Brett led her husband to the car. "Are you sure he can't feel anything? There's a lot blood coming from his mouth where you hit him. Maybe you could take him to the hospital?" Biting her lip, the woman faltered. "I changed my mind. Just let him go. I shouldn't have called the cops. He's really a nice guy except when he drinks."

Brett gritted his teeth. "Lady, you should have thought about that before you made the call. He hit an officer, so he's going to jail. You can come down tomorrow and bail him out."

Brett twisted the man's arm to get him to bend over and get in the car.

"Ouch! You're breaking my arm."

"Quit complaining and get in. Don't puke in my car either, or you'll be the one cleaning it up. Got it?"

Once they were driving, Brett glanced at Al. "Hey, I have a question. Why couldn't you hit my prisoner—not that I wanted you to?"

Al shrugged. "One of the many rules that's in my handbook. You're the only one who can see or talk to me. You're the only who can actually touch me. I knew I couldn't make contact with the guy, but it felt good to take a few swings at the asshole."

"Handbook?" Brett choked out.

Al grinned. "Gosh sonny. I'm pulling your leg."

For the third time that night, Brett took a prisoner to jail. The desk sergeant looked up and frowned. "O'Shea. Don't you ever get tired of all the reports and paperwork?"

Brett shrugged. "Well, at least I keep busy." Glancing at the clock, Brett smiled. "You won't be seeing me again tonight. Twenty minutes and I'm out of here."

Shuffling through paper at the printer, the disinterested jailer quipped, "Yippee. Now get out of here and leave me alone."

Brett slid behind the wheel and found Al glaring out the window. "Now what's the matter?"

Al's stomach rolled. He knew something was going to happen. His hand tightened on the door handle until the ends of his fingers turned even whiter.

"Start driving!" Al barked.

Brett turned and gaped at him.

"Are you deaf? I said start driving." Al pointed to the street.

"Okay, okay. What's your problem?" Brett pulled away from the jail. "Any particular direction?"

Absently, Al shook his head. "I don't know. Just keep going until I tell you to stop."

Lights from passing buildings illuminated their profiles, creating misshapen shadows. Brett muttered, "Something weird is going on. The hairs on the back of my neck are standing on end. It's as if electricity is in the car."

Al's voice sounded hoarse even to his own ears. "I have a gut feeling that something bad is about to happen."

"What are you talking about?"

"Murder!" he murmured.

Brett's eyes grew wide. "How do you know? Do you have a sixth sense or something?"

"Listen to me. There's going to be a murder tonight, and we have to try to stop it."

CHAPTER FIVE

B rett stared at the road in front of him. He felt the heat of Al's gaze. What was he supposed to do? There was a damn ghost telling him what to do. This wasn't how things were done. Brett flexed his fingers, trying to ease the stress.

He couldn't report a murder that hadn't happened, but he didn't want anyone to die if it could be prevented.

"Where is this murder going to take place?"

"If I knew that, I'd tell you. You've got to trust me."

Indecision ripped through Brett. He growled as he gripped the wheel tighter. Accepting the inevitable, he snapped, "Okay. You'd better pray that we get there in time."

Al stared out the window. "I'm hoping to see something that will look familiar. Heck, maybe the guy upstairs will send us a signal."

Suddenly, Al yelled, "Turn right!"

Brett jerked the wheel and found himself on the one street he avoided—York Street. It was the street where his grandfather had died. A street in the center of a blue-collar neighborhood where several recent burglaries had taken place.

Al nearly jumped out of the car. "What street is this?"

"York Street. Why?" Brett's gaze darted from left to right, sensing the unseen threat.

"No reason."

Their harsh, labored breathing echoed in the car. Brett stared straight ahead. At the end of the block sat a large two-story house surrounded by empty lots.

"Is this it?" Brett hissed.

"I don't know. Stay here and I'll check it out."

Before Brett could argue, Al's body disappeared from the seat next to him. Unfastening his holster, Brett eased open his door and crouched down next to the car. He took a deep breath and ran toward the side of the house. Glass crunched beneath his feet with each step. Blinds fluttered in the night air through a broken window.

He inched toward the front door, which was cracked open. Using his foot, he nudged the door open and crouched low to the floor, ready to fire.

A loud crash came from the back of the house. Instinctively, Brett ran into the house, heading toward the sound. A lithe figure, dressed in black, leapt out a large window, shattering the glass. Brett saw the figure quickly jump to his feet and race down the alley. Brett jumped through the opening and followed.

"Stop or I'll shoot!"

The man glanced over his shoulder at Brett before jumping into a parked car. Brett's stride slowed as the car sped away. His chest heaved up and down as he fought to draw in air. The license number was obscured by the darkness. Frustrated, he marched back to the house. Al suddenly materialized at the back door.

"Put the gun away. You won't be needing it."

Breathless from the adrenaline pumping through his body, Brett panted, "Well? Did we do it? Did we prevent the murder?"

With his head bowed, Al's voice cracked. "We're too late. There's a body upstairs."

"Damn it!" He squeezed his eyes shut. "I need to call it in."

Brett waited outside the bedroom where the body lay. A short time later, detectives swarmed through the house, snapping pictures of the crime scene.

Sergeant Taylor suddenly appeared in front of Brett. "How in the hell did you end up here? Your shift ended an hour ago. You weren't authorized to work over."

"I had a hunch."

"A street cop with a hunch. Hell, do you think your name is Sherlock Holmes or something?"

Brett relaxed his fist. "I lost track of time; otherwise, I would have called in earlier."

The sergeant grimaced. "Are you sure it was a hunch? Maybe someone told you this was going down tonight?"

Brett shook his head. "No, it was a hunch."

"Hunch my ass. Damn it, O'Shea! Who's your source?"

There was no way Brett was going to reveal his source. He'd be laughed out of the department.

"Sergeant, there is no source! I was driving by, and something didn't sit right with me. So I stopped to investigate. End of story."

Now, thanks to Al, Brett was resorting to half-truths and lies. Something he had never done before.

Taylor's bushy brows drew together. "By-the-book O'Shea took it upon himself to ignore procedure, all because you had a hunch?"

"Well, obviously it was a good hunch, because I almost caught the guy. A few seconds earlier and I would have had him." Brett tensed, taking a step toward Taylor. *Little weasel!*

It was clear to Brett that Detectives Kane and Donnellson, standing nearby, were straining to hear the conversation. Everyone knew that Taylor had it in for him, but no one knew why. Donnellson winked in commiseration with Brett. He and Donnellson had gone through the academy together.

Taylor studied Brett. "Yeah? It could be your body lying on the floor. From here on out, if you get a hunch or a tip or a premonition, I want to know about it before you do anything crazy. Do I make myself clear?"

"Got it. Is that all, sir?"

"Submit your report before you leave—and it better be good."

Brett stormed downstairs. Every decent cop had gut feelings or hunches about things, such as driving past a building and thinking that you saw something. Just recently an officer had driven by a used car lot and thought he saw something. He turned around and came in the back way and surprised a guy breaking into a car. It was just one of those things every cop experienced from time to time. There was no rationale as to why it happened; it just did.

He opened the car door and saw Al sitting in the front seat with his head bowed. Brett felt a flash of sentimentality. "The guys inside are good. They'll catch the bastard."

Al shook his head. "It's not that. I should have been here. It's happening again. Just like before."

"What's happening again?"

"The burglaries and murders, just like what happened before."

Brett turned to study Al. "Before?"

"Yeah, but don't ask me when. I just know this feels familiar." Al stared out the window.

"I'll admit that you freaked me out knowing that there was going to be a murder tonight. You're not omniscient, are you?"

Brett was silenced by the hopelessness that clung to Al's slumped body. Not sure if he could say anything to make it better, he silently finished his report on the laptop. After submitting the report, Brett drove home. He regretted the snide remarks he had made to Al earlier. He was not trying to put Al down, but this ghost thing was unnerving. He wanted to become a detective, not be investigated by one. If he had any more 'hunches' like tonight's, he'd be the prime suspect.

Brett showered and headed for bed, relieved that Al had disappeared.

CHAPTER SIX

The afternoon sun peeked around the blinds. Brett rolled over and stretched. A glance at the clock showed it was past noon. He clicked on the TV to listen to the midday news. Sure enough, the murder the night before was the top story. Reporter Lisa Winslow stood in front of the house on York Street. She brushed back a blonde strand blowing about her face. Her crisp voice announced that the suspect remained at large. The segment must have been filmed the previous night, as residents in the neighborhood were standing about in their pajamas. Those who were interviewed said they never heard or saw anything.

Al still had not reappeared. *Surely he doesn't need sleep*, thought Brett. *Where is he?*

Brett threw a load of laundry into the dryer and checked his answering machine. He picked up the phone and quickly dialed his mom's number.

"What's up, Mom? You sounded upset when you called."

"I was listening to the scanner and heard the call come in last night. I had a feeling you were involved and just wanted to make sure you were okay."

His mind raced. Would she believe that a ghost had helped him? He wanted to tell her, yet something held him back.

"Brett, are you sure you're fine? You sound different."

"Yeah, I'm fine. I have a lot on my mind right now." After a brief pause, he blurted, "Do you believe in ghosts?"

Sandy chuckled into the receiver. "Like ghosts and goblins that haunt ancient castles?"

"Never mind. I'll talk to you later."

Brett started to hang up, but his mom's voice came across the line. "Brett! I was teasing. I thought you were trying to be funny. I'm sorry."

He sighed. "I can't tell anyone but you. I have a real ghost following me around. It started a several days ago. He showed up at the house and has been popping in and out for the past few days. He says we're supposed to solve great-grandpa's murder. He's got this weird sense of when things are going to happen. He knew the murder was going to happen last night. We tried to stop it. I didn't want to believe what he told me. But, Mom, he was right."

Sandy softly murmured, "You know, Grandma always liked to exaggerate. I think the story of seeing her father's ghost was her way of teasing you. I'm sure that she never saw his ghost. You've been under a lot of stress with her death and worrying about the promotion. Can you get some time off? You and I could take a vacation. Let's go somewhere and have fun. How about Vegas?"

Feeling like an idiot for bringing up the topic, he mumbled, "We'll see. I've got to go, Mom. I'll talk to you later." He didn't want to argue with his mom.

On the way to the gym, he wondered if he was crazy; really crazy. Throughout the day, he kept glancing over his shoulder, thinking that Al would show up. Brett didn't know if his absence was a blessing or a curse.

The rest of the day passed in a blur until he went to work. Sergeant Taylor waited in the parking lot as Brett pulled in. Taylor motioned to Brett. Brett's gut tightened. From the time he first joined the force, Taylor had been a pain in the ass.

"O'Shea, I want you to know that I'll be watching you. Make sure you stay in your own territory and clock out on time. I don't want to work late because of you not showing up. Got it?"

Brett bit the inside of his lip. He really wanted to tell Taylor to fuck off. Instead he pulled his cap down over his brow. "Got it." He started to turn away, but he paused. "Let me ask you something. Did I do something wrong? Ever since I started the force, it seems that you have had a problem with me."

Taylor hesitated. "Yeah. I got a problem. You think because your name is O'Shea and your relatives were on the force that you can just waltz in and apply for a promotion and get it. I've been here years, and things don't work that way. You need to put in your time like everyone else."

"Well, I guess anything that I say to you is like spitting in the wind." Brett kept his face immobile—no frown, no snarls, nothing. He was not getting into a pissing match with Taylor. He'd end up losing. He turned and walked to the squad car, feeling the heat from Taylor's gaze on his back.

Once on the streets, Brett relaxed. He made his regular stops at the convenience stores and picked up his free coffee. The store managers liked the officers to stop by. The stores were less likely to be robbed with a cop inside the store, unless the criminal was a complete pothead.

The night was slow, so Brett pulled off into an empty parking lot. Rainy weather kept most of the crazy drivers off the street. Sitting in the car, he flipped through a *Sports Illustrated* magazine. The hum of a revved up engine passed by. The streetlights glistened off a familiar Mustang. Brett stared at the receding taillights as the car drove out of sight. *The hell with it*. He wasn't chasing anyone. The previous night had been enough excitement to last him for several weeks.

He tossed the magazine into his bag and leaned his back in the seat. How had Al known a murder was going to happen? What was it about the previous night that seemed so familiar? He remembered reading old newspaper articles discussing his grandfather's murder. He was missing something, but for the life of him, he didn't know what.

When Brett entered the station to report in for the night, Taylor glanced at the clock. Brett bit back a smile.

"What's wrong, O'Shea? No jokes or smart comments tonight?" Taylor growled.

"Not tonight." Brett strode past the sergeant and headed to the locker room. He didn't care what Taylor thought or did. He had more important things on his mind. He knew his Mom had boxes of articles and newspaper clippings about his great-grandfather. Maybe he could find a clue.

The next morning, Brett drove to his mother's house. She was at work, so he let himself in. In the basement, he quickly found a box for labeled "Mike O'Shea." He dumped it out on the floor and sifted through the pile. Article after article hailed Michael as a hero for solving the toughest cases. Hidden at the bottom were several articles describing Michael's ongoing feud with the brass. He was probably the most suspended officer in the history of the department. Brett felt a strange sense of admiration. The man had balls!

A black folder peeked from beneath the papers. Brett picked it up. Inside were yellowed newspaper clippings about the string of burglaries preceding Michael's death. The pinnacle of violence came when his grandfather was murdered. After his death, the killings mysteriously stopped. There were no answers in the stack of papers, only more questions. With the absence of forensics at the time of the crime, leads were nonexistent. The case was cold—dead cold.

Was there a connection between Michael's death and the recent death on York Street? Logically, the answer would be no. Something was missing, but what? He started arranging the clippings in chronological order. Rummaging through the closet, he found a roll of brown wrapping paper. He cut off several feet and laid it out on the floor. With a black marker, he began listing each robbery on a time line. He felt that if he could visualize each crime, perhaps a common thread would become evident.

Hours later, Brett tossed the papers aside. He had been at this for hours and found nothing. He rubbed his tired eyes. Wearily, he reached for the scattered papers. His gaze lit on the dates of the crimes. He jerked, knocking his coffee across the floor. His pulse raced. Could this be significant? The length of time between crimes decreased by a week, up to the time of the Michael's murder. Applying the same logic, the next murder would occur in three weeks. Brett rose to his feet. His head bowed as thoughts raced in his mind. He couldn't take this information to Taylor. Taylor would laugh and ignore any theories that Brett presented. He didn't want to involve his mom. The less she knew, the better he could protect her. That left Captain Miller. As an old friend of the family, he was the best option.

That evening after roll call, Brett knocked on Captain Miller's door. As he stood in the doorway, Miller motioned for him to come in and sit down. With the phone stuck to his ear, Miller smiled before turning his chair away from Brett. Obviously it wasn't a pleasant conversation. Miller's short gray hair was messy, as if the captain had run his hands through it.

"Yes, sir. I've got my best detectives working on the case." Nodding his head, the captain acquiesced. "I know the public thinks we're not doing enough, but sir—"

The captain's leathery neck turned red as he hung up the phone. He swiveled toward Brett with an artificial smile on his face. Brett felt empathy for his superior.

Hastily jumping to his feet, Brett grabbed his hat. "I'll come back later, when it's more convenient."

"Nonsense. Sit down. You wouldn't have stopped in unless it was important. Now tell me, how's your mother? I haven't seen her since your grandmother's funeral."

"She's fine. No matter how you try to prepare for someone's death, you're always surprised when it happens. How's your wife, Joan, and Candace? I see Joan around town every once in a while."

"Joan's fine. According to her, she loves spending my money. Candace just got engaged, so now I have a wedding to pay for. Well, enough of that. What's on your mind?"

Clearing his throat, Brett met Miller's curious gaze. "I'm not quite sure how to say this, but I think I may have a lead on the murder that occurred earlier in the week."

Captain Miller studied him as he popped open a bottle of Tums. Crunching the tablets, he folded his hands together and rested them on the desk. "Why do I think I don't want to hear this?"

"Sir, trust me. You want to hear this. I grew up with all the stories about my great-grandfather's murder. Around my house, Mike O'Shea was a hero. My grandmother had boxes of stuff from the paper and information from the detectives' investigation. After the recent break-ins and murder, I did a little research. From what I can see, there are quite a few similarities between the old case and the recent break-ins and murder. If the past is any indication, then we should be able to predict when the next murder will occur."

Miller leaned back in his chair, reaching to the bottle of Tums again. "Why do you think your grandfather's case is even relevant?"

Brett shrugged, fighting back his doubts. "I've asked myself that same question. All I can say is that I know they are related." In a rush he added, "All the old-timers say that a good cop has the instinct to know certain facts or to be able to predict when something is going to happen. There's nothing logical about it. I feel there is some connection between the cases. We just have to find out what."

"You think it's a copycat? No one even remembers that case anymore except your family and a couple of us old-timers."

"I know it's a stretch, but someone has the information. I laid out facts from the 1933 murder, thinking it would help to predict what will happen next."

Miller smiled. "You know, I've also heard the stories surrounding Michael O'Shea. He had an extraordinary knack for being at the right place at the right time. He broke more cases in his short career than most detectives do in their entire career. Maybe you have inherited the same ability. Why don't you leave what you have with me? I'll take a look at it and get back to you tomorrow. No one else has come up with anything, so it can't hurt to take a look."

Brett shook the captain's hand. As he headed toward the patrol car, it was hard to keep from smiling. He slid behind the wheel, tossing his hat on the passenger seat.

"Watch it, sonny. You almost hit my privates."

Brett jumped, banging his elbow on the steering wheel. "Damn it! Where have you been? You know I hate it when you just pop in and out."

Al chuckled. "Simmer down. I was staying out of the way until you had time to figure out what was going on. And I was right! I knew you would figure it out on your own."

"Why didn't you just tell me what was going on?"

Al grimaced. "It's one of the rules. I can't tell you things you should be able to figure out on your own. You don't know how hard it was for me to stay away. Sometimes I think God is challenging me by expecting me to follow the rules. I really don't think ghosts need rules, do you?"

Brett studied his companion, who seemed upbeat. "I agree. Who ever heard of ghosts having rules?"

Both of them laughed. Brett slowly left the police lot, noticing that Taylor sat in a nearby squad car, watching him. *Crap.* Here he was waving his hands and talking to Al. Taylor was obviously suspicious; Brett could tell by the way he was staring at him.

"Well, what are we going to do tonight?" Al rubbed his hands together. "Run that gun thing you call radar? Close down a meth lab?"

Brett checked the address on the paper beside him. "Nothing so exciting. We don't handle meth labs. There is a special team to do that. I do have a warrant for a guy I've busted several times. I plan on swinging by and catching him at home tonight. I've spoken to his wife on the phone, and she swears he's not there."

After a dinner break, they pulled up to a ranch-style home. The torn screen on the front door fluttered in the breeze. Brett walked to the door, careful not to trip over the various bicycles parts and dented beer cans that cluttered the yard. Using his flashlight, he rapped on the door. Hushed voices and the sound of scurrying feet came from inside. Finally, the door inched open. A woman glared out at them.

"What do you want? It's late and I don't appreciate you bothering me this late at night."

"Sorry Mrs. Black, but I have a warrant for your husband, Henry."

"Henry ain't here. I don't know where he is, and if I did, I sure in the hell wouldn't tell you." She took a puff on her cigarette and blew smoke toward him.

Brett tried not to smile. The woman's bony chin jutted upward, challenging him to say otherwise. He almost felt sorry for Henry. "I know he's in there. Why don't you tell him to come with me down to the jail? It will save him and me a lot of trouble."

She flicked the cigarette butt through the hole in the screen. "I've got nothing else to say."

Brett turned to leave and then paused. "I'll be stopping by later tonight to see if Henry showed up. We wouldn't want any lawbreakers lurking about the neighborhood, now would we?"

The woman screeched obscenities as he returned to the car. As they drove away, Al threw up his hands. "Is that it? Just go in there and grab the guy. There are way too many rights for criminals nowadays."

"No, that's not it. Just watch, and you might learn something about strategy."

Every hour they drove by the Black house and shined the spotlight on the house. At every half hour, Brett called the house and got the answering machine. "Henry, I know you're there. You're not going to get any sleep until you turn yourself in. So how about it?"

As dawn broke through the clouds, Brett made the last call of the night to Henry. Instead of the answering machine, Mrs. Black's screeching voice tore at his eardrum. "Damn it! I want to get some sleep. Henry is coming out. You take his sorry ass to jail and leave me alone."

A smile lit Brett's face as he pulled up to the house. Mrs. Black shoved her husband out the door. Henry struggled to keep his balance as he yanked up his pants. He ducked as his shoes sailed out onto the lawn.

Aware that Brett was watching him, Henry straightened and tucked his T-shirt into his pants. "Damn woman. Don't know why she's mad at me. *I* didn't keep her awake all night."

Brett sauntered toward Henry, his handcuffs dangling from his hand. Brett started to recite his rights, but Henry interrupted. "Yeah, yeah. I know my rights." Turning toward the house, he bellowed, "Can't wait to go to jail and get some peace and quiet. A place where there aren't any bitchy women!"

Brett chuckled as he assisted Henry into the car. With his prisoner secure, Brett hopped into the car whistling a merry tune. He hadn't felt this good in days.

Al sat with his arms folded across his chest. A wide grin was plastered on his lower face. "Sonny, you know how to get things done all right!" Al held up his hand. "How about a high five?"

Instinctively Brett slapped his palm against Al's. Feeling Henry's gaze on him, Brett lowered his voice. "How'd you know what a high five was?"

"Who knows? Probably on the thing you call a TV."

In the rearview mirror, Brett saw Henry shaking his head. Brett laughed out loud. Great! Another person who thought he was crazy.

CHAPTER SEVEN

As Brett was turning Henry over to the jailer in the booking room, a familiar, sultry voice caught his attention.

"Officer O'Shea. Can I have a moment?"

Brett neatly stepped away. A quick glance confirmed that she was as attractive as he remembered. Her blonde hair was twisted up in some kind of knot; it accentuated her long neck and determined jaw. She looked very professional in her navy suit and short skirt. He loved short skirts. He was a leg man. Her plump lips were pursed together, probably because she realized that he was trying to ignore her.

"Oh, come on. You could at least be friendly."

With barely a glance, he grunted, "Hello." With that, he proceeded down the hall, her footsteps echoing behind him. His pace quickened. *Shit! Can't the woman take a hint?*

A shrill screech brought him to a halt. He turned in time to see her leg fly up into the air and watch her land with a thud on the polished marble floor.

Her embarrassment quickly turned to fury when she saw his smiling face above her. Ignoring his hand, she struggled to her feet. "I don't think this is funny. I suppose you enjoy seeing people in pain, Officer O'Shea!" She ducked her head, brushing dust from her skirt. With flaming cheeks, she raged on. "I don't know why government buildings can't have carpet. These floors are a lawsuit waiting to happen."

"If you'd wear more sensible shoes, you wouldn't have slipped. How do you women even walk in those things? I bet the heels are at least four inches."

Glaring at him, Lisa snapped, "Apparently you do not understand the meaning of politically incorrect. For your information, we're in the twenty-first century and women have been liberated." Taking a breath, she paused. "You know what? Forget that I even said anything to you." She swung her purse over her shoulder and marched down the hallway.

Brett stood and watched her hips sway provocatively. The corners of his mouth turned upward. Maybe he should reconsider. He could have been more sociable. When she flashed one more scathing glance his way, his smile faded. No, it was better this way. She was definitely high maintenance. Besides that, he didn't need her poking around.

Brett checked in and headed home. He was mentally exhausted and needed some sleep.

He flipped on the hall light as the front door clicked shut behind him. It was quiet. He had forgotten what it was like to come home to a quiet house, with no ghost. Automatically, he switched on the television. He went to the kitchen and grabbed a beer before parking himself in front of the TV. How long would it be before Miller got back to him? Sometimes the brass could be so anal when it came to going through channels. Oh God! Was he beginning to think like Al? Nothing was sacred to Al. Suddenly the lever on the recliner jerked backward and his chair fell back several inches. Foaming beer dribbled down the front of his shirt.

Al stood over him, grinning from ear to ear.

"Damn it! Quit scaring me. You're worse than a five-year-old child."

Al plopped down on the sofa, resting his feet on the coffee table. "Me? You're the one always whining. By the way, who was the high stepper I saw you talking to at the jail?"

"No one."

"No one? By the way you were looking at her, I'd say she was someone."

Brett stripped off the wet shirt and tossed it to the floor. "She's a reporter. I think she suspects something. She's always asking questions about my great-grandfather's murder. I sure don't want her finding out about you. Not that anyone would believe me if I said I had a ghost living with me. My own mother doesn't believe me."

"You're a worrier. But we've got bigger problems than worrying about whether people find out about me. Have you heard back from Miller?"

Returning to an upright position, Brett shook his head. "I thought I would catch him tomorrow and see if he heard back from the chief."

"Good idea. Something is going happen soon. We can't afford to wait around for the next body to show up." Al stretched and adjusted his hat once again. "You look beat. Get some sleep, and I'll see you tomorrow." With that, his form shimmered and dissipated in the air.

Brett rose early the next day. After breakfast, he sat down and flipped through the channels on the television. He paused when he heard a familiar voice. Lisa Winslow. She was doing another segment on the police department. Why was he not surprised? This time she talked about the numerous upcoming retirements and how the department would be short staffed. Had she given up talking about Michael's murder? Her sparkling blue eyes seemed to be looking right at him. She looked especially attractive in a light-colored brown suit. She was wearing her hair down. She was a damn good-looking woman. After flicking off the TV, Brett tossed the remote aside. He needed to think about what he was going to say to Miller.

That afternoon, Brett waited outside of Captain Miller's office, jostling from one foot to the other. Finally the secretary nodded for him to go in. With his cap in hand, Brett sat down. Miller was only a few years older than his mother, but today he looked older. More haggard. The captain definitely appeared to be preoccupied. Miller's frown didn't bode well for his timing.

"Sir, have you reviewed the material I left with you?"

Miller assessed Brett before expelling a sigh. "I have. I admit that I really thought you had something. Unfortunately, the chief thought otherwise. I was told to shelve it."

"Are you saying that they aren't even going to look into it?" Brett leaned forward in the chair with his hands clasped tightly together.

"My hands are tied. I appreciate the effort you made, but we cannot afford to use our limited resources to go off on another investigative path." He held up his hand, cutting off Brett's reply. "Don't say it! It doesn't make any difference what you or I think. As long as the chief thinks it's a goose chase, then that is what it is."

Brett grabbed his hat and surged to his feet. "Understood. For the record, I tried to warn you and the chief. The next death is on your conscience, not mine."

Brett let the door slam behind him. His heart hammered in his chest. If the information had been any clearer, it would have jumped up and bitten them in the ass. Brett rushed outside into the fresh air and stopped. He ran his hand through his hair with his eyes squeezed shut.

"Damn it!" He shouldn't have exploded like that. Miller was a good family friend. Reality set in. It was the chief's decision, not Miller's. Brett owed the man an apology.

Taylor rubbed his chin. He had heard O'Shea's words as he left the captain's office. Why would O'Shea believe that there was going to be another death? Taylor knocked and walked into Miller's office.

"My answer hasn't changed, O'Shea," Miller warned without looking up from the pile of paperwork.

"Excuse me, Captain."

"Oh, it's you. How did you get past my secretary?"

"She was away from her desk. I happened to hear O'Shea say something about another death. Do you know how he came up with that information?"

Tossing down his pen, Miller stood. The muscle in his cheek twitched angrily. "Sergeant, I don't recall your presence in my office while I had a private conversation with Officer O'Shea. I suggest you not read anything into bits of conversation that you happen to overhear."

Taylor bit back a retort. Shrugging, he turned toward the door. "I only mentioned it since I am his immediate superior."

"Don't worry. I will tell you what you need to know. Was there anything else?"

Taylor shook his head and closed the door. He wasn't fooled. He knew what he had heard. O'Shea knew something. The chief would be interested in learning what he had heard. Miller was too close to the O'Shea family, and it affected his judgment. His gut told him that O'Shea was deeply involved in the murder.

CHAPTER EIGHT

Brett slumped over, resting his head against the steering wheel of the patrol car. How could he convince Captain Miller of what was about to happen? With his hands tied, Brett wasn't sure of how to proceed.

A draft of cool air brushed across the back of his neck. Sitting up, he saw Al smiling at him.

"Buck up! We're not beat yet."

"Please. There is nothing else I can do." Brett revved up the engine and pulled out of the lot.

Brett felt Al's stare. His chin jutted forward, daring the ghost to say anything else. Brett should have known by now that Al could not keep his mouth shut.

"Based on what you've told me about your great-grandfather, I don't think he would have given up. We can still work the case and get enough evidence that the chief will have to change his mind."

Brett shook his head, continuing to dart in and out of traffic. "You just don't get the big picture. I am not even assigned to work on the case. I'm a street cop, not a detective."

"Oh thee of little faith. How do you think I got here? It wasn't on my own power. For whatever reason, the guy above thinks that I can help you. So why don't you start thinking about how we can solve the case?"

A feeling of guilt engulfed him. Brett pulled into a McDonald's parking lot and shut off the engine. He sighed. "Okay, maybe you have a point." When Al's smile grew wider, Brett growled, "I said maybe."

Al slapped Brett on the shoulder. "I knew you would change your mind. Even if we don't have police support, we can still investigate on our own. We have a suspicion of where and when the man will strike next."

Brett's hope was fueled by Al's upbeat attitude. "I really don't have much of a choice, do I? I'm off tomorrow night. Let's start then."

The next morning, when his shift was over, Brett hurried home. He needed to get some sleep before he and Al started their investigation later that night.

The doorbell echoed throughout the house. Groaning, he clutched a pillow and pulled it over his head. Minutes later, the bell sounded again. He peeked at the clock. It was only 11:00 a.m. Who in the hell could be at his door? He had been asleep for only three hours. He jerked on his boxers and stomped toward the door. As he peered through the peephole, the last person in the world he expected to see was standing on the steps. *Lisa! What the hell did she want?* He turned to go back to bed. When the bell rang again, Brett's frustration level skyrocketed. He yanked open the door.

Lisa's mouth opened, but no words came out. Standing in his underwear, Brett glared at her. He glanced at his reflection in the glass doorway and saw that he had a case of bedhead. Tufts of brown hair stood on end. His brow rose as she smiled at him. His eyes narrowed. "What do you want?" He felt slightly uncomfortable as her eyes raked over his exposed chest. "Do you like what you see?" he leered.

"In your dreams, O'Shea."

Her smile quickly faded. It was replaced by a withering glare. Her mean look didn't detract from the fact that she was beautiful. A fact that he had pointedly ignored.

"Fine. If you don't want anything I'm going back to bed." He began closing the door.

"I thought maybe ..."

Brett folded his arms across his chest. Shit! Couldn't the woman take a hint?

"You thought what?"

"If you'd let me finish, I would tell you. It would be easier if we could sit down rather than standing here in the doorway. Besides, maybe you would like to get dressed."

"Why? We don't have anything to talk about. If this is about police business, call the station."

Brushing past him, Lisa strolled into the living room. The scent of her perfume wafted past him. She shoved aside some empty beer cans and laid her cell phone on the table. She then sat down on the sofa and adjusted her skirt as she looked at him. "I'm starting the recording now. Are you ready?"

Brett growled, "Does it look like I'm ready?"

"Really, Officer." She flashed him a sly smile. "Now, since you were the first officer at the crime scene, can you tell me if there is a lead on the recent murder?"

Brett sat on the other end of the sofa and stared at her crossed legs. Short skirts had always been his weakness. "What?"

She flashed a coy smile. "I can help in the investigation, if you'd let me. The TV station won't air anything until the police give them the green light."

Brett knew that Miller hadn't said anything, so who could have leaked the info? "I don't know what you're talking about. Like I said, call the station. You need to leave. I need my beauty rest."

"Hmmph." Lisa scooted closer to Brett on the sofa. She tossed her head, flipping her hair over her shoulder.

Brett choked as Al appeared behind Lisa. Al peered over Lisa's shoulder, staring at her curvy legs, and winked. "I told you she liked you."

Pretending to cough, Brett covered his mouth with his hand. "You're crazy."

Lisa's hurt gaze met Brett's. "You don't have to be rude," she snapped.

"Not you, I'm talking to ... Never mind." Flustered, Brett jumped up and paced the floor. It was hard to ignore Al as he ogled Lisa. Brett had to get rid of Lisa before Al did or said something else.

Instead of leaving, she leaned back and looked about the room. His leg began twitching. Why should he be worried? She couldn't see Al.

Shivering, Lisa rubbed her arms. "It seems chilly all of a sudden."

"Really? Doesn't seem that way to me." Brett turned, trying to keep an eye on Al, who now sat only inches from Lisa.

"Why are you acting so nervous? Even though I'm a reporter, you can trust me. I have lots of connections that may be useful."

Brett sighed out of relief that she couldn't see Al. "No thanks. I don't want to be rude, but I'm going back to bed. You can stay and talk to yourself if you want. Your call."

She grabbed her phone and stuck it in her bag. "You're running away, O'Shea. In my job, people who run away have something to hide. I warn you that I excel at ferreting out secrets." Rising, she smoothed the wrinkles from her skirt and adjusted her leather jacket before heading to the door. She flashed an inviting smile as she closed it behind her.

Brett let out a deep sigh before dropping to the sofa. His heart pounded. He turned to Al, who sat next to him. "Satisfied?"

Al's smile faded. "What? I didn't do anything."

"Shit! You're lucky that she can't see you. I don't think we need any complications in our plan, do you?"

"You really need to learn to relax, sonny. She is quite a looker. How come you're not interested?"

Scratching his head, Brett headed down the hall. "None of your business. Now go where ever you go, so I can get some sleep."

Instead of driving back to work, Lisa gave in to her instincts. She walked down the street before cutting back through the neighbors' yards. She skulked along the side of Brett's house, peeping in each window. Normally she didn't resort to this type of illegal behavior, but under these circumstances she would do whatever was necessary. She hoped that she could sway Brett into not pressing charges if he caught her.

Having spotted a side window, she crawled through the flower bed, crunching dried stems and flowers as she inched along on her hands and knees. She finally reached the side of the house and the window. She grinned. Brett still sat on the sofa with his boxers on.

She glanced around the room. He was carrying on an animated conversation with someone. Lisa leaned even closer. She heard a rip and glanced at her leg. A branch from a rosebush had attached itself to her tights. *Damn.* She tugged on the offending limb, causing a thorn to cut her palm. *Geez!* she thought. *This should qualify for hazardous duty.* Pressing her ear against the glass, she could faintly hear a few words. One word was quite clear: "plan." Brett waved his arms and shouted angrily before disappearing down the hallway. A scan of the room revealed that no one had been in there except Brett. She looked again. *He had to be talking to someone!* She turned and ran back to her car. Officer O'Shea definitely needed watching.

Al stood on the front porch and watched the woman reporter pull away in her car. He had seen her peering in the window. He'd bitten the inside of his mouth to keep from laughing aloud. He didn't want to stir up a hornet's nest, so he didn't tell Brett. The girl had spunk. He liked that. The short skirts and knee boots would take some getting used to, but Miss Lisa looked out of this world.

Rubbing his eyes, Al took a deep breath. If only he could remember what his life was like before he died. At times, he raged about his lack of memory. When that happened, someone above always seemed to rattle his brains to remind him of his purpose with his assignment. A hot wind gusted around him, picking up a pile of dry leaves. The leaves became stuck to his body, filling his mouth and covering his eyes. His hat fell to the ground. Unable to see, he stepped to the side, flattening the hat to the sidewalk. Growling, Al spit pieces of leaves and twigs out of his mouth. "Okay! I get it, I get it." The wind disappeared, leaving Al as frustrated as ever. He picked up his hat and punched the crown, attempting to push it back into shape. Flakes of broken leaves fell to the ground.

"Can't lose my favorite hat," he mumbled to himself. He didn't know why it was important, but it was.

A lone ray of sunshine broke through the autumn clouds, creating a spotlight on Al. Glancing up to the sky, Al straightened. "That doesn't make me feel any better, you know."

CHAPTER NINE

B rett flipped the TV on as he dressed. There was Lisa Winslow, doing a live shot outside the police department. She updated the public on the latest break-in victim. The way she looked at the camera, it was as if she were talking directly to him. With a smile, she reminded the audience of the unsolved break-ins and murder from 1933 and how the city lost one of their own, Mike O'Shea, many decades ago.

Gripping his shoelaces, he pulled them tight. He planned to run this morning. Al materialized next to him.

"What's up, dude?"

Brett cocked his head and stared at his ghost. "*Dude?* What are you doing?"

"Trying to fit in. Your generation speaks a different language. I don't understand half of what is said."

"Hmm. Just be yourself. You creep me out when you talk like I do."

"Whatever, sonny."

Brett shook his head. "Stay here. I'll be back in an hour."

Brett glanced back one time before leaving the house. Al was holding the TV remote and flicking through the channels.

Brett stood in the front yard, doing his warm-up exercises. He caught sight of a motorcycle parked in front of his house. The rider was talking on a cell phone.

Brett switched on his iPod and took off on his five-mile run. He loved running. It was a chance to meditate. When he was almost home, he slowed to a walk on the final block to cool down. The motorcycle was still parked in front of his house. Brett didn't recognize the rider as any of his neighbors. *Probably a boyfriend of the high school girl next door,* he thought. As Brett cut across his yard, he hesitated for a brief moment, staring at the cyclist. The rider was unremarkable except for the red skull emblem on the side of the helmet. It was a garish design.

Brett opened the front door and was greeted by the sight of a sprawled out ghost on the sofa. His hat was pulled down to cover his face. Soft snores echoed about the room. Brett couldn't resist and tossed his empty water bottle at Al.

Al jumped to his feet as the bottle hit him in the stomach. "What the hell!"

"Hey, my vacation time starts today. As soon as I shower, let's figure out our plan for tonight." Brett kicked off his shoes and headed to the bedroom.

Rubbing his stomach, Al walked to the window. "Hey, who's the motorcyclist outside the house?"

"Never saw him before. The neighbor girl is probably dating him," called Brett from the other room.

"He's giving me the heebie-jeebies. He's just staring at your house."

Brett joined Al at the window in time to see the cyclist drive away.

"It's probably my imagination, but the way he stared at the window, it was as if he could see me standing here watching him. It gave me the creeps! Are you sure you've never seen him before?" Al asked.

Brett shook his head. "Yes, I'm sure. You seem a little obsessed about the guy. Why?"

"Just curious. He seemed quite fixated on your house."

Brett shrugged. "I'll ask the neighbors if you're so curious."

After lunch, they sat down with Brett's papers that he had shared with Captain Miller spread out on the table. Brett leaned back in the chair, balancing on the back legs. With his arms folded behind his head, Brett closed his eyes. "Now that the chief has shelved my idea, Captain Miller isn't really able to help us. What exactly do you have in mind?"

Al smiled. "Here is what we're up against. You did a good job of identifying a time line. We lost a week waiting for Miller to get back to you. Now we're down to two weeks until the next murder."

"What if we're wrong on the date? I was estimating those dates based on what happened in the thirties."

Al tapped the time line with his finger. "Don't be second-guessing yourself. Your information is solid. So far, the break-ins and attacks have occurred on the eastside. Just as you discovered, that's what happened in the nineteen thirties. The homeowners targeted so far are wealthy or notable figures in local government. All we have to do is identify who is rich or influential and lives on the east side."

The front legs of Brett's chair hit the floor with a thud. "The east side is mostly a blue-collar area. Back in the early part of the twentieth century, there were lots of influential people living on the east side. Now most of the movers and shakers live south of Grand or in West Des Moines. Some people joke about the east side and the number of junk cars found in the front yards of homes."

"Blue collar doesn't mean lazy or poor. From what I've seen, there are a lot of honest, hardworking folks there," Al lectured.

Brett raised his hands in mock surrender. "Okay, okay. I'm sorry I said anything. We can't escape the fact that the east side is a working-class neighborhood. Why would a madman target that part of the city?"

"I don't know, but we need to accept the facts. We will patrol the area ourselves, focusing on the area around York Street. It will be a start."

Twilight was fast approaching. Brett grabbed his gun. He slipped on a jacket, and he and Al began driving in their search for the unknown: unknown killer, unknown motive, and unknown target.

They covered over a hundred miles that night. Much of their time was spent near York Street, searching for anything out of the ordinary. Near dawn, Brett yawned and rubbed his eyes.

"I don't know about you, but I think tonight is a bust. We haven't seen anything, and I'm beat."

After they arrived home, Al did his disappearing act as Brett headed to bed.

This became the pattern for the next ten days. Brett questioned his original theories and his faith in Al. After all, how could a ghost help solve an ongoing case? There had not been any further attacks. Maybe the threat was gone. Everything would be normal again.

His time off work flew by with no results. In a way, Brett was glad to be back to a normal routine.

"Officer O'Shea, wait up." Lisa Winslow came hurrying down the hallway.

Brett's shoulders slumped forward. Pasting on a smile, he turned. Her cashmere sweater clung in all the right places. He forced his gaze up to her face.

"I haven't seen you around the station lately. Been on vacation?" she smilingly asked.

"Yeah, I was." He turned and started walking.

Her heels clicked on the marble floor, indicating that she was following him. "What's wrong? You're acting kind of pissy about something."

Brett turned his face to rein in his anger. "Pissy?"

She placed her free hand on her chest, looking somewhat bewildered. "Well, I don't know how else to describe it. Can't you stop so we can talk?"

"Talk? I think you do enough talking for everyone. What is your problem? You seemed obsessed with reporting my great-grandfather's death. Every year since you started working here, you've done a story on his murder. Why? What is it to you?"

Her cheeks flushed red. She had the decency to take a step back, as if she wanted to retreat. "I thought you would appreciate the fact that I honor your grandfather by doing the story. Even I know that he was a legend."

"Did you ever stop to think that the family doesn't want to be reminded?" With his eyes narrowed, he leaned toward her, his fury uncontainable. "I am trying to live my own life. I don't want to be compared to him. He and I are nothing alike. He was suspended several times, and the last time I checked, I have never been suspended. He picketed in front of the station during one suspension. I am the exact opposite of him. I follow the rules. He didn't. Your stories only encourage other officers to compare the two of us."

Her shoulders sagged. "I'm so sorry. I didn't mean to hurt you. I read all the old stories about Mike. He was quite a character. I really admire him."

"Admire him? Didn't you hear anything I just said?" he bellowed.

"Yes, admire him! The man had principles!"

Tossing his hands in the air, Brett marched away, ignoring the stares from fellow officers. He stopped at his locker and jammed his tablet into a backpack. The metal door clanged as he slammed it shut. He slid into a chair as roll call began. Sergeant Taylor barely glanced at him. *At least something is going right*, he thought. He was the first out of the room. He slid into the front seat of the squad car, and his tires squealed as he pulled onto the street.

A whiff of pipe tobacco filled the car. He turned to see Al sitting next to him. The infamous hat was pulled even lower tonight than it normally was. Brett could barely see the lower part of his face. They drove along for several miles.

Not wanting to take his anger toward Lisa out on Al, Brett cleared his throat. "You're quiet tonight."

"Hmm. Maybe I don't feel like talking." Al turned to look out the window.

Brett broke out laughing. "Since when?"

In a low voice, barely audible, Al answered, "I was at the station tonight when you were talking to the woman reporter."

"Don't remind me. She can be a bitch."

Al leaned over and punched Brett in the shoulder. "Watch your mouth, sonny. Actually, I kind of like her. She seems somewhat impressed with your great-grandfather who was murdered years ago."

Brett gripped the wheel tighter. "She doesn't know what she's talking about."

"I wouldn't say that. I've read all the articles you have lying around the house. He was a one-of-a-kind. That doesn't make him bad or wrong."

Surprised, Brett looked at Al, who was staring straight ahead. "She is romanticizing a dead cop—someone she never knew or understood."

Al turned to Brett. "And you knew Mike O'Shea, did ya? It doesn't seem to me that you understand him at all. Have you thought about how times were different eighty years ago?" Al slowly shook his head. "You are embarrassed by what he did decades ago?"

Brett squirmed in the seat. He was glad it was dark; Al wouldn't see the flush of heat on his face. "Hell, I don't know if 'embarrassed' is the right word. If someone breaks the rules and gets suspended, then he got what he deserved. I believe he was a good detective, but who knows why he was always up against the brass."

"Would it make any difference?" Al turned away, his head tucked to his chest.

Brett thought about Al's question. "Honestly, I don't know."

Al reached up to pull his hat forward. "Well, I guess we'll never know why he did certain things."

Brett glanced over at Al. For some reason, Brett felt like a teenager who had been reprimanded. Brett tapped the steering wheel, trying to think of something to say to break the uncomfortable silence.

"So, have you been able to remember anything about your life? I was wondering what career you had before you became a ghost."

Al didn't glance his way. In fact, he had the nerve to turn and look out the window. Okay, this was awkward. Brett sighed.

Forcing a lighter tone of voice, Brett suggested, "I'll call Lisa later and apologize. I probably overreacted a bit."

Al continued to ignore him. *Shit!* Brett squirmed in the seat. He wanted to reach over and throttle Al. He made a mistake. With a growling stomach, Brett pulled into the diner parking lot.

"I'll be right back. I wish I could bring you something." He strolled into the restaurant. It was going to be a long night. A really long night!

Minutes later Brett returned with a sack full of burgers, fries, and a large chocolate shake. As he slurped the shake, Al started laughing. Brett took a bite from the bacon burger and muttered, "What?"

Al flashed a big smile. "Nothing. You remind me of a time when I was young. I could eat like you did and never gain a pound."

Brett felt relieved. Al's mood had improved.

"See! There is something that you remember."

Al shrugged. "It's about the only thing that I remember," he growled.

After eating, they resumed driving around the east side. The pink-tinged sky in the predawn hours signaled that his shift was almost over. On the way back to the station, Brett impulsively turned down York Street. The turn-of-the-century homes sat far back from the street. While many of the homes had been restored over the past two decades, there were still several that looked dilapidated. He would love to live in a big house like them someday, but he'd never live on York Street.

Al's curt voice snapped Brett out of his reverie. "Turn off your lights now!"

Brett immediately hit the brakes and cut the headlights. A couple of hundred feet ahead, a motorcycle was parked along the curb. It had not been there a couple of hours ago when they drove by.

Brett radioed in his location and indicated that an attempted burglary was in process. He pulled out his Glock. Staying close to the trees and bushes near the houses, Brett advanced to the house where the motorcycle was parked. A quick glance down the driveway revealed a lone dark figure standing by the doorway with a tire iron in his hand.

Brett stepped out from the shadows and yelled, "Police! Drop your weapon and put up your hands!"

The man turned to face Brett. Brett couldn't make out any features, as the man was wearing a dark helmet. He appeared to be around six feet and slender. Brett could see the tire iron still held in his hand.

"Drop the iron now!"

The clang of the metal hitting the driveway rang in the air. Brett moved closer. "Hands against the wall. Spread your feet apart."

The suspect stiffened and crouched. He instantly lunged at Brett, grabbing his hand that held the gun. A shot rang out inches from Brett's head. With his ear ringing, Brett slammed his free hand into the stomach of the other man. As they struggled, the gun fell to the cement. When the man reached for the gun, Brett kicked it out of reach and quickly wrapped an arm around the man's neck. He continued to apply pressure until the man's body slumped forward. Taking a breath, Brett loosened his grip.

In that moment, the man's fist whipped back and made contact with Brett's forehead. Brett fought the blackness that threatened to overwhelm him. Sweat dotted his brow, and his stomach threatened to heave up the remains of his supper. Afraid he was going to pass out, Brett locked his arms around the man's waist. If he was going down, then so was this guy.

Lights from inside the home brightened the driveway. Al wanted to help but could only stand helplessly aside and watch. Brett's eyes fluttered shut as blood ran down his nose. He had to do something. Al picked up a rock and heaved it through a nearby window. Amazingly, the glass broke. A woman screamed. Al heard voices from inside.

As Brett lost consciousness, the man crawled out from under his body. Appearing dazed, he stood and looked around. The sound of distant sirens filled the silence. When the man passed by Al, he hesitated, looking straight in Al's direction. It was as if he sensed something. Al raged when he saw the red skull emblem on the side of the helmet. This was the man that he had seen in front of Brett's home only days before. The man quickly mounted the cycle and tore down the street as the red lights from several squad cars lit up the neighborhood.

Detectives, officers, and medics soon filled the yard. Brett was sitting on the ground and did not appear to have any serious injuries.

Al leaned over Brett's shoulder. "How are you doing?"

Brett rubbed his lowered head. He covered his mouth with his hand. "Splitting headache. Taylor will want to interview me soon. They'll take me to the hospital since I lost consciousness.

"Got it. At least the guy didn't get inside the house. The residents are an elderly physician and his wife."

"Thank God they weren't hurt."

Al glanced up. "Heads up. Here comes your favorite reporter."

The homeowners walked across the yard to shake Brett's hand. The woman hugged him tightly. Al felt a strange emotion build in his chest as he watched Brett. Brett had done a brave thing.

As Brett hugged the woman, the camera crew crouched off to the side so they could get the shot. Al looked around the crowded yard. Sure enough, there was Lisa, interviewing the husband. *Uh oh!*

As he had predicted, Brett walked by Lisa without a word. He hopped into the ambulance and lay back on the stretcher as the technician checked his vitals. Al popped into the ambulance, watching the activity. His eyes widened. He didn't recognize hardly any of the devices being used by the person checking out Brett. He reached out to touch some type of cuff with a rubber tube attached and knew that it looked familiar. It was something to check blood pressure. He wasn't sure how he knew.

He jerked when Brett loudly cleared his throat. Brett was shaking his head, looking like he wanted Al to leave. Al sighed.

As the ambulance doors were closed, Al waved to Brett. "I'll catch up with you."

Al materialized next to Lisa and pulled out his pipe. He could think better with it. Even though it appeared that Brett didn't care for Lisa, Al wanted to learn more about her.

She stood in the shadows, watching the ambulance pull away. She bit her lip, obviously thinking about something. She pulled the collar of her coat up around her face, shivering from the cool air. Looking anxious, she glanced around the yard. Her crew and the officers stood nearby.

Al moved closer. She raised her head and sniffed the air. *Can she smell the smoke from my pipe?* Al moved to stand in front of her. She tensed and moved to stand by the crew as they packed up the cameras. Interesting.

Al followed Lisa. He wished he could talk to her. He did like her. The fact that she approved of Mike O'Shea was a bonus. She had wife potential. Too bad Brett couldn't see that.

Brett lay in the emergency room, waiting to be released. He was growing more anxious by the minute. He couldn't wait to talk to Al to see what he had learned. The door to his room slowly opened. Brett's body tensed as he reached for his weapon. Captain Miller and

Sergeant Taylor entered the room. Brett released his breath. Miller walked to his bedside, placing a hand on his shoulder.

"O'Shea, it's good to see that you don't have any serious injuries. How are you feeling?"

"Pretty good for having been jabbed in the face."

"Good. If it's all right with you, I'd like to hear from you about what happened tonight."

Sergeant Taylor's lip curled as he stepped forward. "What happened, O'Shea?"

"I'll handle this, Sergeant," Miller said in rebuke.

Brett glanced between the two men, catching the twinkle in Miller's eyes. "We were … I mean, I was heading back to the station when I turned down York. I wanted to make one more drive by because of all the recent trouble there. I saw a parked motorcycle in front of a house that wasn't there when I drove by a few hours before. I called in for backup before approaching the house. I spotted the suspect trying to gain entry into the house. As I identified myself, I yelled out and ordered him to drop the weapon in his hand. He was holding a tire iron. He dropped it, and I ordered him against the wall so I could cuff him. He lunged, and we struggled. Somehow he got a hand free and punched me in the face. I must have blacked out. When I came to, the suspect was gone."

Taylor folded his arms across his chest and stared at Brett. "Did you have someone riding with you?"

"No." Brett met Taylor's stare.

"Why did you say 'We were heading back to the station' and then changed it to only you?"

Brett cursed his carelessness. How stupid. Laughing, he touched the huge lump on his head. "I got hit in the head and passed out. Sorry, the words just didn't come out right."

Miller glanced at Taylor, his gruff voice filling the room. "Don't worry, O'Shea. We understand. Submit your report, then go home. I want you to take tomorrow off and rest up." Miller patted Brett on the back. "Great police work tonight. You were on your game and prevented a crime. I'm proud of you, and I'm sure your grandmother would be too."

Brett shook hands with the captain. "Thanks, sir. I appreciate your support."

"You're a good officer, O'Shea. Don't ever forget it. C'mon, Taylor, let's get out of here so O'Shea can go home."

Brett watched the men leave. Taylor turned and glared at Brett, who caught the silent threat. With the room empty of visitors, he could finish dressing and get out of here.

After stopping at the grocery store for Tylenol and frozen dinners, Brett hurried home and collapsed on the sofa with an ice pack. With one arm folded over his brow, his eyes closed and he easily drifted off to sleep. When he woke in late afternoon, his head still pounded from the punch to the face. As Brett turned toward the window, he noticed it was getting dark. He had slept all day. He rubbed his hands through his matted hair. He needed a shower. Stretching, he went to the kitchen for a drink of water. After showering, he grabbed a T-shirt and jogging shorts and came back to the sofa to turn on the television.

Brett glanced outside to see the twilight sky streaked with red and gold. He sighed. He was restless and had no idea what he was going to do tonight. His poker buddies called. There was a game that night. But since he was on medical leave, he passed. He really wanted to be on the streets to find the punk that slugged him.

When his stomach growled, he decided to order a pizza and bread sticks. While lying back waiting for supper, the sound of a motorcycle caught his attention.

Brett jumped to his feet and rushed to the front window. A lone cyclist sat in front of house. The rider, clad in solid black leather, appeared to be staring at him. When the man turned his head slightly, Brett spotted the skull on the side of the helmet. Intuition told him that this was the suspect from the previous night. But why was he here? How did the man know who he was and where he lived?

Frozen with curiosity, Brett watched as the rider raised his arm, making his fingers into the shape of a gun. The man pointed at the window where Brett stood. *Shit!* His heart pounding, Brett turned to grab his gun and cell phone. By the time he returned to the window, the rider had disappeared.

"I knew it!" Al bellowed.

Brett nearly dropped his gun. "Crap! Quit creeping up on me. What do you mean you knew it?"

"I saw that guy in front of your house almost every day for the past week. I wondered why he was watching the house."

"You could have said something earlier, you know."

The doorbell rang, interrupting their conversation. The pizza delivery boy shoved the boxes into Brett's arms, bopping to the music coming from his iPod. After paying for dinner, Brett went to the kitchen with Al following close behind.

With his thoughts racing, Brett absently chewed the lukewarm pizza.

Al's fingers thumped against the table. "Well, what are we going to do?"

Brett shoved the half-eaten pizza to the middle of the table. "I'm trying to figure out who that guy is. Why is he watching my house?" He lowered his head to the table, his arms folded over. "What am I missing? Shit."

Al glanced over his shoulder. "This may be bigger than the both of us. Something is at play here. I think we need to hit the streets tonight and find the guy. Maybe he can give us some answers."

Brett raised his head, staring at Al. "Are you fricking serious? I'm on medical leave. How will it look if I'm involved in something tonight? I already have Taylor breathing down my neck."

Al kicked back the chair and stood over Brett. His usually pale complexion was even whiter than normal. "How could it be any plainer? It's a sign, a connection. Do you need an invitation?"

Brett slammed his fist on the table. "What do you want from me? You've turned my life upside down. I'm involved in all kinds of stupid shit. I don't even know what I'm doing anymore. Why is this happening?"

Al reached up to place a hand on each side of Brett's face. "Listen very carefully. We need to think about what happens next. The cyclist is a link, a clue to what is going on. You and I need to solve this case."

Brett closed his eyes. He knew what he should do. His life was unraveling, and he couldn't stop it. A broken sob escaped from him. Could he ignore years of training? Years of following the rules? Was it more important to solve the mystery of his great-grandfather's murder or to become a detective? Minutes passed. The coolness of Al's hands slowed Brett's ragged breathing. Peace filled his mind.

Stepping back, Brett opened his eyes and reluctantly smiled. "Okay. Let's find our cyclist."

CHAPTER TEN

Richard quietly lowered the garage door, hiding the motorcycle from view. Glancing over his shoulder, he looked around, making sure none of the neighbors were watching him. Seeing nothing suspicious, he opened the door and quickly slipped inside. The house sat at on a dead-end street. He had carefully picked this location. Most of the neighbors were elderly, meaning they stayed indoors and went to bed very early. Traffic was almost nonexistent in the neighborhood. No one monitored his comings and goings.

He opened the fridge and grabbed a beer. Tossing the cap in the sink, he slumped in the recliner. His head throbbed. He saw his medicine sitting on the table. His head didn't hurt when he listened to the voice. He wasn't sure what to do now. Maybe he should take his meds. His doctor was always harping that he had to take his meds. What would the voice want him to do? His hands twisted together. One leg twitched nonstop. It was as if it weren't part of his body.

Nervously, he glanced about the empty room. He needed something to take away the splitting pain. He whimpered as the pounding in his head increased. He begged aloud, "Please come back. I need you to help me." He slid from the chair and collapsed on the floor in a motionless heap.

Hours later, Richard woke on the cold linoleum. He rose, dusted off his clothes, and smiled. The answer to his problem had come in his dream. Officer O'Shea needed to be taught a lesson. A serious lesson. Grabbing his jacket and tools, he went to his garage.

Minutes later, Richard roared down the dimly lit street on his motorcycle. Light glistened on his black helmet. Bent over the handlebars, he stared ahead. His headache had gone away. The voice had provided a plan. He had to follow the plan; make the voice happy. Otherwise, the voice would leave and he would have nothing—nothing but sickness.

He weaved in and out of traffic, seeing nothing. He was intent upon pleasing the voice so he would feel better. All he had to do was follow instructions and all his troubles would be over.

He slowly turned down York Street. It was the dead of night. A lonely owl sat watching him from a barren tree as he cut his engine and pushed the bike behind a shrub. The owl tilted his head as if trying to figure out what he was doing. Richard hissed and flapped his arms. Unease coursed through him. He didn't like the way the owl was staring at him.

A sharp pain tore through his head. Bent over from the pain, Richard whimpered. "Please stop. I'm doing what you want." His soft cries ended several minutes later when the pain diminished.

Determined to complete the plan, Richard crouched near the cop's house. Dressed from head to toe in black, he blended with the dark of the night. Pressing against the outside wall of the house, he waited and listened. Nothing. With a slight smile, he lifted a small crowbar. The handle of the door cracked and gave way. The door edged open. Richard peered around the door into the darkened kitchen. The smell of baked cookies filled the air. He paused. His mother used to bake cookies for him when he was young. He had always liked coming home from elementary school and enjoying warm cookies and milk with his mom. He growled. No use thinking about the past. Nothing could bring her back. She was dead. She had left him, just like everyone he had ever known or cared about.

The darkened hallway stood in front of him. The bedrooms were only feet away. His footsteps were silenced by the plush carpet beneath his feet. Slumberous snores came from the master bedroom. Using his foot, he edged the door open and stood watching the sleeping couple.

The bedroom reminded him of his grandmother's. Lace curtains fluttered above the furnace registers. Slender Victorian lamps graced nightstands by the bed. A large dresser was adorned with numerous pictures of family members.

The woman lay closest to the door. Richard crouched down near the floor and pulled a knife from his jacket pocket. He inched toward the sleeping woman. Her glasses sat on the nightstand. Tiny wrinkles surrounded her eyes. Tufts of her hair stood on end. She didn't look really old. Maybe in her sixties? Richard leaned closer to study her face. The faint scent of roses filled his nose. His mother had smelled like roses. A frown marred his brow. He wondered if she was a good mother to her children. Did she hug and kiss them every day? Tell them that she loved them? Bake them special birthday cakes? His hand shook as raised the blade toward her neck.

A tear rolled down his cheek. He blinked and rubbed the offensive tears from his eyes. There was no time for emotion. He had a job to perform. He opened his eyes and saw the woman staring at him.

She was fully awake and opened her mouth to scream. Richard dropped the knife and quickly picked up the crowbar. He raised it above him and brought it down on her head. Her body slumped toward him, falling to the floor.

Her husband mumbled something as he rolled over. His hand reached out to find his wife. Finding the bed empty, he opened one eye and he saw Richard standing there. Suddenly alert, the man scrambled to the other side of the bed, trying to reach his revolver that lay on the nightstand.

Richard jumped on the bed and swung the crowbar at the man's head. Fighting to remain conscious in the wake of the blow, he called out, "Joan, Joan, are you okay? Answer me!" His head dropped back on the pillow.

"Whew! You almost had me, Captain Miller. I'll be taking that gun of yours."

Richard quickly cut the sheet into strips and tied the Millers' hands to the bed frame. He glanced in the mirror, smiling as he stared at himself. He wet his finger, wiping the blood spatter from his cheek. His hair fell about his gaunt face. His sapphire eyes glittered dangerously, twitching with excitement. He sighed, remembering that he must pace himself. After the first strike, it was hard to think about the plan. His pulse increased as adrenaline raced through his body. He could barely keep still. The excitement of the kill was better than any high. He paced the room, waiting for man to come to.

Miller moaned as he opened his eyes. "What do you want? I don't have much money in the house, but in the bottom drawer there is a cash box with a few hundred. Take it all." He pulled on the restraints.

"Oh, don't worry, I will take the cash box. Now let's get down to business." Richard smiled, tapping the knife against his thigh. Miller kicked out, trying to injure him.

"Tsk, tsk," Richard admonished. "We can't have you escaping." Richard plunged the knife deep into Miller's leg. Blood squirted across the bed. A scream rent the air. "Well look at that. I think I hit a major blood vessel. Damn, I can't have you dying too soon."

Richard jumped up on the bed, towering over Miller. He jumped a couple of times to see if he could touch the ceiling. A chuckle escaped him as he bounced down on his victim's leg.

"God, help me. Please, have mercy," Miller wailed. He was close to going under again.

Richard gripped Miller's chin and twisted his face toward him. "You shouldn't ask God for mercy. You need to ask me." Richard slammed a fist into the man's face. *That felt so good*, he thought.

"Who are you?"

"You won't need to know my name where you're going. You and your wife are nothing but a piece in a puzzle. I've been chosen to carry out the mission."

Miller sobbed, "You're crazy. I can help you, get you anything you want. I have money. I'm a police officer. I can help you get away. Just let me live. Please!"

Richard straddled the man, pressing the tip of the blade to his neck. "Please? Why should I let you live? I have everything I need. Everything! The voice gave me the power. Me! I can do anything. No police can stop me. No one can stop me. I'm invincible!"

Fear widened the man's eyes as the blade cut into his skin. Deeper the blade plunged, twisting as it cut through his neck. Blood pulsed out from the cut. The light slowly dimmed from the man's eyes as dark liquid spread across the bed.

Richard didn't know how long he sat on the man as his life drained away. He moaned, leaning back to stare at the ceiling. He watched the man's soul float above him, studying him. Each time it was the same. The image disappeared and he was filled with power and elation. He had completed the mission. O'Shea would regret disrupting his mission the other night. He couldn't have any more screw-ups. The voice might go away and he'd be left incapacitated.

He reached down, smoothing the man's hair back. A wry grin lit his face. They seemed to be a nice couple. They would be grateful to know that their death had meaning. He had no regret, no doubts.

Darkness gave way to morning. He yanked out the drawer and grabbed the cash, stuffing it into his pocket. He picked up his helmet from the kitchen table. Spotting a cookie jar on the counter, he peered inside. Sure enough, it was full of fresh chocolate cookies. He grabbed a handful, munching as the door latched behind him. It had been a good night.

CHAPTER ELEVEN

After deciding that they needed to trap the cyclist, Brett and Al spent several hours debating and arguing about what they should do. Brett grabbed extra ammunition as they loaded the car. Al believed that the cyclist was linked to the earlier robberies and maybe the murder. Brett couldn't wait to confront the cyclist and find out why he was watching his house.

"Let's get over to York Street," Al barked. "Something is happening. Hurry!"

Brett pressed the accelerator down. As they started to make the turn down York Street, a lone motorcyclist roared toward the stop sign. When he neared the cyclist, Brett stopped the car. Only the sound of purring engines broke the silence. Brett reached for his pistol.

"Pull over, now!" Brett yelled, jerking his gun up. He trained his gun on the cyclist.

Al's gruff voice hissed in his ear, "Shoot him!"

Brett ignored Al, never taking his eyes off the helmeted man. The man made no move to turn off the cycle. There was no doubt that he was going to make a run for it. Brett put the car in park and carefully opened the door, his aim never wavering.

The cyclist watched him approach. The man's hand tightened on the throttle.

"I said pull it over. Turn it off now! I'm not asking again." Brett tensed.

The cyclist gunned the engine. A muffled voice responded, "Officer O'Shea, what a surprise."

"Who are you?"

The man shook his finger at Brett. "No, no. You will find out soon enough. How did you know I'd be here tonight?"

Brett shrugged, keeping his gun trained on the cyclist. "Can't say. Let's just say that I have a secret weapon. Why have you been sitting outside my house?"

The man shook his head. "Why would I sit in front of your house? I will admit that I'm having fun trying to figure you out. Your secret weapon isn't working too well, is it?"

Brett pulled out the handcuffs. "You're under arrest. Shut it off."

Brett saw Al walk around the car toward the cyclist. Al studied the cyclist as he walked around the bike. He reached out to wipe something off the man's jacket. His finger came away with blood on it. Al held up his finger for Brett to see.

The cyclist shivered when Al touched him. He turned as if he had felt Al touch him.

With his cuffs in hand, Brett edged toward the cyclist. Suddenly the cyclist kicked out his leg, narrowly missing Brett's stomach. Brett jumped back to avoid being hit and was thrown off balance.

The cyclist turned the throttle, and the cycle roared down the street. The rider glanced back at Brett and flipped him off. Brett ran back to his car. Looking at Al, he yelled, "Get in."

"Never mind him. We need to go down the street." Al pointed to the destination.

Torn with indecision, Brett yelled, "Fuck! Fine. I hope you know what you're doing."

Al shimmered and appeared in the front seat next to Brett. Brett drove slowly down the street, looking for anything out of the ordinary. Just when he wondered if they were on another wild goose chase, Brett saw a light shining from Captain Miller's kitchen window. He slammed on the brakes.

Brett stared at the Miller house. "Looks like the captain is up early today."

Al leaned his head back against the headrest and closed his eyes. "I don't think that's it."

Fear gripped his heart. His stomach rolled with nausea. "I'll call it in."

Al got out of the car and walked toward the back door, looking like he knew where to go. Brett followed as quickly as he could. They saw that the lock on the door was broken. Brett pulled his gun as they walked into the kitchen. A light above the sink lit the room. The lid to the cookie jar sat on the counter.

Al led the way down the hallway. Brett called out, "Captain Miller, it's Officer O'Shea. Are you okay?" Brett heard Al cry out as he entered the bedroom. He rushed into the room and slid to a halt. Joan's body lay on the floor, closest to the door. Miller's body was almost unrecognizable. Blood splatters covered the bed and walls.

Brett's knees folded as he sank to the floor. He leaned against the door, staring with disbelief. A sour taste rose in his mouth. He turned at the last second and grabbed a wastebasket. When he had finished, he staggered to his feet, trying not to touch anything or disturb the crime scene.

He knelt beside Joan to check her pulse. It was faint, but she was alive. He pulled out his police radio and quickly called for an ambulance. He gently touched her shoulder. "Mrs. Miller, its Brett O'Shea. Help is on the way. Don't move." She moaned and reached up to grip his hand.

Al walked around the bed and stood near them. He shook his head at Brett's unasked question. Brett soothed Mrs. Miller until help arrived. He heard a loud crash as the front door was kicked open. Officers flooded the scene, yelling as they entered the house. Brett called out, "Down here! Hurry." The sound of heavy footsteps filled the house.

Medics made the captain's wife as stable as possible before loading her in the ambulance. Brett followed the stretcher outside. Detective Donnellson was the first detective on the scene. Once the ambulance left for the hospital, Donnellson approached Brett. "O'Shea, let's go inside so I can start taking your story."

Brett sat at the kitchen table, slumped in the chair. He would never forget the terror on Miller's face as he lay frozen in death. How could anyone be so brutal? For what reason did he die? Maybe he should have shot the cyclist, as he was the most likely suspect in this murder. *Hell!* He was starting to think like Al.

Brett barely heard the other officers speaking to one another. As he clenched his fists, his mind rehashed the conversation with Miller in his office. It was horribly ironic that only weeks before, he told Miller he would be responsible for the next murder. He'd had no idea that Miller would be the next victim. Brett was sick. How he wished he'd never uttered those words. Now it was too late to take them back

"Well, well. What do we have here?" Sergeant Taylor announced as he entered the room. "If I'm not mistaken, you are on medical leave, O'Shea. What are you doing here in the middle of the night?"

Brett stared at his superior with burning eyes. He bit back the sarcastic remark he wanted to make. "After sleeping all day, I couldn't sleep, so I decided to take a drive. When I saw the light on at the captain's house, I thought I'd stop and visit. When I saw the lock had been broken, I called for backup and came inside to investigate."

Taylor sat down across the table, glaring at him. "You decided to take a drive in the middle of the night? You expect me to believe that, O'Shea?" Detectives Jake Foster and Kevin Donnellson stood nearby, listening to the exchange and taking notes.

"As I said earlier, I decided to take a drive. Captain Miller has been a friend of the family since I was born. I've been to this house many times for dinners and parties. I don't recall ever seeing you here, Sergeant?"

Taylor flushed. "You have always been a smart-ass, O'Shea. Just because you got some college degree, you think you're smarter than us cops, who have put in years on the street." Taylor grabbed a glass out of a cupboard and filled it with water before taking a sip. "You know what I think? I know that the captain shot down your ideas about the recent break-ins and murder. I think that made you mad. Made you so mad that you had all this anger building up inside of you and you snapped. Is that why you killed Captain Miller?"

Brett jerked to his feet, causing the chair to crash on the floor. The detectives standing in front of him straightened, their hands immediately on their guns. "No! He was like an uncle to me." Glaring back at the sergeant, Brett's jaw tightened. "You're a sick son of a bitch, Taylor. I suggest we wait until Mrs. Miller can tell you the truth. She will tell you I was not here when this happened."

"If she recovers?"

Brett stepped toward Taylor. Donnellson placed a hand on Brett's arm. Brett glanced at the man, knowing he was trying to defuse the situation. "Are you always such an ass, Taylor?"

Taylor's cheeks turned bright red. He growled and lunged toward Brett. Foster grabbed Taylor to restrain him. Brett took a step toward Taylor but felt Donnellson's grip tighten.

Turning, he saw Major Terry Anders standing behind him. Anders was nearing fifty, but he was a large man most men didn't mess with.

Anders rolled his eyes. "Knock it off, O'Shea. Are you trying to get written up?"

Brett glanced at Anders. His calm demeanor reminded Brett that the men were just doing their duty. Except for Taylor. Brett sighed. "You're right. I understand that you need to ask these questions. I want you all to know that I will help in any way that I can. I want the son of a bitch who did this caught."

Anders nodded at Foster, who escorted Sergeant Taylor outside. Anders took out a notebook and started writing. Without looking up, Anders snickered. "You need to work on your people skills, O'Shea. Taylor is a prick, but he's your superior. I'd watch my back if I were you."

"You can count on that. I've never understood what his problem is."

"I heard a rumor that you're going to apply for the opening in our unit?"

Brett stiffened. *Shit! Does everyone at the station know?* "I'm thinking about it. Is that a problem?"

Anders flashed a wry smile. "No, no. Just thought I'd ask. I wanted to let you know that I think you would do a good job."

Glancing about the room, as if to check that they were the only ones present, Anders lowered his voice to a husky whisper, "I've never told anyone, but when I started with the department, the patrolman who trained me used to work with your great-grandfather, Mike O'Shea. I can't tell you the number of stories that I heard about that guy."

Brett groaned and hung his head, shaking it slowly. He'd never get the detective job now. Even though the man had been dead for decades, Brett was still reminded of his escapades.

Anders's chuckle filled the room. "I guess by your reaction that you've heard those stories too. One of my favorites was when O'Shea got a complaint from the downtown businesses about a few drunks pissing and puking on the sidewalks. Apparently they were driving away the paying customers. I heard that your grandfather and his partner took several of them down to the train tracks. When the train stopped, they found an empty car and loaded all the drunks inside." Anders's grin grew wider. "When the drunks woke up the next morning, they found themselves in Chicago!"

"I've heard that story. Luckily none of the drunks froze to death during the train ride."

"Oh, let me tell you another one! This is a good one. Now, let me know if this one is true. O'Shea and his partner went rabbit hunting down by the tracks. After gutting the rabbits, they put the guts in the sergeant's car. I guess they froze, and the sergeant had a heck of a time getting them out of the car."

"That's one I haven't heard before." Brett glanced up and saw Al standing near the door, glaring at him. "Well, if there's nothing else, I should get going."

Anders clapped him on the shoulder. "Don't worry about Taylor. We may have a few more questions, but we'll let you know. Go home and get some sleep."

The morning news focused on the murder of Captain Miller. Joan Miller was in serious yet stable condition. The entire police department was on edge. The chief was on a rampage and ordered twelve-hour shifts for everyone until the suspect was caught. Brett was not surprised by the sideways glances and whispers that followed him into the station. Several news crews were set up in front of the building.

As everyone took a seat, Brett was surprised to see Chief Ellison march into the room. Sergeant Taylor stepped aside so the chief could take center stage. Ellison had the look of an old bulldog. His protruding stomach and fleshy jowls jiggled as he walked past the patrolmen. Chief Ellison surveyed the room. His beady eyes made Brett nervous. What was he doing?

Ellison cleared his throat. "Men, as you've heard Captain Miller was murdered last night. He was an experienced and well-respected officer. His wife is holding her own. We have a guard outside of her room for protection. We are utilizing every tool to catch the killer. I want you to keep your ears and eyes open. You will report any lead to Major Anders. He is leading the investigation." His fingers gripped the podium, turning white. "I want this guy caught now! Any questions?"

A few patrolmen nodded. Chief Ellison turned and stormed from the room. *What an A-hole! Ellison was the one who shelved my idea and timeline. Now he wants the murderer caught? Why didn't he do this weeks ago?*

Brett got in his car, surprised that Al was still ignoring him. His first stop would be the hospital. He wanted to check on Mrs. Miller.

As Brett walked toward her room, the guard outside the room straightened and watched as he approached. Nodding to the officer, Brett slowly opened the door. A few family members sat near the bed. Mrs. Miller's daughter, Candice, rose and gave him a hug.

Whispering, Brett asked, "How is she doing?"

Candice wiped her nose with a tissue. "They think she'll make it. She has a severe concussion. They removed a piece of the skull to relieve the swelling on the brain. I can't believe that my father is gone. Brett, who would want to kill him?"

Brett draped an arm over her shoulder. "I don't know. I wish I had gotten there earlier. I'm so sorry. If you or the family need anything, please call me or my mom."

Brett returned to his car a couple of hours later. He sighed and rested his head on the steering wheel. He wished he had run down the cyclist and asked questions later. His heart raced. He balled his hands into fists and pounded the dash, screaming until his head throbbed. He couldn't believe the captain was dead. His whole world was going to shit. What had happened to the carefully laid plans he had had only a few weeks before?

Brett opened his eyes and saw Al staring at him. Brett gasped in surprise.

"Hey, sonny, are you okay?" Al asked.

Brett turned on the car and slammed it into gear. "Nice of you to make an appearance."

Al's left hand tipped his hat at an angle, giving him a rakish look. "Listen, sonny. You're getting on my nerves again. A good cop was murdered last night, and you and Anders stood in the kitchen and joked."

"But I—"

"No buts! We've got to find the cyclist before he finds you. Understand?"

"Well, you need to understand how cops deal with death and things that the public wouldn't think of dealing with. Cops need to cope in their own way. If Anders wants to joke and reminisce, who am I to call him on it?"

Al held up his hands. "Fine. I guess I never thought of it that way."

Still annoyed with Al, Brett asked, "Can't your friend upstairs help us?"

"Sure, he is going to direct a ray of sunlight down on the guy and the angels in heaven will join in song."

Brett couldn't respond, afraid of what he would say, although he did have the urge to reach over and slap his ghostly friend on the cheek.

They drove in uncomfortable silence for several hours. Brett pulled in to his favorite barbecue joint for dinner. He liked to get his meals to go and eat in the car. Al watched as Brett stirred a large french fry in cheese sauce.

"Boy, you do like to eat."

As Brett finished off two beef sandwiches and the fries, Al fiddled with Brett's iPod. "How do you find any decent music on this thing?"

"Define 'decent.' I have a feeling that we like different styles of music."

"You've got that right. What does this song called 'Creep' sound like?"

Brett grabbed his iPod and set it in the cup holder. "Nothing you would like."

Al bit back a laugh as a familiar green Mustang roared by. He turned in the seat and waited for Brett's reaction.

Brett slammed his soda into the drink holder and gunned the car. They thundered out of the lot with lights flashing. Brett drew up on the Mustang and tripped the siren. A block later, the car slowed down and stopped. Brett grabbed his hat and walked over to the driver's window.

The driver looked up, his smile fading as he saw Brett. "Good evening, Officer. How can I help you?"

Brett slipped out his ticket book and started writing. The driver's eyes widened.

"Sir, what are you doing? Am I getting a ticket?"

"Yes, you are getting a ticket. The instructions for paying the ticket are on the back of the ticket. If you disagree with my actions, your rights are explained on the back of the ticket. Please sign the ticket. By signing the ticket, you are not admitting to any wrongful action." Brett ripped the ticket out of the book and handed it to the confused-looking driver.

Brett opened his door and tossed his hat inside. Al was still smiling and was using Brett's iPod again. With his luck, Al would probably screw up the iPod and he'd never get music to play on it again.

Al removed one earplug and turned toward him. "Did that feel good?"

Brett hesitated and broke out in a grin. "You know, it did."

The two laughed so hard that tears ran down Brett's face. The laughter cleared the air.

"Have any ideas where we should look for the cycle guy?"

"I think we need to check out the York Street area and the rest of the east side."

Brett nodded and turned around, heading east. For once, York Street was not deserted. An unusual amount of traffic was on the street. Probably family members and visitors at the Miller house.

Brett pulled over and turned off his lights. They sat for a couple of hours in the darkened car, watching the house, but not even a mouse stirred. As dawn broke over the horizon, it came time to go home.

As Brett was preparing for bed, Al suddenly popped into the kitchen, doing a lighthearted dance, the earphones still intact.

Brett pulled out an earphone and yelled, "Earth to Al, come in."

"What? I really like all this technology. Do you mind if I borrow your iTod?"

"IPod! How many times have I told y—"

With that, Al vanished, taking the iPod with him. Brett groaned. There was no way to win with a guy who could just disappear.

CHAPTER TWELVE

I t was midafternoon when Brett woke to a ringing phone.

"Hello." He didn't even bother to open his eyes, hoping it was a sales call and he could hang up.

"Hello, Brett? It's Lisa."

The lighthearted tone in her voice made him sit up. Why was she calling this time?

"Lisa. What do you want?"

She giggled. "Nothing like getting to the point. I was wondering if you would have some time today. I'd like to talk to you about Captain Miller. How about dinner? My treat?"

Brett ran his fingers through his hair. Could he stall her? Did he want to? One part of him wanted to tell her to get lost. He had no intention of talking about the Miller case, especially to some damn reporter. But, if he was honest, he did want to see her. Maybe dinner wouldn't hurt.

"You know that I cannot talk about the case. But I would like to do dinner."

"Sure, where would you like to go?"

Brett had developed a flair for cooking and could grill a mean steak. "Why don't you come here and I'll put some steaks on the grill?"

"You can cook?"

Brett growled, "Why don't come over and find out?"

"A dare? I never could resist a dare. See you around six. I'll bring the wine."

Brett hung up the phone and rolled onto his back, tossing the blanket aside. What had he just agreed to? His feet hit the floor while he scratched his head. No use procrastinating. He had errands to run. He stopped by the store and went to the local bakery to buy a fresh baguette. When he returned, he tackled the house, giving the bathroom a thorough cleaning. He didn't want her to think he was a slob. An hour before dinner, he hopped in the shower. After dressing, he headed to the kitchen and started chopping produce for a salad. Without warning, Al appeared at the table as Brett pulled out the dishes.

"What's going on?"

"Company is coming over."

Al's brow arched. "Hmm. It must be a woman. You're not wearing your gym shorts and T-shirt."

Brett laughed. "Maybe I dressed to impress you."

The doorbell rang. Al jumped to his feet.

"Hey, old man, why don't you go entertain yourself somewhere else tonight?" Brett yelled to the empty room.

Brett opened the door and ushered Lisa inside. She glanced around the house while taking off her coat. Brett felt a moment of awkwardness but quickly brushed it aside.

"Let's go in the kitchen. You can keep me company while I grill the steaks."

Lisa grabbed a bottle of wine and popped the cork. "Wine?"

"Just one glass. I'm on duty later tonight."

They took their glasses outside to the deck as the meat cooked. Lisa perched on the edge of the chaise lounge, twirling her glass. Brett could feel her watching him as he flipped the meat.

He was also doing his share of checking her out. Her slim-cropped pants hugged her slender hips and thighs. The V-neck top she was wearing revealed ample cleavage. Brett had to remind himself to look at her face.

"So I heard you were the one to report the Miller attack. I imagine it was quite a shock to see the body. His poor wife. Have you heard how she is doing?"

Brett tensed. He had told her this topic was off limits. "I visited Mrs. Miller yesterday. She is still unconscious, but holding her own."

Lisa peered at him over the rim of her glass. Her tongue darted out, catching a drop of wine. *Damn! Did she do that on purpose?* He forced himself to look at the cooking meat.

Determined to get through dinner and get Lisa out of the house, Brett flopped the steaks on the plate. The sexual tension had him on edge. As they sat down to eat, an uncomfortable silence grew.

Lisa picked at her food. Setting her fork aside, she folded her arms and watched Brett continue to eat. "This is awkward, the silent treatment. What's wrong?"

Brett froze, his mouth open as if he were about to speak. Al stood behind Lisa, smiling like a clown. Brett placed his elbows on the table. "I can't believe that you would even bring up the Miller case. I told you it was off limits." He waved his hand as he talked, motioning for Al to leave.

Lisa glanced over her shoulder. "I was only making a general comment. I wasn't trying to get information." She twisted a strand of hair around a finger. Shrugging, she mumbled, "I'm sorry. I wouldn't do anything to jeopardize the case. Do you smell something? It's like tobacco or something burning."

Al leaned over Lisa, peeking down her décolletage. Brett jerked, nearly knocking over his glass. "I don't smell anything." He flapped his hand, hoping Al would take the hint and leave.

With a hint of a smile, Lisa stood and walked to Brett's side. She placed an arm on his shoulder, leaned down, and in a husky voice, whispered in his ear, "I don't know what you're doing, but it is so cute. Why don't I clear the dishes; then we can sit and chat."

Brett nodded. Right now, he couldn't trust his voice. He was ready to pop Al in the face. They quickly put everything away. Lisa grabbed the bottle of wine and glasses and headed to the family room, where the fireplace warmed the air. Brett sat on the sofa. Lisa sat near him. Al chose to sit in the lounger near the window. Brett grabbed a throw pillow and tossed it at Al's head. Al chuckled as he dodged the pillow.

Lisa looked puzzled. "You threw that pillow really hard, like you were trying to hit something. You should be careful; they can fall apart. My four-year-old nephews destroyed my pillows."

Al placed his hands over his heart and adopted a pathetic face. Brett snorted.

Surprised at Brett's reaction, she nodded. "It's true. In five minutes, my living room was demolished. How about some more wine?"

"No thanks. One glass is enough. Remember, I have to work later."

With turned-down lips, Lisa scooted closer. "Okay. I want to make sure there are no hard feelings tonight."

Brett froze as her hand came to rest on his thigh. His body tensed. Unconsciously, he pressed nearer to her. He watched her pink lips part ever so slightly. Her gaze made his blood notch up a couple of degrees. Placing a hand behind her head, he angled his face before capturing her mouth. He smothered her excited moans. His body came alive with emotions. He began pushing her down on the cushions. One of her legs wrapped around his hip. Where was this going? She was sexy hot, but she was also trouble. She was more interested in the story than in him. He broke away, trying to calm his ragged breathing. Looking around the room, he was glad to find that no one had watched them. *Thank god Al had the decency to leave.*

Lisa laughed nervously. "Wow. That was nice."

"Yes, it was." He glanced at the clock.

Lisa jumped up, looking for her handbag. "It's getting late. I'm sure you need to get ready for work, so I'll get out of here. Thanks for dinner."

"Hey, slow down. I've got plenty of time. I'm really glad you called. Maybe we can do this again."

They were standing by the door when Brett heard the sound of a motorcycle outside. Lisa turned the knob and opened the door.

CHAPTER THIRTEEN

Brett jerked Lisa's hand off the knob and slammed the door closed, locking it. Shoving her behind him, he hissed, "Stay here." He shut off the lights and crawled to the side of the window. He peeked outside and saw the cyclist watching the house. Lisa, sensing Brett's fear, slid down the wall until she was sitting on the floor.

"What's going on?"

"Nothing. Just stay down and be quiet."

Lisa crawled over to Brett's side. He glared at her. "Don't you ever listen?"

"Don't be so bossy. Why are we hiding?" She tried to stand and look out the window, but Brett pulled her back to the floor. "I saw a guy on a motorcycle. Is he dangerous?"

Brett cracked a smile. "Are you always this curious?" Not waiting for an answer, he half rose and made his way to the bedroom to grab his gun. Lisa followed him.

"This guy has been watching my house for the past couple of weeks. I don't know why, but I'm going to find out." Upon reaching the back hallway, Brett straightened. "I'm going out the back door to try to circle around to the front. If you hear shots, call nine-one-one."

Lisa grabbed his arm. "Please, Brett, don't go outside. Let's just call for backup now and let them find out who the guy is. I don't want you to get hurt."

Brett leaned over and kissed her cheek. "Stay inside, please."

As he darted out the back door, he caught sight of Al.

"I wondered if you two were going to play kissy-face all night. I didn't want to interrupt you when I heard the cycle coming."

Brett planted a fist in Al's shoulder. "Shh."

"Ow. No one can hear me, remember?"

"You can't feel any pain, remember? Just stay out of my way."

Brett crept toward the corner of the house. The cycle remained parked in the street, but the rider was gone. *Where did he go?* Brett headed inside to call the station. Before he could reach the door, a scream rent the air. *Lisa!*

Brett ripped the door open and rushed into the kitchen. A flash of silver whizzed by his head. Twisting to the side, he saw a large butcher knife sticking out of the wall, inches from his head.

Al yelled from the front room. Careening into the corner wall, Brett skidded to a stop staring at the scene before him. Lisa was slamming a shoe with a five-inch spiked heel into the neck and shoulders of the cyclist, who wore a mask. The guy had one hand wrapped around her wrist. Al jumped around the struggling pair with a knife and was trying to cut the man's hand. It would have been almost comical seeing a knife floating in the air if the situation hadn't been so dire.

"Let her go!" Brett demanded.

For a split second, all movement ceased and then chaos resumed. The man shoved Lisa across the floor. She slid over to Brett's feet. A bloody scratch graced her cheek. For the first time, the cyclist appeared to notice the knife hanging in midair. His eyes widened.

Brett lunged and grabbed the man's waist, pulling him down. A lamp from a nearby table crashed to the floor, shattering glass over the two of them. They rolled across the floor, each planting hard punches. Grunts of pain filled the room.

"Lisa, call nine-one-one!"

She crawled away to escape the fighting men, grabbing her phone that lay on the floor. Brett grasped his cuffs, intending to secure the man to the leg of the sofa. He surprised Brett, however, by slamming a fist into his stomach. Brett fought the urge to vomit as pain gripped his midsection. Scrambling out of reach, the man twisted to his feet. Brett grabbed a hold of an ankle, fighting to maintain his hold.

The man's army boot smacked into Brett's shoulder, causing him to lose his grip. Before Brett could open his eyes, the door slammed. Minutes later, the motorcycle roared away.

Brett rolled to his side in order to push himself to his feet. He slumped into a chair, waiting for the patrol cars to arrive. Lisa leaned against the wall, bedraggled yet smiling.

"You throw quite a dinner party, O'Shea."

Brett grinned in response. "Is your shoe okay?" He nodded to her broken heel lying next to her.

She picked up the open-toe shoe, studying the dangling heel. "I think you owe me a new pair of shoes."

Brett laughed, holding his shoulder. "Not a problem. Seriously, I'm sorry you were here when this happened."

Lisa rose to sit on the sofa. Lifting her legs, she stretched out. "He came in through the front door. I was sitting in the corner and about died when he snuck in. I decided to surprise him with my shoe. By the way, did you see anything odd going on during the fight?"

Brett tensed. "No. Did you see something?"

Lisa let loose a snort. "If I tell you, you'll think I'm crazy."

"Give me a try."

Lisa sighed, "Well, it looked like a knife floated in the air and was jabbing at the guy who broke into the house. Didn't you see it?"

"No, when I came in, I saw you pounding the heel of your shoe into the guy's shoulder and neck. By the way, it looked like you were winning."

"It was the only weapon I had on me. What did he want?"

"That's the million-dollar question, but I'm going to find out."

Detective Kane was the first to arrive. He glanced about the room and started chuckling. "Geez, O'Shea, what trouble did you get into this time?"

Brett groaned as he rose to his feet. "Hey man. Thanks for getting here so quick. A guy broke into my house."

"You're lucky I was driving home when the call came in."

Soon police filled his house. Luckily Taylor wasn't on duty yet, so Brett didn't have to deal with him. Brett reported that he had seen the cyclist watching the house in the previous weeks. When the detectives on duty arrived later, Brett repeated the story to them.

Lisa was interviewed by the detectives and corroborated Brett's story. Major Anders took one look at Brett and ordered him to take the night off. Two hours later, the house finally emptied. Lisa stood and picked up her purse, stifling a yawn. "I've had enough fun for one night. Brett, thanks again for inviting me over. Dinner was great. Maybe next time we won't be interrupted." She leaned over and kissed him on the cheek.

Brett walked her to her car. "Be careful, and lock your car door."

He stood in the empty street, watching the taillights disappear in the night. After entering the house, he locked the door and walked directly to the fridge and pulled out a beer. The cold brew took the edge off.

Al walked into the room. "Well that was quite a brouhaha."

"Ya think?" Brett set down the empty bottle and grabbed another beer.

Al shrugged. "Don't be pissed at me. I didn't invite the jerk here."

Brett shook his head. "We still don't know any more than we did yesterday."

Al walked directly to Brett and grabbed Brett's shirt. "Sonny, use that head of yours. Think!"

Brett took a deep breath and removed Al's hands. "He has to be getting desperate if he broke in to my house. But why? Are we getting close to identifying who he is? That has to be it."

Al nodded, patting Brett on the shoulder. Brett took his beer and went to his room. The world as he knew it was spiraling out of control.

CHAPTER FOURTEEN

The lead story on the morning news was the attack on police officer Brett O'Shea. It also noted that a guest in his home at the time, a local reporter, was injured during the attack.

Richard shut off the TV and tossed the remote aside. Nothing was going as planned. When he had entered the house, he thought he could catch Brett off guard. Instead he found that crazy reporter. He had twenty half-circle cuts on his cheeks and neck from her damn shoe. She was a raving maniac. *Stupid, stupid bitch!* He would make her pay.

After catching a glimpse of the morning news, Brett knew he'd be getting lots of calls. His phone rang all day—mostly other officers and relatives checking to see if he was okay. His mom gave him an old-fashioned tongue-lashing for not calling the night before. He had turned down her offer to stay with her. Now that he knew the killer was targeting him, there was no way he was going to put his mom in danger. He knew that the Miller case and what happened the previous night were connected. He had to prove it before he ended up like Miller.

Brett decided to head to work early. At least that way he wouldn't have to answer his phone every ten minutes. Sergeant Taylor stood near the doorway as he approached the station. Brett forced himself to unclench his hands while meeting the gaze of his superior.

"O'Shea, congratulations for making the news again."

Brett tried walking by Taylor, flashing a glare at his sergeant. Instead, Taylor reached out and put a hand on his chest. Brett drew a deep breath and clenched his fists.

Taylor's beady eyes glittered. "Getting one of ours killed wasn't enough for you. Now you're putting an innocent woman's life in danger. I know you're hiding something, and I'm going to find out what it is. I'm going to be your shadow until Miller's death is solved."

Taking a step forward, Brett pushed Taylor's hand into his own chest. As the two stood nose to nose, Brett made a guttural sound—a sound of fury. "Tell me something. Is it because I am young that you don't like me, or is it something else? What have I ever done to you?"

Taylor's thin lips curled in a snarl. "I treat you the same as any other officer under my command. I may not have the education you have, but I have street experience. I know cops. And I know that something isn't right with you."

Brett wanted to smash a fist into Taylor's face. His reply was interrupted by a loud laugh in close proximity to his ear. Detective Anders stood to his side. "Hey guys. What are we doing? Standing that close to each other is going to start rumors. Get my drift?"

Taylor pushed Brett aside and marched into building. Anders cocked his head, staring at Brett. "O'Shea, what are you doing?"

Brett shook his head. "Nothing. Just clocking in. Thanks, though. I was ready to knock the shit out of him."

Tapping his foot, Anders stood with folded arms across his chest. "I could see that. I thought you might appreciate some interference. Unless you want to forget about any future promotions?"

"I'm glad you stepped in. After last night, I am not sure of anything right now."

"I heard about that. I read your statement from last night. You indicated that this guy has been watching your house for some time. Why didn't you report it earlier?"

"At first I thought he was dating the neighbor girl. Then it became too suspicious. After last night, I know that guy is after me."

"You really don't have any idea why the guy is targeting you?"

"I wish I did." Shaking the detective's hand, Brett added, "Well, I've got to go. Maybe we can meet for lunch sometime."

Anders rubbed his ear, staring at Brett. "You're a shit magnet, O'Shea. All this trouble lately seems to be tied to you somehow."

Walking away, Brett glibly remarked, "A shit magnet? Gee, I wondered what was wrong with me. Maybe you should give me a hand, Anders, and help me figure out what's going on."

Once Brett got into his squad car, he smelled the all-too-familiar faint smell of tobacco.

"Wow. I thought you were going to pop Taylor. I like Anders. He seems like an all right guy," Al acknowledged.

"Yeah, I'm glad it turned out the way it did."

As they turned down York Street, Brett's phone rang. Before he could say hello, he heard Lisa's voice.

"Brett, I think I'm being followed."

Brett pulled off the street. His fingers tightened around the phone. "By who?"

"I think it's the guy from last night. He's on a motorcycle. What should I do?" Her husky voice cracked.

Brett's grip threatened to crush the cell phone.

"Where are you now?"

She tearfully responded, "Uh, on sixth street, driving north out of downtown."

His brows drew together as he tried to think of options. "Okay, here's what you're going to do. I want to you to keep heading north until you get to University Avenue. Then turn right on University. Can you do that?"

"Yes, I've got it."

"Good! Now once you go over the river bridge, I will pull out and get behind the cyclist. When he starts to run, I'll follow him and you head somewhere safe."

"I'm afraid to go home. I don't want to be alone." She choked back a sob.

"Hey, I know you are scared. Why don't you go to my house? The code for the garage is three-three-three-three. Be sure to draw all the blinds before you turn on any lights. Be sure to call me on my cell if there are any problems."

Lisa sighed with relief. "Thanks, Brett. I really appreciate your help. The sooner you get this guy off my ass, the better I'll feel."

Brett couldn't help but smile. She was scared shitless and she still had an attitude. "Don't worry, in ten minutes this will be over and you'll be safe."

He dropped his phone in the center console and quickly turned the car around.

Al grunted, "So, are you going to tell me what's going on or not?"

"The cyclist is following Lisa. She is going to lead him past us. Then we can drop in behind them. Hopefully, when the guy sees us, he will take off and we'll be right behind. Lisa is scared, and I don't blame her. I told her to crash at my house tonight."

Al smiled. "Sonny, you have yourself a plan." He held up the palm of his hand, and they slapped a high five. Brett had to smile. Al looked absolutely gleeful.

As the squad car tore down the road, Sergeant Taylor followed closely behind Brett's car. He saw O'Shea raise his hand as though he were hitting something. He kept turning his head as if talking to someone. Taylor squinted, rubbing his eyes. No one was in the car, so what was O'Shea doing? The bigger question was, why was he tearing down the road? He wasn't on a trip. Taylor decided he would follow O'Shea and see what he was up to.

As he neared the bridge, Brett pulled into an abandoned parking lot. The place used to be a car lot, but now the small office building would be the perfect place to hide beside. After quickly shutting off the headlights, Brett grabbed his phone and dialed Lisa. "Hey, we're in place. Where are you?"

"I just crossed Second Avenue. I'll be going by in a minute."

Brett waited. His foot rested on the gas pedal, ready to fall into place. Al shifted in the seat, looking as nervous as Brett felt. Lisa's silver SUV passed in front of them. The cyclist still followed her car. Brett pulled out on the road and roared up behind the cyclist. With the flick of a lever, the lights and siren filled the night. The noise obviously startled the rider ahead. His head whipped around, catching sight of the black-and-white on his ass.

"Get his license number, Al!"

Just as he expected, the rider tore past Lisa's vehicle as she turned off. Brett followed the cyclist. His speed quickly approached eighty miles per hour. Hearing another siren, Brett glanced in the mirror. "Damn it! Taylor is right behind us."

On the radio, Brett heard Taylor calling in the chase. He knew he should have called it in himself. Another ass-chewing was coming. By now they were tearing through the east side, coming up on the fairgrounds. Brett could see that one gate to the grounds was lopsided and a gap of four feet existed. The cyclist roared through the small opening. Once inside, he braked hard and stared back at the approaching squad car. Brett didn't hesitate.

Al leaned forward in his seat. "C'mon, sonny. You know what needs to be done," Al murmured.

Brett floored the accelerator. The broken gate flew into the air, soaring over the hood of the squad car, and slammed into the windshield of Taylor's car.

"Yeehaw!" roared Al. "Taylor's out. His entire windshield is gone. Don't you dare stop to check on the asshole. We can't lose the cyclist."

The cyclist was on the run. They tore through the winding roads in the fairgrounds. They circled around the cattle barn several times. Pieces of turf dotted the windows of the car. Brett narrowly missed a large bench cemented into the ground. Al's hand gripped the dash to prevent being thrown over onto Brett's lap.

"I'm getting dizzy," Al wailed.

"Stop whining. You think I like this?"

Brett could hear Taylor calling in their location at the fairgrounds. Within seconds, there would be a swarm of cars. They continued to follow the cyclist to the southeast area of the fairgrounds, where the campsite was located. They turned a corner and found that the road ahead was empty. Brett stopped and rolled down the windows, listening for the roar of the cycle engine.

"Shit! Where is he?"

Al's shoulders slumped forward. His head bowed. "We need to search the grounds. He probably ditched the cycle and is making a run for it."

Headlights caught Brett's attention. A line of several squad cars barreled toward them. Taylor jumped out of the first car and walked to him.

"Uh oh," chirped Al. "This is my cue to disappear for a while. I'll go look around and see if I can find the cyclist."

"Thanks for the vote of confidence," Brett muttered under his breath as he walked toward the sergeant.

"O'Shea! I can't tell you the number of violations you committed tonight. When we get back to the station, we're going to have a long, long discussion."

Rather than say something that would get him into trouble, Brett nodded.

Taylor peered inside Brett's squad car. He opened the back door, glancing down on the floor.

"Can I help you look for something, sir?"

"No. Earlier tonight I saw you talking to someone in your car."

Brett bit his lower lip. He wouldn't smile. No matter what. "No sir. I've been alone all night."

"Why were you chasing the cyclist?"

"Ms. Winslow called me tonight to ask for my help. We think this is the same guy that broke into my house last night. He was following Lisa—I mean Ms. Winslow—tonight. She can corroborate my story."

Sergeant Taylor smirked at Brett. "I bet she can. She will need to come down to the station so we can take her statement."

An unmarked car pulled up beside them. Detective Anders quickly got out. He took one look at Taylor's smashed windshield and burst out laughing. "Taylor, what did you hit?"

"Nothing. O'Shea went through the gate, and it flew up and hit my windshield," Taylor growled.

Anders glanced at Brett, his brows arching. "I should have known. Well, now that I'm here, I'll take O'Shea's statement. Thanks, Sergeant."

Brett was impressed with the way Anders took control and dismissed Taylor. Anders walked several feet away and leaned against Brett's squad car. Brett took off his hat and scratched his head, ruffling his hair. With his hands on his hips, Anders stared at him.

"Like I said earlier—shit magnet. Do you hear me, O'Shea? What the hell happened this time? I heard you were involved in a chase."

"It was the cyclist. He was tailing Ms. Winslow, the TV reporter. She called and asked for my help. It was the same guy who broke into my house."

Anders straightened, pulling out his paper and pen, and took some notes. "Did you get a license number?"

"Yeah, we ... I got it."

"Well, what is it?"

Brett paused. Al hadn't told him the number yet. *Damn.* "I scribbled it on a piece of paper. It's in the car somewhere; I'll get it to you."

Anders stepped forward and stood inches from Brett. His eyes glittered with suspicion. "O'Shea, what are you up to?"

Before Brett could respond, his cell phone rang. It was Lisa. "Hello."

Breathless, Lisa asked, "Did you catch him?"

"No, he got away. Did you park your car behind the garage so no one can see it from the street?"

"No, I'll go do that as soon as I hang up."

"Good. I have to finish up here. I should be home in an hour or so. Remember to draw all the blinds. Call me if you hear anything."

Anders smiled. "Ms. Winslow?"

Brett, feeling defensive, gave a clipped response. "Yes. She was afraid to go home. I told her to go to my house. If that's all, I should head home to check things out."

"By all means. But I want that license number first."

Brett opened the car door, pretending to look in the console and on the floor. He glanced up and saw Anders closely watching him. Brett hated lying. He had to tell Anders the truth. He turned and came face-to-face with Al. Al held out a piece of paper with the plate number.

Al grinned at him. "I figured you might need this."

"Thanks. Your timing is perfect," Brett murmured.

After backing out of the squad car, Brett gave Anders the piece of paper. He wiped a bead of sweat from his forehead.

"Great. We'll get this out. Hopefully we'll have this guy locked up by morning. Why don't you go home and make sure your reporter is safe and snug."

"She's not my reporter."

"Whatever. I'll let Taylor know. Call me if you think of anything else."

With Anders gone, Brett climbed back into the squad car, where Al waited. Brett was mentally exhausted. Why had he told Lisa to go to his house? She probably had several friends she could go stay with. His carefully orchestrated life was disintegrating.

CHAPTER FIFTEEN

When Brett opened the door, he jumped. Lisa stood in the shadows with a canister of mace aimed at his face.

"Whoa! It's me."

Lisa threw herself into his arms, sobbing with relief. "I'm so scared. I'm glad you're here."

Untangling her arms from around his neck, Brett took a step back. "What a night, huh?" Conscious of Al standing nearby, Brett hurried to grab clean bedding for the spare room. Lisa followed him down the hall.

He opened the door to the spare bedroom. "Here you go. A room all to yourself."

Lisa bit her lip, looking perplexed. "Where's your room?"

"Just next door. I'm close if you need anything." With his eyes downcast, he closed the door. "See you in the morning."

Blowing out a puff of air, he went to the kitchen and grabbed a beer. With a quick kick, his shoes went flying across the room. He headed to the living room and sat in his recliner. Sitting in the dark was conducive for thinking.

Clearing his throat, Al appeared on the sofa. The resident ghost stretched out, filling the space. Brett saw that Al's hat was covering most of his face.

"Don't you ever take off that hat?"

"Nope."

Silence reigned again. Hours passed. Brett woke with the beer bottle dangling from his fingertips. He set the bottle on the floor and stood.

"I'm going to bed. See you in the morning."

"Are you going to check on your guest?" Al muttered.

"I didn't know ghosts could be smart-asses." Brett chuckled as he closed his bedroom door.

Lisa lay in bed, unable to sleep. She was amped up from being followed earlier. She had never been so terrified. Thankfully, Brett had literally saved the day. Ever since she had been attacked by the cyclist, she jumped at every shadow and noise. Knowing that Brett had a gun and was nearby made her feel safer.

She was somewhat put out that he had put her in the guest room. She had assumed that she would sleep with him. She cared for him, but maybe he didn't return those feelings. She would definitely like to see where their relationship would go.

Hearing a voice, she sat up. Brett's voice was clear, but who was he talking to? She thought she heard a low, rumbling voice responding. Minutes later, Brett closed his door. She lay back down and waited. The house was quiet again. She pulled the covers up about her neck and sighed. She quickly drifted off to sleep.

Hours later, she felt someone sit down on the edge of her bed. Brett? She had wondered if he had any romantic interest in her. Apparently he did. Smiling, she rolled over, expecting to see the handsome officer staring down at her with longing.

Instead, she saw nothing. Glancing around the room, which was bathed in moonlight, she found that no one but her was in the room. Had she imagined it? Moving her legs, she felt something odd. There was a slight indentation on the edge of her bed, as if something or someone were sitting there. She reached out in that direction and waved her arms back and forth. Other than a slight chill in the air, she felt nothing. *Okay, this is getting too weird.* She turned on the small lamp sitting on the nightstand and looked about the room. Nope, there was nothing. Should she go wake Brett, or would that look like she was hitting on him? "Quit being a fraidy cat," she said, chiding herself. With that, she shut off the light and jumped back into bed.

It was late when Brett woke. The smell of bacon and eggs filled the air. He quickly dressed and brushed his teeth. After donning his gym shorts and T-shirt, he shuffled down the hallway in bare feet. He leaned against the doorway, watching Lisa flip the eggs. Pancakes were cooking on the griddle.

"I didn't know I was going to get a great breakfast like this when I offered you a place to stay."

Lisa turned with a spatula in her hand. "Why don't you grab the syrup and sit down. Breakfast is ready, and I'm starved."

As they devoured the stack of pancakes and pile of bacon, Brett enjoyed getting to know her better. He watched her spread jelly on her pancakes.

His nose wrinkled. "What are you doing?"

She waved the jelly-coated knife toward his face, laughing when he jerked back. "I like jelly."

"I can see that. It looks like you have half the jar on your plate."

She winked at him. "And I'm not sharing. You can use the syrup."

Brett leaned on the table as Lisa talked excitedly with her hands. She was fun and definitely a good cook. He could get used to breakfast like this every day. They cleared the table and loaded the dishwasher. As she went to shower, Brett flipped on the TV. Another break-in had occurred over night. Thankfully, the homeowners had been out of town, but their home was severely vandalized. Had the cyclist done this? Or was it a random burglary?

Lisa came back from showering wearing one of his T-shirts. As she combed out her long, wet hair, Brett became fixated on her slender legs. She watched the news, setting her legs on the coffee table.

Nonchalantly, she glanced at him, twirling a strand of damp hair. "I hope I'm not being nosey, but I thought I heard you talking to someone last night."

Brett shook his head. "Sorry, I didn't mean to wake you. I was on the phone." *Shit! Had she heard Al and him talking?*

Leaning forward, she bent over and ran her fingers through her long blonde hair. She smiled as she sat up. "Sorry, I probably look silly."

Feeling warm, Brett forced his gaze back to the television. "Nah. You're fine."

When Brett looked back at her minutes later, Al was sitting next to her. Brett wanted to roll his eyes.

"I shouldn't say anything, but I swear someone came into my room last night."

Brett calmly met her questioning gaze. Then his eyes darted to Al, who shrugged back at him. "Really? It wasn't me. I fell asleep as soon as my head hit the pillow."

Looking flustered, Lisa apologized. "No, I wasn't insinuating that it was you. It's just that I felt someone sitting on the bed. I got up and turned on the light, but nothing was there. It was weird; there wasn't anything there." Her nervous laugh filled the room.

"Hmm. That is strange." Brett ignored Al, who wore a lopsided smile.

"What about you? Do you ever feel like someone is watching you?"

Brett shook his head. "No, can't say I do."

Lisa drew her knees up to her chest, covering her legs with Brett's shirt. "Last night, I could have sworn … Have you ever wondered if your place is haunted?"

Brett started to choke. His eyes watering, Lisa jumped up and patted his back. "Are you okay?"

Nodding, he wiped his eyes. "You say someone was sitting on your bed?" His eyes narrowed, glaring at Al. "Why would *someone* go into your room?"

Al began whistling and stared at the ceiling. His innocent look didn't fool Brett. He wanted to go over and shake Al.

Looking uncomfortable, Lisa stood. "I'm sorry for bringing it up. It was probably my imagination. I'm going to get dressed. I need to get home."

Hearing the door close in the spare room, Brett stood over Al. "What were you doing?" he hissed.

"Nothing. I was just curious about her. You seem to like her, and I wanted to know more about her."

Brett grabbed the pillow and swung it at Al's head. "You perv! You can't get to know someone by watching them sleep."

"Watch it, sonny. Are you jealous?" With that, Al disappeared.

Before Brett could scream with frustration, Lisa returned with all her belongings.

"I'll get out of your hair. I need to get ready for work later today." She walked to his side, leaned in, and pressed a quick kiss to his cheek. "Brett, I really appreciate your help last night and letting me stay here."

"No problem. If there is anything else I can do, please call me."

He walked her outside and watched as she drove away in her silver SUV. Storming back into the house, he yelled for Al. He was disappointed that Al had spied on Lisa. It was just plain creepy. Yet Al's words lingered in his mind. Why was he so protective of Lisa? Sure, he liked her, but was it jealousy?

CHAPTER SIXTEEN

Still unable to sort out his feelings for Lisa, Brett decided to hit the gym. After grabbing his bag, he quickly left. Although it was a short drive, Brett saw a car following him. One man in a dark sedan.

As he pulled into the parking lot at the gym, the sedan kept going. Once inside, Brett called Anders.

"Hey, it's O'Shea."

"What's going on? Is there a problem?"

Bret hesitated. "I'm not sure. I think I was tailed on my way to the gym just now. Do you know anything about it?"

"Could it have been the guy who broke into your house?"

"I don't think so. The driver of the car looked bigger. Maybe I'm being paranoid."

Brett heard Anders ask someone else about him being followed.

Back on the line again, Anders lowered his voice, "No one in my unit knows anything about a tail. I'll do some checking and get back to you later."

Brett did his workout and returned home, with the mystery car following again. He looked at his phone to see if he had missed a call from Anders. Nothing. After fixing a sandwich, Brett took a tray into the living room and sat down to find a good movie on TV. Anything to distract himself for a couple of hours. Al was standing in the front window, watching the parked unmarked car outside.

Al tilted his head, scratching his chin. "Is someone tailing you?"

Taking a bite out of his ham sandwich, Brett shrugged. "I'm trying to find out. Anders is looking into the matter for me. I'm wondering if Taylor ordered it."

"Hmm. I think I'll go investigate."

A second later, Al was gone. Brett set the tray aside and went to the window. "No, he's not doing that."

Sure enough, Al was sitting in the front seat of the car. Al saw Brett in the window and waved. *Good God!* The guy was always so impulsive. Yet this time it may prove to be useful.

An hour later, Al popped up next to Brett. "Quit doing that! Well, what did you find out?"

"You were right. Taylor is up to something. It seems that there are several of your coworkers who wonder why you are always at the scene when the Eastside Shadow strikes."

Brett stared at Al. "The what?"

"The Eastside Shadow. The murderer has earned a moniker."

"Shit! He doesn't deserve any recognition. Who in the hell came up with that name?"

Al grinned. "That TV station your girlfriend works at."

Brett grabbed his cell phone and pressed Lisa's number. "She's not my girlfriend."

"Whatever you say, sonny."

"Quit calling me sonny. Hey Lisa, it's Brett. What is up with naming the murderer? I can't believe it—the Eastside Shadow."

Brett paced the room as Lisa told him that the producer had come up with the name, wanting to spice up the news. Snapping the phone closed, Brett groaned.

"The producer wants to get more of us to watch the evening news. What an idiot."

Al barked, "It's going to scare people. There have been so many break-ins and two murders; we don't need to give that guy any publicity."

Brett threw up his hands. "Hey, you're preaching to the choir." Clicking off the TV, he muttered, "I need to get ready for work."

Somehow the evening hours always flew by. He had a quiet dinner with Al, who watched him eat a thick pork chop and a baked potato.

Al never seemed to mind him eating in front of him, but Brett tried to hurry nevertheless. Lisa called a couple of times, indicating that she would also be working that night. Brett was bound to run into her.

The car following him pulled into the police parking lot next to his car. Detective Kane got out of the car and shrugged at Brett. What the hell was going on? Brett had always thought Kane was a friend.

As he stood next to his car watching Kane enter the station, Al appeared next to him. There was an unusual tenseness around his mouth. "Listen up. You need to be careful tonight. I have a bad feeling."

Brett grumbled, "You and your feelings. What is going to happen?"

"Sonny, if I knew, I'd tell you. You need to be careful. I'm sticking close to you tonight."

"You usually do."

Brett strode into the building, his mind racing. Sergeant Taylor stood at the podium and watched him as he took his seat. Detective Kane, who had been following Brett, whispered something in Taylor's ear. Brett rolled his eyes. Now what?

Brett listened as Taylor reviewed the priorities for the oncoming shift. Even Taylor referred to Miller's killer as the Eastside Shadow.

As Brett rose to leave, Taylor called his name.

"Sir?" Brett turned to Taylor.

Taylor puffed out his narrow chest. His eyes glittered. "Who were you talking to when you entered the building tonight?"

"No one. Why?"

"Office Kane witnessed you carrying on a conversation. Obviously you have some kind of medical issue. You have been acting very strange lately. I am going to recommend that you be placed on medical leave."

Brett smiled and leaned against the podium. "Sergeant, I am well aware that I was followed all day. Do what you need to do, and so will I." Brett turned on his heel and sauntered out of the room. He could feel Taylor's eyes boring into his back.

Once outside, Kane came running out the door. "Hey, O'Shea. Wait up."

Brett bit back a caustic remark, willing to see what his friend had to say. "Kane."

Kane shifted from foot to foot before finally meeting Brett's eyes. "I'm sorry about what happened. Taylor and Ellison didn't give me an option. You know what assholes they can be."

Brett shrugged. "Yeah, I do. I know what Taylor thinks, but do you think I had anything to do with the murders?"

"Hell no. You know me better than that."

Brett nodded, somewhat pacified by the acknowledgment. "Well, I thought I knew you too." Taking a deep sigh, Brett rubbed the back of neck. "I don't mean to be a dick. I want to get this guy more than anyone. Miller was a good friend."

Kane smiled. "Don't worry. Taylor just told me not to bother following you anymore. I just want to make sure we're squared away and still friends."

Brett held out his hand. The men shook hands, clapping each other on the back.

Brett climbed into his squad car, where Al waited. Al shook his head and took out his pipe.

"Taylor really has it in for you. Did you and Kane work things out?"

"Yeah, Kane and I are squared. Taylor wants to put me on medical leave. He thinks I'm crazy 'cause I carry on conversations with myself." Brett roared in frustration. His chance for promotion to the detective bureau would go down the drain if he went on medical leave. Damn Taylor! That's probably what he wanted.

His cell phone rang. Brett glanced at the number to see who was calling. It was Lisa. He really didn't feel like talking right now, so he let the call go to voicemail. A few minutes later, the phone rang again. Lisa.

Frustrated, he ground out, "O'Shea here."

Silence greeted him. Now he was getting annoyed. "Lisa, what do you need? I'm tied up right now."

Lisa whispered, her voice shaky. "Brett, it's me. I was told to call you."

Brett was clearly puzzled. "Lisa, what's wrong? Are you sick?"

Her voice became muffled. Unfamiliar laughter filled his ear.

"Lisa, Lisa!"

"Officer O'Shea, it seems we will meet once again. We haven't had the opportunity to be formally introduced yet."

"Who is this? Put Lisa on the phone now!" Brett demanded.

"I must applaud your courage the night of Captain Miller's death. You almost had me, but you hesitated."

The cyclist! Brett felt the blood drain to his feet. He couldn't think. Why was the cyclist calling him on Lisa's phone? His blood pounded in his ears.

He heard Lisa scream. "Lisa! Are you okay? What's going on?"

The cyclist answered, "I have your girlfriend, the reporter. The game begins now. Tag—you're it!"

CHAPTER SEVENTEEN

B rett sat holding his phone. He couldn't move. Lisa was in danger. He realized that he cared deeply for her. He wasn't sure when his feelings had shifted, but he was scared of what could happen to her.

Al tilted his head, trying to see Brett's face. "What's wrong? You're as white as a ghost."

Brett's throat tightened as he tried to speak. He coughed. "Lisa. He's got her."

Al's lips narrowed. "Who has her?"

"The cyclist," Brett growled. "How the hell did this happen?"

Al reached over and placed a hand on his shoulder. "It's not your fault. How do we find her?"

"Shit. I don't know. I need to report this to Taylor." Brett started to open the car door.

"Wait," Al shouted. "Think for a second. What will Taylor do if you report her kidnapping?"

"He'll report it to the detective unit, and one of them will be assigned to the case." Brett paused before adding, "He'll make sure I have nothing to do with the case, won't he."

"Hell yes. Obviously the cyclist is trying to get to you. We just need to be smarter than him."

Brett nodded. "Right, but we'll need some experienced help. What about bringing Terry Anders in?"

"Good idea. Give him a call."

Brett dialed Anders and set up a meeting in less than an hour. He pulled out of the parking lot, trying to figure out his next steps. He had to get to Lisa before it was too late. He wouldn't think about her getting hurt or dying, not now. He needed a clear mind. He was going to catch the son of a bitch by whatever means necessary. The hell with regulations.

Laughter welled up inside of him.

Al stared at him. "What the hell is so funny?"

Brett rubbed his brow, still smiling. "Nothing. Actually, I was thinking about how I'm becoming like my great-grandfather, Mike."

Al folded his arms across his chest and leaned back against the seat. "I guess I'm missing something. Why is that amusing?"

"All the years I've served on the department, I always swore I'd never be like him. He circumvented the rules all the time. He picketed the station once when he was suspended. He even got his job back, including a promotion. How does a guy like that always end up landing on his feet?"

Al thumped his forefinger against the side of Brett's head. "He used his head and the inborn instinct I told you about. You have the same instinct and are learning how to use it."

"Yeah, but I don't want to end up dead like him."

"Don't worry, that's why I'm here to help you."

The drive to the restaurant was quiet as Brett thought about what he was going to say to Anders. They had to move quickly.

Brett spotted Anders sitting alone in the rear of the restaurant. He slid into the booth across from the senior detective. After giving the waitress their orders for dinner, Brett took a long sip of soda.

Anders gave Brett a quizzical look. "Well, what's going on? I can tell by your face it's serious."

"I got a call from the guy who I think killed Captain Miller."

Anders started to grab his cell phone. Brett grasped his arm. "Wait. There's more."

"You'd better tell me everything right now, O'Shea!"

Brett glanced around the restaurant to ensure no one was eavesdropping. "You know the reporter Lisa Winslow?" Seeing Anders nod, Brett continued, "The guy who called me has her. He called me on her cell phone."

Anders raked his fingers through his hair. "Why you? Why did he call you?"

"I've been kind of seeing Lisa. You know she was at my house when the cyclist broke into my house. You remember she called when the same guy was following her. We set up a trap. That's the night when I chased him all over at the fairgrounds."

Anders frantically scribbled some notes as Brett talked. After pausing, Anders asked, "Why didn't you report this to your superior?"

"I was going to, but I wanted to talk to you first. You know Taylor has it in for me. For some reason, the guy wants my hide, and now an innocent person is involved. You're an experienced detective, the best on the department, so I figured you would know what to do."

"Quit the bullshit. Why did you call me?"

"With your skills, and with me being the bait, I'm hoping that the two of us can nail this guy before Lisa becomes the next victim."

Brett waited to see what Anders would do while the server set their food on the table and refilled their drinks. Anders continued with the silent treatment. Halfway through the meal, Brett looked up to see Al sitting next to him. Brett softly groaned and jerked his head toward the car.

Anders looked up from his plate and looked at Brett and then at the chair where Al sat. "Hmm, they must have turned up the air conditioning all of a sudden." Anders resumed eating, watching Brett. "You know that I would be circumventing department policy. My job will be on the line, just like yours."

"If you're uncomfortable with helping me, that's fine. I can play it straight. But for whatever reason, I'm involved, and Taylor will try to keep me out of the loop."

Anders sighed. "Stop being a martyr. I'm in. I want the SOB who killed Miller." Jabbing his finger in Brett's face, he said, "I'm putting my ass, my career, on the line, O'Shea, so you'd better tell me everything you know, or by God I'll shoot you myself."

Brett glanced over at Al, who shrugged back. "Fine. I want to tell you one more thing. The night that the captain was murdered, I saw the cyclist at the corner. He just sat there and stared at me as I turned down York Street. I knew something was wrong just by the way the guy looked at me."

Anders's eyes narrowed. "I don't recall reading that little tidbit in your report."

"I know," said Brett, "but at the time I didn't realize the significance. What I don't understand is why he has been watching my house. What I do believe is that York Street is a large piece of the puzzle."

"What do you mean?"

"Every break-in, assault, and now murder was centered on or near York Street. I don't think it's the people being targeted. I really think it's because of where they live."

"You may have a point." Anders made some more notes. "Any ideas why York Street? I've lived in this city my entire life and nothing important has ever happened there. It's just a blue-collar area."

Al nudged Brett. "Tell him your theory that you shared with Miller."

Anders flashed Brett an odd look. "Hey, O'Shea, what's going on? If I didn't know better, I'd say it looks like you are listening to someone talking to you."

Brett gave a half laugh before blurting out the truth. "There is a ghost sitting next to me. He was sent to help me solve the case."

Anders's mouth fell open before his fists hit the table as he burst out laughing. He laughed so loudly that most of the other diners turned to look at them. As he wiped away tears from his face, Anders's eyes twinkled with amusement. "Good God, O'Shea. Are you trying to give me a heart attack?"

Brett didn't know why he had expected Anders to believe him. If he had been in Anders's shoes, he would have laughed also. At least he had tried. He wasn't going to belabor the idea now—not with Lisa's life on the line.

Shrugging, Brett forced a smile. "Sorry." He pulled out the paperwork he had shared with Captain Miller. "Here is what I've put together. I don't know if you remember, but back in 1933, Mike O'Shea was brutally murdered in a house on York Street. Back then there was a series of break-ins, attacks, and then his murder. It's the same pattern that we're seeing now, except now we have two murders. The time span between the original incidents shortened with each attack. I believe the same pattern is happening again. If my theory is correct, then there could be another murder in two days."

"Holy shit! Let me see that." Anders grabbed the paperwork and began poring over the time line. "This is good work, O'Shea. I may even rethink the idea that you're a shit magnet."

Brett felt himself blush. "Thanks." Even Al beamed at the unexpected praise.

Anders held up his empty coffee cup as a passing waitress stopped to fill it, and he then resumed analyzing the documentation that Brett had put together. Brett forced himself to sit still and remain quiet. Al stood up and peered over Anders's shoulder. Brett bowed his head in annoyance. Why couldn't Al just act like he had some manners?

"Okay. Here is our plan, O'Shea. I'm going to have my unit cover York Street as much as I can. I know that you will monitor the area when you're on duty. Don't do anything to piss off Taylor any further."

Feeling his stomach twist into knots, Brett nervously glanced around the restaurant. "So you agree with what I've laid out?"

"At this point, yes. I'll see if we can trace her phone. If he calls you again, contact me immediately. If we don't find Lisa in the next thirty-six hours, we've got to bring in the authorities. You'd better pray that we find her. Otherwise, you and I will be out on the street with no job."

After paying for their meal, Brett drove around. All he could think about was Lisa. She was probably scared to death. He didn't think the man would kill her right away. Brett sensed that he wanted to play cat and mouse to torment him further. Brett knew the clock was ticking. He had to find her before it was too late.

CHAPTER EIGHTEEN

Lisa pulled up to her garage and grabbed her purse. She had left work early. Ever since the cyclist incident, she was exhausted from always looking over her shoulder. She'd been checking her car before she got in and doing all the things the safety experts recommended. At the moment, she just wanted to curl up with a blanket and a cup of hot tea. Maybe she'd even read a book.

She pressed the door opener. Nothing happened. She pressed it several more times. Sighing, she tossed the opener in the backseat. The opener had been acting up for the past week. She mentally kicked herself for not getting it fixed.

Sitting in the car, she glanced around. All she had to do was walk around the garage to her back door. She held a small canister of mace in one hand. Realizing she couldn't sit there all night, she quickly got out and practically ran up the sidewalk. Relief flooded through her as she inserted her key in the lock.

The next second, strong arms wrapped around her body, effectively trapping her arms.

"What's—"

A smelly rag was pressed against her mouth and nose. Kicking her leg, she tried to break free. She couldn't breathe. Everything went black.

As she came to, she fought to calm her roiling stomach. Opening her eyes, she was surprised that she couldn't see. Where was she? The smell of old gas or oil drifted around her. Her breath caught in her chest when she found her hands were tied together. Reaching to her face, she discovered that a hood covered her head. Frantic, she ripped it off. She still couldn't see. She tried to stretch, but her feet hit a solid surface. *Oh my God!* She realized that she was in a car trunk.

She wasn't sure how long they had traveled. A tire iron bounced into her head as they went over railroad tracks. "Crap," she muttered. She could feel something warm flowing down the side of the head. She needed to find her cell phone. She reached around the small enclosure but couldn't find it. Her eyes drifted closed. No matter how she fought it, unconsciousness claimed her.

When she opened her eyes once again, she realized that the car had stopped. A minute later the trunk lid flew open. Lisa drew back, suddenly afraid. A hand reached into the trunk and grabbed the ropes around her hands.

"Get out!" the man ordered.

Lisa couldn't move. She bit her lip, choking back a sob.

Using both hands, he yanked her out of the trunk. Her legs crumpled.

He reached into the trunk and held up the tire iron. "Get in the house now or I will bury you."

Lisa willed her body to stand. Somehow, she made it up the four steps leading inside. With every step, she kept waiting to be bashed in the head.

Lisa sighed with relief as the bedroom door closed. Even though she was tied to the bed and had a gag in her mouth, he was gone. The man appeared to be in his early twenties. His eyes were hollow, like those of someone who had lived through lots of pain. She glanced at his face. There was no emotion showing from his eyes. She shivered as she assessed him. His slight frame looked almost skeletal. From the way he had pulled her out of the trunk, she knew he was surprisingly stronger than he looked.

Richard paced restlessly through the house. All the blinds and curtains were closed. He peeked out every window to make sure no one was approaching the house.

He could hear Lisa thrashing about on the bed and was thankful that the gag in her mouth was working. Before she became unconscious, she had cussed and shrieked like a madwoman. He ran his fingers over the scratch marks made when she raked her nails down his cheek and arms. He had to punch her in the face to get her to shut her fucking mouth.

He opened the bedroom door. She stopped moving and glared at him. He reached down and checked the ropes about her wrists. "Stop moving. You're not going to get out of here."

Her head thrashed back and forth in denial. Richard forced himself to walk off, shutting her away from him. He was frustrated. He hadn't wanted to take her to his home. He wanted to kill her slowly. He knew how to kill, not kidnap. Yet the voice had been insistent.

"You have to get to Officer O'Shea. He will lead us to the key," ordered the voice.

Richard nodded. "So O'Shea is the key?"

The voice in his head grew louder, more demanding. "No! He will lead us to the key."

Shaking, Richard lowered his gaze to the floor. "What is the key? A person?"

By now, his head throbbed. The voice raged inside of him. He fell to his knees, grasping both sides of his head.

In a low monotone voice, Richard mumbled, "Must get to Officer O'Shea. I have to hurt the reporter. O'Shea is the link to the key. O'Shea is the link to the key."

Richard knew he had to find the key; the voice had promised retribution otherwise. Rubbing his head, he looked for his pills. When he listened to the voice, his head didn't hurt. Why did he hurt? He was listening to the voice. He gripped his head with both hands. The pain was bad. The voice was punishing him. What had he done wrong?

Lisa glanced around the room. It looked ancient, like something out of the 1950s. Old, peeling wallpaper graced the walls. Tattered lace curtains covered a yellowed shade that blocked the sunlight. The weathered hardwood floors were bare. A lone dresser sat in the corner, with a chipped basin on top.

She tilted her head, trying to learn any details of her abductor or her location. Instead there was no noise in the house. Didn't that man ever talk on the phone? No television, no radio, nothing. Outside was the same. Quiet. No cars, no lawnmowers, no dogs barking. Where could she be?

The knot on one hand was looser than the other. Scooting toward the headboard, Lisa turned her head to see if she could get the gag out of her mouth. As the gag loosened, Lisa paused. What if he came in again? She needed to wait until dark.

She must have fallen asleep, because she awoke to a darkened room. Her stomach growled. She hadn't eaten or drunk anything all day. The gag in her mouth made her mouth feel even drier. Desperately trying to forget about her hunger, she tried humming songs and listing the presidents in order of election.

While she was scooting to sit up, the door suddenly opened. Lisa froze and slowly inched back to her original position. He couldn't know that she was trying to escape. Surprisingly, her captor held a glass of water and a banana. It wasn't the Ritz, but she'd take it.

Eyeing him warily, she watched as he sat on the edge of the bed. His face was drawn and peaked, as if he were in pain. He yanked the gag from her mouth, making her wince.

"Drink." He held the glass to her lips and tipped it. She greedily swallowed, even though the front of her shirt got wet from the dribbling water. He silently peeled the banana and held it up to her mouth.

She leaned forward and took a small bite. He stared at her with no expression on his face. She took another bite and chewed. She thought maybe she should try to talk to him.

"Thanks. I was really thirsty."

He pulled down the peel, offering her another bite. No reaction. "I don't know if you realize who I am, but people will be looking for me. If you let me go now, you can escape."

His eyes narrowed.

Shit! Did I say too much?

He reached down and pulled the gag back into her mouth. "Go to sleep. Don't make me come back in here tonight." He leaned down, his yellow teeth and foul breath making her wince.

The door closed. Lisa's eyes filled with tears. Her body trembled. She had to escape. Now that she had seen his face, there was no way he would let her go.

She waited until she heard another door close nearby. She could hear his footsteps in the room next door. After an hour, all was quiet again. He must have gone to bed. Ignoring the taste of blood in her mouth, she used her shoulder to rub the gag from her mouth. She pulled her arm as far as she could. Then, twisting her body, she bent her head until she could touch the rope with her teeth. Her arm was shaking from the strain of pulling it. Every few minutes, she relaxed her arm and turned her head the other direction. Slowly, inch by inch, the rope loosened.

Beads of sweat dotted her forehead. Her heart pounded. She absently wondered if this was what it was like to have a heart attack. She hoped not. She had to escape this hell, not die here. One hand was almost free. She choked back her cry of excitement.

A loud thud echoed outside her room. She paused, listening for any other sounds. Maybe it came from outside the house. Again her heartbeat sped up. Afraid to move, she waited silently in the dark. Assured by the lack of additional noises, she gave one final yank with her teeth and freed her right hand. She bowed her head, wanting to cry with joy, but she had to work fast. He could reenter the room at any minute.

She somehow managed to untie her other hand. Shaking her hands to restore the blood circulation, she hurried to the window and lifted the brittle shade. She saw an old chain-link fence around the yard. The neighbor's house was only thirty feet away. Squinting at the house next door, she decided it looked as spooky as the house she was trying to escape from. She turned toward the street and saw that there were no lights. *The streetlights must be broken*, she thought. *That might help shield my escape.*

As she pulled up on the window, the old wood frame cracked from disuse. She stopped and listened for footsteps. She had to be quiet. Inch by inch, she pried the window open enough for her to squeeze through. She placed one leg over the sill, stopping when thorns dug into her skin. A rosebush sat beneath the window. It was an easy choice: suffer a few cuts or remain a prisoner and die.

One foot hit the ground as she slowly lowered her other leg. Crouched against the house, she hesitated. With no car and no idea where she was, she didn't know which way to go. Damn it! She was clueless. After taking a deep breath, she stood and started running. If she stayed on the sidewalk, she could hide behind a bush or tree if she saw anyone coming down the streets. She ran until she couldn't go any farther. She took so many turns that she soon wasn't sure how far she had traveled. It had to be at least a mile or two. She stopped, gasping for breath. Leaning against a large oak tree, she took a second to collect her thoughts. She hadn't seen any vehicles since she left the house. Where the hell was she?

Without warning, a dog ran along a nearby fence and began barking and jumping toward her. Saliva dripped from the German shepherd's jaw. The dog lunged at the fence, trying to get her.

She edged away from the fence. "Nice doggy. Quit barking," she calmly whispered. Cursing the dog, she scurried down the driveway toward the street.

Since the dog could still see her, the barking continued. She stood in the street as despair washed over her. She had to keep going. She knew Brett and the police were looking for her. It was just a matter of time before she was safe.

As she started down the sidewalk, the sound of a motorcycle filled the air. She dropped on her stomach and crawled by the bushes that lined the nearby driveway. The motorcycle slowly drove down the street, past her hiding place.

The damned dog kept barking. She continued crawling among the bushes, trying to reach the farthest corner of the house. Rocks and sticks on the ground cut into her skin, but she kept going. The dog raced along the fence, his barking becoming more frenzied, if that were even possible.

Lisa saw the cyclist turn around and stop in front of the house. He took off his helmet and stared down the long driveway where she was hiding. That damn dog was like a red flashing beacon saying "Here she is; come and get her."

She shrunk back into the bushes. She knew she should get up and run, but her legs wouldn't obey. Maybe she could knock on the door. But would anyone even open their door in the middle of the night? She took a quick peek to her right and saw her kidnapper walking directly toward her.

She shrank back farther into the shadows. Covering her mouth with her hand, she tried to muffle her breathing. Without warning, a fist from above grabbed her hair by the roots and yanked upward. Flailing her arms, she slammed her fists into his body. She lunged toward him, throwing him off balance. When he released her hair, she ran, for her life depended on it. She made it to the street before he tackled her to the ground.

Her face it the pavement hard, causing her teeth to slice her lip. Blood filled her mouth. He jerked her over to her back and straddled her. A knife flashed in his hand. She felt the punishing force of the blade bury itself in her shoulder. Excruciating pain ripped into her. She failed to recognize her own voice as her screams broke the silence.

Suddenly, headlights lit the pavement, highlighting their struggle. A car stopped a few feet away. A man opened the door and stood with his cell phone in hand.

"Hey, what's going on? Lady, you okay?"

Lisa yelled, "Call the police. Help me!"

A homeowner came outside and yelled at the dog. When the barking continued, he walked toward the dog. Suddenly he spotted the commotion. "Hey there! What's going on?"

The cyclist jumped off of Lisa and ran and hopped onto his cycle. Seconds later, the roar of the engine faded away. Lisa lay on the cold cement, her eyes closed. She had done it! She had escaped, and more importantly, she was alive.

She opened her eyes and saw a kind-looking man in plaid pajamas bending down to look at her. "Hi. My name is Lisa Winslow. Could you call an ambulance? I've been stabbed."

That was her last coherent thought before darkness claimed her.

CHAPTER NINETEEN

Brett grew more frustrated by the minute. He had been driving for over four hours and hadn't seen anything connected to Lisa or the cyclist. Anders's team also had been looking with no luck. Glancing at his watch, he saw that it was time to head back to the station.

His cell phone rang. Brett saw that it was Anders. "O'Shea."

"It's Anders. You need to get over to Mercy Hospital right away."

Brett turned into the first parking lot he saw and whipped the car around. "What is it?"

"It's Lisa Winslow. She's in surgery right now. Our unit got the call about an hour ago. I'll fill you in when you get here."

"Thank God. I'll be right there." When he hung up, he wiped his eyes.

Al grinned, slapping his knee. "About time we got some good news."

"Anders got the call an hour ago. I don't know much more than that." Brett radioed dispatch that he was heading to the hospital.

After parking the squad car, Brett ran toward the emergency entrance with Al. A crowd of people milled around, including a news crew from the station that Lisa worked at. Several detectives, including Anders, stood in the far corner. Anders waved him over. He stood and looked at his coworkers. "Excuse me, guys; I need to fill in O'Shea."

"Have a seat, O'Shea. You're not going to believe this."

"Okay, but could you hurry? I'd like to see how she is doing."

Anders set his cup of coffee on the table and took out his notepad. He flipped back a few pages. "Calm down. We can't get in yet to see her. Now, down to business. Your reporter friend escaped. Apparently she ran at least a mile or more before the guy caught her. She was stabbed, but she is in stable condition. Luckily, a passing motorist stopped to help her. He saw a man get on a cycle and drive away."

Brett leaned back in the chair, shutting his eyes. He couldn't believe she had escaped on her own. "Where was the house located?"

"We're not sure. We do know where she was found. I've briefly interviewed the motorist and a homeowner who was at the scene."

"Have you seen Lisa yet? Is she in pain?" Brett popped out of the chair to glance down the sterile hallway.

Anders nodded. "Yeah, I saw her but briefly. She's going to be sore for a while. She's one lucky lady."

Brett rubbed his hands together. "I saw the news crew when I came in. I hope they don't plaster this all over the TV. The guy is still out there."

"I agree. I'll call the station manager and see what they're planning."

"Shit. Once he knows she's in the hospital, he'll try to kill her again. We've got to get a guard at her door at all times."

Anders nodded, motioning for one of his detectives to come over. Anders whispered something in the man's ear. Brett watched the detective get on the elevator. Foster looked only a few years older than Brett, but with his brawny six-foot-five frame, he was a guy Brett would want backing him.

"That was Jake Foster. He's my right-hand man. He'll set up a schedule for the guards. My guys will cover it."

Brett relaxed until he saw a doctor approach them.

Glancing around the crowded waiting room full of men in uniform, the doctor asked, "Is there a police officer by the name of O'Shea here?"

Brett stepped forward, removing his hat. "I'm O'Shea, sir."

The doctor smiled at him. "Ms. Winslow is out of surgery and is being taken to a room. The puncture wounds just missed a major artery. She will be out of here in a couple of days."

"Can I go see her now?"

The doctor reached for his pager that was buzzing in his pocket. "Sure, but you might want to wait about twenty minutes. Check at the nurses' station to get her room number."

Before Brett could thank the doctor, he had turned and walked down the hall. After they finally got the room number, Brett and Anders hopped on the elevator. Upon reaching her room, they found a nurse checking Lisa's IV. The nurse frowned as she glanced up. "The patient needs to rest, officers. Perhaps you can come back later."

Lisa weakly raised her hand, waving at Brett. Her face and arms were covered with abrasions. Her left shoulder was wrapped in bandages. Brett smiled down at her. He grimaced when she attempted to smile. Her lips were swollen from a large cut on her mouth.

"Hey there. How do you feel?" He leaned down, lightly kissing her forehead.

She took a sip of water. "Like I've been run over by a semitruck. Did they catch the guy?"

Brett shook his head. "Everyone is looking for him. We'll catch him. You can count on that." Brett didn't want to upset Lisa at this point. She needed time to recover, mentally and physically.

Lisa moaned, wadding a Kleenex in her fist. "I was so scared."

Brett picked up her hand and gently squeezed it. "I know you were. I'd have been scared too. You need to concentrate on getting out of here. We'll have a guard just outside your door. Just go to sleep. You're safe now."

A nurse entered the room to check Lisa's vitals. Lisa's eyes closed as she drifted off to sleep.

Anders nodded to Brett, and the men stepped out into the hallway. Jake was standing outside her room. Anders looked at Jake. "Jake, no one but her family and my unit, including O'Shea, are allowed to enter her room. If there's a problem, call my cell."

Jake nodded at Anders. "Don't worry, sir. There won't be a problem here."

Brett and Anders walked toward the elevators. "Well, it's clear that she's unable to give her story tonight. Let's go home. Tomorrow is going to be crazy," Anders said.

Brett replied, "I want to be there when you interview her."

Anders studied Brett before replying. "Sure. But let me do the talking."

Brett and Al left the hospital and drove to the station to clock in. Brett wanted to get home, take a hot shower, and go to bed. He thanked God that Lisa had escaped the lunatic and survived.

Richard slammed the garage door shut, hiding his motorcycle. He glanced toward the neighbor's house. Mae Wilson, the old woman next door, peered out a slit in the curtain, watching him. *Old busybody.* When she realized that he could see her, the curtain fell back in place. *She'd better mind her own business or I'll be forced to get rid of her too.*

Richard stomped up the wooden steps of the back porch and unlocked the door. Inside, he quickly turned the locks on the door. He flipped on the light switch and sank onto the sofa. The lone hanging light bulb washed the room in a yellowish tone. He didn't even notice the threadbare room today. His anger blinded him to everything but his emotions.

He had never been this angry before. How could she have escaped? He had done everything the voice instructed. The pounding in his head increased. A cry welled up in his chest. He wanted this torment to end. Richard knew that something was wrong with him. There were very few days that he felt like his old self.

Slapping his head with his open hands, he screamed, "Stop it, stop it. Make the pain stop."

The pain in his head suddenly lessened. With a slight smile on his face, he chuckled. A trembling sensation raced up his arms. The pain returned as quickly as it had gone away.

"Richard! What did you do?"

"Nothing. I followed your instructions, but the woman escaped. It wasn't my fault." Fearing the reaction of the voice, he sunk lower on the sofa, hugging a tattered pillow to his chest.

"No, Richard. You failed. You failed me! I cannot trust you anymore."

Richard rolled to the floor, his arms stretched out and his head resting on the oak boards. "I'm sorry. I can do better. You must give me another chance. Let me serve you."

Silence filled the room. There was no response to his plea. No, this wouldn't do. The voice made him feel invincible. Sobbing incoherently, Richard banged his forehead on the floor, heedless of the blood covering his face.

"Please. Let me serve you. I will honor you. Please, please come back."

"Richard, you get one more chance. Do it right or else I will make you suffer. Do you want to suffer, Richard?"

Richard sobbed with relief. "No, sir. Please, no more pain. I will do as you instruct."

The voice had answered him. He had direction again. Everything would be fine.

Crawling to his feet, he wiped away the tears with the sleeve of his shirt. He swallowed another pill for his headaches. He walked into the bedroom, surveying the area where the woman had been. Somehow she had untied the knots and crawled out the window. He had lost his advantage. The damn barking dog had woken his owner and ruined his plans. People had to pay. The voice was unhappy with him. He wouldn't get another opportunity. Officer O'Shea continued to be a problem. He had to figure out who or what was the key. Otherwise, the voice would eliminate him.

CHAPTER TWENTY

As soon as Brett woke, he dressed and hurried to the hospital to see Lisa. There was a huge crowd of people in her room: coworkers, family members, and detectives. Brett peeked around the door and caught Lisa's gaze.

Lisa patted the bed with her uninjured arm. "Brett! Get in here."

Detective Anders smiled at him. "You're just in time, O'Shea. We're getting started with her statement." Turning to the others in the room, Anders ordered, "Listen up. If you're not family or in law enforcement, I want you out of this room now."

Brett went to Lisa's bedside, where she gripped his hand. Anders's brow raised. It looked as if he bit back a smile. He felt himself flush as the detectives in the room saw them hold hands. Even Lisa's mom looked surprised.

After clearing his throat, Anders asked, "Well, Ms. Winslow, can you tell us what happened? Let's start with the beginning."

Lisa's smile faded, and she gripped Brett's hand tighter. "Uh, sure. I was coming home from work when he grabbed me from behind. He held something to my nose that made me pass out. When I came to, I was in the trunk of a car. He took me to a house and kept me locked in a bedroom. I never really got to look around."

Anders gave her an encouraging look before asking, "But you got a good look at the guy, right?"

"Sure. He was young, early twenties. Probably five-ten, if that. He looked sickly. Very thin. He couldn't have weighed a hundred sixty pounds. His hair was thin and shaggy, about chin length."

"Good job, Lisa," Anders said as he wrote his notes. "Any tattoos or markings?"

Lisa closed her eyes, shaking her head. Anders started to close his tablet. Suddenly, Lisa's eyes flew open. "Wait. I heard him talking to someone, but I don't think there was anyone else in the house. He always had a funny look about him. Something wasn't right with him. It was like he was mentally off. When he gave me a drink of water, I saw a number written on his wrist. I didn't think anything about it until now."

"What was the number?" Anders brusquely demanded.

"One-nine-three-three."

Brett looked at Anders, who shrugged his shoulders.

Foster, who stood by the door, asked, "Could it be an address?"

Lisa had let go of Brett's hand, so he moved back against the wall. He was so busy watching Anders that he jumped when Al materialized next to him.

Al hissed, "Did you hear that? Nineteen thirty-three!"

Brett pretended to cough, covering his mouth with a hand. "Hmm. I have a theory."

"I knew there was a reason you and I were assigned to do this."

Brett rolled his eyes but didn't respond. Anders glanced at Brett with a quizzical look on his face. After a minute, Anders returned to writing.

"Your grandfather was murdered in nineteen thirty-three," Al mumbled.

"Mmm hmm," Brett softly murmured. Couldn't Al wait until they were alone to discuss the matter?

Al took out a pipe and lit it. Luckily no one but him could see it. Anders stopped and took a deep breath. Brett fought to keep a straight face. Al was worse than a child sometimes. Brett swore he did things just to get attention.

Anders held up his hand. "Hold on a second." Anders stuck his head out the doorway, looking down the hall. Scratching his head, he wondered aloud, "Does anyone else smell a cigar or pipe?"

Brett quickly spoke up. "I don't smell anything."

Anders stared at Brett, his brow crinkling. "I'm sure you don't."

Brett avoided meeting Al's gaze. He didn't want to see the ghost's antics. From the corner of his eye, he saw Al trying to smother his laughter. Everyone in the room was watching Brett. Heads turned as Sergeant Taylor entered the room. Brett could hear several of the other men groan, mimicking his thoughts.

Anders nodded to Taylor and turned toward Brett. "What do you think?"

Brett straightened. "About?"

Al jabbed Brett in the ribs. Brett's gut told him he was on the right track. "I do have a theory. I don't believe it's an address. My family has served on the police department since the late eighteen hundreds. When my great-grandfather was murdered, it almost destroyed our family. Some of you may not remember that he was murdered on York Street."

Brett paused as several detectives jerked to attention.

"Everything that has happened in the past six months has centered on York Street. My research has shown that the break-ins and murders appear to be following the same pattern as in nineteen thirty-three. My great-grandfather died in nineteen thirty-three. Somehow these two cases are connected."

Before anyone could respond, Sergeant Taylor burst out laughing. "O'Shea, you don't have a clue what's going on. You need to sit down and shut up. Let the professionals, like me and Anders, handle things."

Brett's fingers clenched together. At that moment, he hated Taylor. He walked toward Taylor until Anders stepped in between them. Gritting his teeth, Brett leaned around Anders to glare at Taylor. "What's your theory, Taylor? I'm sure everyone here would love to hear it!"

"You watch yourself, O'Shea." Holding up two fingers an inch apart, Taylor barked, "You're this far from insubordination. Just keep it up."

Brett had never been so pissed off. He lunged forward with the intention of wiping the smile off Taylor's face. Anything to shut up his fat mouth. Anders reached out and gently pushed Brett back from Taylor.

Wide-eyed, Lisa spoke, "Actually, I agree with Brett. I have studied the history of the department for the past five years. I don't know why I didn't think of this earlier."

Brett saw Foster and Anders glance at each other. Anders smiled at Lisa before responding. "I happen to agree with O'Shea on this one. Foster, O'Shea, and I will head to the station. O'Shea, I want to flesh out all the details of your idea. It definitely has merit."

When Taylor began to bluster, Anders pointed a finger at him. "Careful, Sergeant. I outranked you the last time that I checked."

"Chief Ellison has already rejected O'Shea's idea."

"Yeah, and now Captain Miller is dead," Brett angrily muttered.

Anders growled, "Enough! I am in charge of the case. I will be the one to decide how we proceed. Understand?" His flinty gaze skirted the room.

Taylor whipped around and stormed out. Minutes later, the other officers and detectives filed out of the room. Anders leaned over to Brett, whispering, "Take a few moments here. Foster and I will meet you at the station."

Appreciative of the support in front of Taylor, Brett shook the major's hand. Lisa quietly asked her parents to give her a few minutes alone with Brett.

"Well, that was interesting," Lisa murmured after they were alone.

"Sorry, I let my temper get the best of me. Now, how's your shoulder?"

Flipping her long strands over her shoulder, she smiled. "I don't feel a thing. Great meds."

Pulling up a chair, he sat down next to her bed. "I hope you don't mind talking about this again, but I was sick when I heard your voice on the cell that night. I'm really glad you're okay."

Tears welled up in her eyes. She reached for a tissue and dabbed at her face. "It was horrible. When I was tied to that bed, I knew I had to escape. He had such a crazy look in his eyes. I've never seen anything so scary. He was going to kill me. I know it."

"Did you see anything that looked familiar when you escaped?"

She shook her head. "I was scared. The houses in the neighborhood were very small and old. It reminded me of houses built back in the forties or fifties. They looked pretty dilapidated."

Hanging his head, he mumbled, "That could be several neighborhoods. At least we know the house is within a two-mile radius of where you were found."

Lisa reached over to pat his leg. After taking a long sip of water, she sank lower on the pillows. She looked tired. "After they let me out of here, why don't you and I drive around and see what we can find? Who knows, we might find something."

He stood and pressed a kiss to her forehead. "We'll see. I've got to go, but call me later. I don't want to call and wake you."

As he walked down the hall, he nodded to Lisa's parents as he passed them in the hallway. Once in his car, he drove toward the station to meet with Anders.

Anders instructed his secretary to order in lunch. He was going to be working late today. He growled when one of the younger detectives told him that the chief was on the line.

"Tell him I'm gone and take a message," he bellowed.

The door to his office opened. Brett stood there looking unsure of himself.

"I don't bite. Get yourself in here and sit down," Anders ordered. "Grab some coffee if you want some. Lunch will be delivered in a while."

Brett glanced around the detective war room. Whiteboards lined the room, listing potential suspects and a time line of events. His eyes darted everywhere. Anders bit back a smile.

"I like you, O'Shea. You've got the balls to speak up and take a risk. Now, tell me everything you know about this killer."

Several hours later, Anders felt his hand begin to cramp from all the writing. Brett's debriefing was thorough. Although he had been skeptical at first, when he looked at the entire picture, pieces did start to fall into place. Anders hadn't forgotten that there were key questions still unanswered, but today they discussed strategy.

When Brett stood to leave, Anders waved for him to sit down. "Where are you off to?"

Brett glanced at his watch. "Well, my shift begins in two hours. I need to go home and grab my uniform."

Anders slid a piece of paper across the table and watched the young officer read the form.

Brett's eyes grew wide. He looked completely dumbfounded.

"Is this what I think it is?"

Anders couldn't hold back a chuckle. "Damn straight. I told the chief that I needed you on our team and that you were the best thing we had to solve this case."

"I guess the chief is taking a lot of heat about the killings and now the kidnapping of a reporter."

"Yeah, the mayor and city council have been unmerciful. Not that I blame them. People are scared, afraid to go out at night. Businesses are starting to suffer. That means less tax revenue. So you do the math."

Brett shook his head. "I don't know how to thank you, sir. I won't let you down."

Anders stood as the secretary brought in brownies for dessert. "I know you won't. My reputation is in your hands. Now, let's eat. Then we're all hitting the streets in teams."

CHAPTER TWENTY-ONE

Brett grabbed his bag from his locker. As he slammed the door shut, he saw Sergeant Taylor walking toward him. Taylor's eyes glinted with disapproval.

"It's time for roll call. Why aren't you in uniform, O'Shea?"

Brett paused and scratched his chin. "Did you get the memo from the chief's office? It appears that I've been temporarily reassigned to the detective unit."

Taylor's cheeks puffed out, like a volcano ready to explode. "We'll see about that." He turned and stormed down the hall to the elevator.

Brett whistled as he headed in the opposite direction. He hadn't been this optimistic in weeks. This opportunity to work with Anders would show that he had the skills and ability to be a detective. He and Anders were going to start where Lisa was found and work their way out until they found the suspect's house.

As he walked through the parking lot, Al appeared next to him. The infamous hat was pulled down, leaving only Al's nose and mouth exposed.

"Am I ever going to see your face, Al?"

"It depends. Can you solve the murder of your grandfather?"

Brett sighed. "Enough with the riddles. I don't have time for this."

Al crowed, "You don't have time! What about me? My spirit can't pass on until we solve your great-grandfather's murder case."

Brett felt a twinge of guilt. "Sorry, I was being petty."

Al grunted. "Never mind. At least you're working with the detectives. You'll have a better chance of solving the case now."

Brett glanced at Al. He was smiling, which was encouraging.

The pair approach the unmarked car they would be using that night, and Brett threw his belongings in the backseat. He saw Anders heading toward him.

"Thanks. I think. Hey, Anders is coming, so I won't be able to talk to you tonight. I'll meet you at home in the morning."

Al's smile faded. "Well, sonny, I've been told to stay close to you. Sorry, I'll try not to cause any trouble, but I feel safer knowing that we're together."

Brett glanced to the heavens and raked his hand through his hair. "Really? Are you trying to make me grow old before my time?"

Al tapped him on his shoulder. "Uh, I wouldn't do that if I were you. He doesn't like to be challenged."

A loud clap of thunder seemed to echo Al's words. Brett shook from a sudden chill. "Great. Just don't get me in trouble with Anders. Got it?"

Brett straightened as Anders called out to him. "O'Shea, you ready?"

"Yep. I've got everything you asked for. Let's go."

It would take a week to cover the area they were searching. That night, they would head north from where Lisa was found.

As they drove, it took some effort for Brett to ignore Al sitting in the backseat. Al kept poking his head between Brett and Anders in the front seat.

Even though it was fall, the temperature was unseasonably warm. Brett had his window partially down. A full moon lit the night sky. As they drove there were fewer and fewer working streetlights. Apparently they made for good target practice. The houses grew shabbier with each block. Garbage littered front yards. Eventually the lights of the city became distant beacons behind them.

Anders slid the car into park and turned off the headlights.

"What do you think?" he asked.

Brett looked out his window. Although it was near midnight, there was no activity on the streets. Eerily quiet. He glanced back toward Al, who shook his head. Brett assumed that according to Al's divine knowledge, this was not the right neighborhood.

"I haven't seen anything that fits Lisa's description. Maybe we should drive around a bit longer. We might find something."

Brett's unease grew as Anders turned and looked in the backseat.

"Humph. You're right. I don't see anything here." Anders started the car and checked his rearview mirror.

Brett bit his lip, worried that he had screwed up. One of Anders's staff called on his cell phone. From the one-sided conversation he was listening to, it sounded as if Lisa was going to be released from the hospital the following day. Her parents were going to stay with her for a while until she was released to return to work. Thank God she wouldn't be alone.

Driving down another street, they continued to study the neighborhoods. Anders spotted a convenience store ahead and pulled in.

"I don't know about you, but I need some coffee. Do you want anything?"

Brett shook his head. "No thanks. I'll wait here."

As soon as Anders went into the store, Brett whipped around.

"See, I told you this was a bad idea. Did you see the way Anders was looking around the backseat? I know he suspects something."

Al leaned against the backseat, appearing to be sleeping. Brett hated that damn hat.

"Chill, sonny. He doesn't suspect anything. You're being paranoid."

"Sometimes you are a pain in my ass. I know what I'm talking about."

Al's lips curled into a full smile. "Uh, I'd turn around if I were you. Here comes your boss."

Brett jerked forward in time to see Anders frowning at him. Climbing into the car, Anders placed his cup in the holder and turned toward Brett.

"O'Shea, what is so damn interesting in the backseat? Every time I look, you're turned around. When I came out of the store, it looked like you were talking to someone."

Brett pasted a smile on his face. "I'm just looking around. I don't want to miss something that will help us. I guess I talk to myself."

"Are you bullshitting me?"

Shrugging, Brett shook his head. "Why would I do that? There's no one in the car for me to talk to."

Anders grabbed his cup and took a sip. "You know that you can tell me anything, don't you? Whatever happens between us will be confidential. We've got to trust each other. Got it?"

Brett nodded. He wanted to sink down in the seat and disappear. He felt like a traitor for not telling the truth.

The rest of the night was uneventful. By dawn, neither man could keep from yawning. After checking in the car, Anders patted Brett on the shoulder.

"See you tomorrow night. Maybe we'll be more successful then."

"Thanks, sir."

Brett marched to his car. He glanced around. Al was nowhere to be seen. Brett drove home and entered the house to find Al sitting on the sofa watching TV with his feet up on the table and his shoes off. That just added fuel to the fire stewing in Brett.

Tossing the keys on the table, Brett snorted, "Comfortable?"

"Yeah, now that you mention it. I sure wish I could enjoy a beer. Could you move a little to the left? You're blocking my view."

Brett stopped himself before he complied with the request. "Are you even aware of what you've done?" Brett exploded.

Al rose to his feet, clicking off the TV. He faced Brett. "Maybe you should take his advice and tell him the whole truth, including about me."

Brett plopped on the sofa. "Are you kidding? I already told him once, and he didn't believe me. Why would he believe me now?"

"Listen, Anders is a good guy. He's got your back. Think about it. I'm going to bed."

With that said, Al evaporated into the air. Brett threw his hands up and lay on the sofa, resting his arm over his eyes. Ghosts didn't need to go to bed, did they? Why did he even care? Al was going to do what he wanted, when he wanted.

Brett wanted to kick himself. His first night working with Anders and he had made a fool of himself. His cell phone vibrated in his pocket. He pulled it out and glanced at the number before answering.

"Hey, Lisa. I heard you're getting released," Brett answered, trying to sound upbeat.

"Yeah, tomorrow. I can't wait to sleep in my own bed."

"How's your shoulder?"

"Oh, it's much better. I've got physical therapy scheduled for the next few weeks. My parents are staying with me. They want me to move home until they catch this guy."

Brett closed his eyes. "Do you blame them? If you were my daughter, I'd just pack up your stuff and move you home."

Lisa giggled. "God, you sound just like my dad. Sorry, that attitude doesn't work on me."

Her yawn told him she needed her rest. "Why don't you call me when you get home tomorrow? You are tired, and so am I. I'm afraid that I'm not good company tonight."

"Don't be so hard on yourself. You probably just had a bad day. Talk to you later. Bye."

Afterward, Brett forced himself to get up and take a shower. The steamy, hot water helped him relax. Lisa was right. It had just been a bad day. The following day would be better.

Anders watched his new partner get into his car. Chewing on a plastic toothpick that hung out of his mouth, Anders grunted his annoyance while thinking about a recent conversation with the chief. Ellison sure had a burr up his butt about O'Shea. What did Taylor and the chief have against this guy? His family had maintained a stellar record with the police department since the late nineteenth century. Anders had done his research on the O'Shea family before asking Brett to work with him.

Brett's father, John, also a police officer, had died of a heart attack. Poor guy. He'd only been retired a few months when he died. From what he had read, John O'Shea and Michael O'Shea had a lot of similarities. Both were characters. Even their cases were unusual. One of Anders's favorites was when John sat in a squad car outside a convenience store after purchasing a soda. Some guy walked up, right in front of the squad car, and jimmied the newspaper machine. He took a paper without paying for it. According to the report, the officer couldn't believe what he was seeing. Before he could set the soda aside and get out of the car, the guy came back and took several more papers and proceeded to sell them to other customers for half the price. This arrest even made the local papers.

Anders was pushing fifty. He swore he had seen every bizarre crime that could be committed. Now that he was working with O'Shea, he wasn't sure. Brett knew something that he wasn't telling him. He had to figure out how to break through O'Shea's reserve and earn his trust. Anders was more than curious about what Taylor and the chief had against O'Shea. He was going to find out what it was.

CHAPTER TWENTY-TWO

B rett woke to a quiet house. There was no TV blaring throughout the rooms. No music rattling the windows. After getting dressed, he grabbed a quick breakfast. He opened the blinds and looked around outside. No motorcyclist sitting by the curb. Maybe today would be better than the day before. Anything had to be an improvement.

After the gym, he came home to relax. Very seldom did he have time to do nothing. After eating, he flicked on the TV. His lids slowly lowered as he faded away for a nap. He didn't know how long he dozed, but he jerked awake as the trailer of a movie played on the TV. Stretching, he glanced at the clock. He had a couple of hours before work.

A shadow fell over him, causing him to clench his muscles, preparing for an attack. Instead boisterous laughter greeted him.

Al patted his head as if he were a child. "I thought you were going to roll to the floor again. I hope I didn't scare you."

"Shit! Do you enjoy trying to give me a heart attack?"

"Oh c'mon. I left you all alone for most of the day. What are your plans for tonight?"

Brett sat up and clicked off the TV. "The plans haven't changed. I'm riding with Anders again."

Al tilted his head to study him. "Kind of crabby, aren't you? Maybe you need to get laid. My wife always used to tell me that she could tell when we men needed sex. She said we got crabby when we were horny."

Brett growled, "Urgh! Stop it. I do not want to hear about your sex life."

Al chuckled. "Okay, okay."

"Do you have any leads from the guy upstairs or new information to help us solve this case?" Without waiting for an answer, Brett took the tray and dirty dishes to the sink.

Al followed Brett. "No, but I still think you need to confide in Anders. I think the problem is bigger than you or I expect it to be. I don't want you hurt."

Brett glanced at Al, surprised at the somber tone in his voice. "Don't worry about that. With you at my side, I'll be fine. I'm a crack shot."

Al's shoulders slumped as he shook his head. "We're on a downhill slide, sonny. There's no way we can stop the circumstances that are already in motion. I will try everything in my power to protect you."

Brett felt chills run up his back. Why was Al so melodramatic today? "I know you will. Now, will you take off that damn hat or pull it back off your face so I can actually see you?"

Al's lips turned up at the corners. "Nice try, sonny.

As Brett walked down the hall to get dressed for work, he shouted so Al could hear him. "I don't know how you even see with that hat down so low."

When he came out of the bedroom, Al was leaning against the wall with his arms folded across his chest. "Seriously, you need to be careful. Catch ya later."

With that, Al disappeared. Brett's jaw clenched. "Do you have to do that?" Brett clicked his fingers together. "Look at me. Poof! I can disappear."

Al could drive a saint to start drinking.

On his way to work, Brett's cell rang. It was Lisa. "Hi. How is it going with Mom and Dad?"

Lisa moaned. "If you lived with your parents, how would you be doing?"

He laughed. "Yeah, I get it. I love my mom, but I sure couldn't live with her."

"Physical therapy is going well. The doctor says I should be back to normal in a couple of weeks. I really can't wait to get back to work. Do you have any update on the kidnapper?"

Brett hesitated. He wished he could give her positive news. "Unfortunately, no. Finding him is our number-one priority."

Lisa sighed. "I know. It's just that I hate looking over my shoulder all the time. I don't want this to become the way I live for the next umpteen years."

"I know it sucks right now, but don't get discouraged. I just pulled into the station. I'll give you a call tomorrow. If you need anything, just let me know."

"Thanks, Brett. I can't wait to see you again."

Her sultry voice reminded him of the hot kisses they had shared. He did look forward to seeing her again. "Me too. Get better, and I'll see you soon."

He saw Anders pull up next to his car. Nodding, he got out. The men walked to their unmarked car. Anders was carrying a large Starbucks coffee and a bag of goodies.

Anders held up the bag. "My wife thought we needed something to sustain us tonight."

Brett grinned. "I love homemade cookies. My mom doesn't bake anymore, so this is a real treat."

"Let's go clock in and get started." Anders marched ahead of him.

As he followed the detective, he saw Taylor walking toward them. Taylor's eyes narrowed as he approached.

"Well, well," Taylor sniped. "What do we have here? It's the Mounties off to save the world."

Brett opened his mouth to reply, but Anders replied first. "Knock it off, Taylor. You need to remember that you never know who your boss will be someday." Waggling his eyebrows, he snickered. "Hell, it could be me."

Taylor's mouth opened and closed like that of a big fish gasping for air. He sucked in his protruding stomach and straightened. "Shit, do you really think you're going to be chief? There is no way in hell that you'll even be here next year, Anders."

Anders ignored the sergeant, looking at Brett. "C'mon O'Shea. Let's go do our job."

Brett couldn't help but smile as he walked past Taylor. He'd never seen the man at such a loss for words. The two men quickly checked in and tossed their gear in the car.

The plan that night was to cover the area south of where Lisa was recovered. What had been a booming mining area at the turn of the last century was now a neighborhood with numerous vacant lots and older two-bedroom homes. The area fit Lisa's description, so maybe they'd get lucky tonight.

Several hours later, they stopped for another coffee break. Anders was addicted to his coffee. By this time of night, Starbucks was closed. Luckily there were convenience stores open. After purchasing a large Cherry Coke, Brett hurried back to the car where Anders waited.

As he slid into the seat, he saw motion in the back. Al had joined them. His smile faded. "What are you doing?"

Shit! He had forgotten that Anders sat behind the wheel, watching him like a hawk. How was he going to recover from this one?

Anders turned to look at the backseat. Setting his coffee aside, he furrowed his brow. "Okay, O'Shea. What the hell is going on?"

Brett bit the inside of his cheek. He needed to think, but it was damn difficult with Anders glaring at him. Al had moved forward, and his head was now leaning over the front seat.

Smiling at Brett, Al asked, "Yeah, what is going on?"

Feeling completely unnerved, Brett pointed at Al. "You be quiet."

Bending forward, Brett rested his head on his knees. No one spoke. After several minutes, Anders's gruff voice announced, "We're not moving until you tell me what's going on. So take your time; I have the rest of the night."

Al whistled as he leaned back and waited. How was Brett going to explain this one? He hadn't planned on creating a problem for Brett, but considering the circumstances, maybe it was time for the truth to come out.

Brett's face was unusually pale. Al almost felt sorry for the young man.

"Sonny, tell the man and quit stalling."

Brett straightened and turned toward Anders. After taking a deep breath, he started talking, "Okay, here goes. You will not believe what I am going to tell you."

Anders's eyes narrowed. "Why don't you let me be the judge of that? Keep talking."

"Right after my grandmother died, something strange happened to me. I woke up one night and saw a ghost standing over me."

CHAPTER TWENTY-THREE

Anders glanced in the backseat again and turned back to Brett. Brett looked uncomfortable. This was bullshit. Yet there was no reason the officer would pull his leg.

"O'Shea, I don't know what your game is, but we don't have time for this now."

"Sir, I'm not joking." Brett collapsed in the seat as if all the air had gone out of him. "I knew you wouldn't believe me."

Anders rubbed his throbbing temple. "Tell me again what you saw."

After twenty minutes, Anders was still torn. His mind could not comprehend that supernatural beings existed. O'Shea was convinced ghosts existed. It was too convenient that only O'Shea could hear the ghost.

"Let's keep driving around. I need to think about what you've said."

Brett nodded and sat quietly, unsure of what to say at this point. He had laid out the truth, and Anders thought he was a nut case. Good-bye promotion. Good-bye career.

"Sonny, don't worry; I'll take care of things."

Brett caught himself before he turned to yell at Al. *Crapola!* The guy was driving him crazy. Brett held his breath as Al reached between the front seats and lifted Anders's coffee cup in the air.

Anders's eyes grew wide when his cup began floating in the air. He hit the brakes and pulled over to the curb. Pointing to the moving cup, Anders yelled, "What's that?"

In a resigned tone, Brett said, "Major, meet Al, my ghost companion."

"Well, tell him to put my cup back. I don't like anyone messing with my coffee."

Al chuckled. "Tell him that I can hear him just fine."

Brett grumbled, "Tell him yourself. I'm not getting in the middle of you two."

Anders watched Brett as he carried on a conversation with Al. Brett almost laughed at the confusion on Anders's face. The poor guy looked like Brett had felt when he first met Al.

"Sir, maybe I should drive. You look like you're going to pass out."

Anders wiped his brow. "You're serious, aren't you?"

"Yes. Welcome to my world."

Anders got out of the car, leaning against the side of the car. His chest heaved as he took deep breaths. Brett got out and stood next to his superior. Al stood on the other side of Anders.

Anders paused, raising his head. "I just felt something cold. Is he near me?"

Surprised, Brett nodded. Even Al looked amazed. Al leaned nearer, blowing into Anders's ear. Anders quickly rubbed at the side of his head.

"Did you blow into my ear, O'Shea?"

"How could I when I'm on this side of you? Al did it."

Anders's eyes widened. "Damn! Could it be true?" He slapped the side of the car, his face lighting up with amazement.

A light from a nearby house came on. "Sir, we'd better get in the car. People are watching us." As they climbed into the car, Anders was literally bouncing in his seat. Either the caffeine had taken hold or he believed what Brett had told him.

Anders drained the cold coffee left in the cup and faced Brett. "So why is Al here? I mean, why did he show himself to you?"

Brett thought back to the first night he met Al. "Al was sent here to help me solve Mike O'Shea's murder and catch the serial killer."

Anders thoughtfully scratched his chin. "No offense, but how can a ghost solve a cold case?"

"I have no idea, but Al has access to the man upstairs. Who knows what we can accomplish."

"Man upstairs?"

Brett nodded. "Yeah, you know, the man up in the sky. God."

Anders stared back at him, his eyes blinking rapidly. "God?"

Brett turned to Al and muttered, "Can you help me out here?"

Al grinned back at him. "Sure. Repeat what I tell you to Anders. Al is a spirit. To go to heaven, Al has to help Brett. As a bonus, we've been asked to solve the current case. We know the killer will strike soon, so we've a lot of work ahead of us."

By the time Brett finished relaying Al's speech, Anders looked as pale as Al. It was almost funny.

Anders started the car and drove a few blocks to a convenience store. He parked the car and exited without saying a word. Brett and Al looked at each other. Minutes later, Anders came out with another cup of coffee and a Coke for Brett.

"I can't think without coffee."

All of them agreed that the priority was to get the killer. However, Anders agreed to do some research on Brett's great-grandfather's murder. As a major, he could get access to old files that were off-limits to Brett. He would assign someone from his team to start work right away.

By the end of the shift, Brett's good mood continued. Al had done his disappearing act again, leaving Brett to drive home alone. When he pulled down his street, he spotted something at the end of the block that made the hair on his arms stand up. Was it a motorcycle? He couldn't tell if it was someone's parked bike or whether someone was sitting on it—someone like the killer! Instead of turning into his driveway, he flicked off his headlights and slowly rolled down the street.

A second later, the roar of the engine signaled that someone was on the cycle. *Shit! It has to be the killer.* Brett sped up, hoping to cut off the cycle's escape. Instead of retreating, the cycle rumbled straight toward him. Son of a bitch! The guy wanted to play chicken. Fine!

He'd mow the bastard down. When they were within twenty feet of colliding, the cyclist flipped on his headlight, shining it directly in Brett's eyes.

Instinctively, Brett knew the cyclist was not going to veer away. Brett yanked the wheel to the left, avoiding a collision. A shot rang out, shattering the windshield of his car. He ducked while hitting the brakes. Before the car could come to a complete stop, he opened the door and rolled out to the ground. Brett whipped out his gun, aimed at the cyclist's back, and pulled the trigger. He wanted to see that dirtbag on the ground and bleeding. The man jerked as the cycle slowed to a stop. Did he get him? Brett ran toward the cycle, noticing that several homeowners now stood in their doorways, watching the scene play out before them.

Afraid that someone innocent would get hurt, Brett waved his arms. "Get inside your homes. Someone call nine-one-one!"

He hoped at least one person would heed his words. As he approached the cyclist, he paused. Something was wrong. The man sat astride the cycle, his head leaning forward. There was no gun in the hand that Brett could see, but what about the other hand?

Brett saw a dark stain on the man's left shoulder. Pleasure ripped through Brett, just knowing the bastard was hurting. As Brett walked up behind the cyclist, he tensed. The only sound Brett heard was his own harsh breathing. Adrenaline coursed through him.

"Stop right there or I'll shoot," Brett ordered. The sound of sirens filled the night air. The man sat unmoving on the cycle. Brett stared at the man's back. "Get off the cycle now!"

Brett crouched slightly and eased to the side. One mistake and this guy would kill him.

"Officer, I can help you. I've got my gun trained on him," called an elderly man. Brett turned his head and saw a neighbor standing next to him wearing only Hawkeye boxer shorts and a pair of fuzzy slippers.

In that single moment when Brett was distracted, the cyclist raised his right arm and trained a gun on him. Brett lunged toward the elderly man, knocking him to the ground as a hail of bullets flew above their heads.

Brett's gun landed several feet away. The man beneath him moaned in pain.

"My head. My head." The man held up fingers coated in blood.

Hearing the cycle start up, Brett rolled over the man and grabbed his gun. Aiming toward the tires, Brett fired off three shots, but he missed as the cycle sped out of sight.

Holstering his gun, Brett rose and helped the older man off the ground. The man weaved, unsteady on his feet. Blood was running down the back of his head. By now most of the neighbors were outside, milling around Brett and the man. Several squad cars came skidding up to the curb. Officers ran up to Brett. He yelled for someone to call an ambulance.

The older man grabbed Brett's arm. "I'm sorry, officer. I thought I could help you. Instead I ended up allowing the guy to get away."

Brett patted the man's shoulders. "Not a problem. Not many men would have tried to help. I appreciate it. The detectives will want to get a statement from you."

Brett groaned as Taylor marched across the lawn.

"I should have known that you were involved, O'Shea. I can't wait to hear how this all transpired."

"It was the cyclist. The one that murdered Miller and kidnapped the reporter. When I came home tonight, I saw something suspicious in the street. So I drove toward him. The next thing I knew, the guy shot out my windshield."

The older man stepped forward. "That's right, sir. I heard the first shot and looked out my window. I saw this young officer jumping out of his car and shooting at the cyclist."

"Thank you for helping our men," said Taylor. He turned toward Brett. "Did you hit him?"

"Yeah, got him in the left shoulder. We should put a call out to all the hospitals and clinics."

"No shit, Sherlock," growled Taylor. "I've been on the department longer than you, O'Shea. I don't need you telling me how to do my job." Taylor glanced around at the neighbors standing in their yards. "You could have shot one of these civilians. Internal Affairs will be following up with you."

Watching Taylor join the other officers, Brett kicked the dirt at his feet. He had been so close in getting the killer. If only the old guy hadn't distracted him. After talking to the detective assigned to the case, he was released to go home.

Once inside, he called Anders and updated him on the latest events. Anders stated that he would talk to the detective on the case and update him in the morning. Once off the phone, he jumped into the shower. His hands trembled. He hadn't shot a person before. During the heat of the moment, he had wanted to kill the asshole. Now he didn't know how he felt. These conflicting emotions were unexpected. He was so wound up; it would be hard to sleep. After he slipped into his shorts, he grabbed a pillow and headed to the sofa. He flicked on the TV and let the mindless chatter lull him to sleep.

CHAPTER TWENTY-FOUR

Richard quickly hid the cycle and ran into the house. His arm throbbed with pain. After locking the house, he flipped on the light. He cut off his shirt so he could examine his wound. It appeared that the bullet had gone through the fleshy part of his upper arm. A sob escaped him as blood trickled from the wound. He was furious. He had missed an opportunity to kill the officer. *Damn it.* He had been so close until that stupid old man came out to help. He had to stop the bleeding. Putting pressure on the wound, he made his way to the bathroom. A glance in the mirror made him pause. His vision dimmed as a ferocious headache brought him to his knees.

"Stop it, stop it." Richard knew what the pain signaled. His voice had returned.

"Quit your blubbering, crybaby. You failed me again."

Using the sink as leverage, Richard pulled himself to his feet and stared into the mirror. His eyes glazed over as he saw a shadowy reflection behind him. The soulless eyes pierced him. The facial features contorted from human to those of an indescribable creature. His pain forgotten, Richard trembled with fear.

"I'm sorry. I followed your plan. Everything would have worked fine if some old guy hadn't come out to help. As I turned to shoot, O'Shea jumped on the old man to protect him."

Vapor rolled out of the creature's mouth. "In other words, you failed. It seems my trust in you has been misplaced, Richard. Perhaps I should put my trust in another needy soul."

"No, you were right to choose me. I can do it." Richard's voice trailed off.

A bright flash of light pushed him to the floor. He cowered in the corner. It was as if a sword pulsed in his wound. Whimpering like a child, Richard turned away, afraid to look at the shadow any longer.

"How many chances should I give you, Richard? How many?" Vibrations shook the house as the monster vented his fury.

As Richard pressed his face to the floor, his body trembled. Screams ripped from his throat until no further sound could be uttered. He collapsed in a heap.

When he woke the next morning, he rolled onto his back. His shoulder no longer ached. He turned his head and saw that the bleeding had stopped and the wound was healing. Tears seeped from beneath his lids and coursed down his cheeks. He had to kill O'Shea or he would die. There could be no more mistakes.

Although it was difficult to maintain any coherent thought, Richard reflected on the image he had witnessed in the mirror last night. He didn't believe in heaven or hell, but the entity in his house the previous night was becoming more real every day. Was it Satan? His confused mind couldn't comprehend that Satan even existed. However, the thing he saw the night before was how he would imagine Satan looking. Richard sensed that his life was spiraling out of control and he had nowhere to turn.

He rose to his feet and staggered to the kitchen. He needed to take his medicine. As the effects of the medicine flowed through his body, he became drowsy. He shuffled to his room and lay on the rumpled yellow sheets. Pressing a hand over his eyes, he willed his mind to slow the chaotic thoughts and focused on one thing. He had to kill O'Shea.

CHAPTER TWENTY-FIVE

Major Terry Anders glanced at the scattered folders on his desk. His staff had been thorough in their research. Several boxes of documents on Detective Mike O'Shea lay before him. Report after report showed the range of hijinks that O'Shea had pulled. As he picked up another yellowed report, Anders's eyes began to water. He buried his head in folded arms while his shoulders shook. A loud chuckle broke from his chest.

This was one he hadn't heard before. O'Shea had picketed the station during one of his many suspensions. Hell, he had even carried a sign bearing a message about the unfair conduct of the brass. That man called it like he saw it. Anders shook his head. O'Shea always got reinstated and promoted. If police pulled shit like that today, they'd be fired. End of story!

Shoving the papers aside, he picked up his cellphone to check messages. One text from Brett. They were on tonight. They were going to scout out another neighborhood, trying to find the killer's house. Too bad nothing ever came from the license number on the motorcycle.

Terry picked up some of the papers and stuffed them into his briefcase. He'd take them home to review. He still didn't know how they could solve a cold case with no evidence. Maybe he'd find one clue that could help them.

Brett peeked out the window to see who had rung the doorbell. Lisa stood outside, nervously twisting her hair. Grinning, he opened the door, and she rushed past him.

"Hey, what—"

She tossed her purse to the floor, turned, and threw her arms around his neck. She pressed her lips against his. His eyes widened while his arms helplessly wrapped her in a tight embrace. Her tongue wound its way in between his lips. Her hands gripped his hips, pulling him to her. His dick jumped to attention. It obviously liked the attention.

He pulled back, glancing at her flushed face and plump lips. "Hello to you too. What's going on?"

"You know, we never got to finish our dinner date here at your house. Even though I know it's important, you've been so busy with work that I missed you. So here I am."

Brett smiled and took her by the hand, leading her down the hallway. "Yes, here you are. What am I supposed to do with you?"

A blush stained her cheeks. "Well, I do have a couple of ideas, Officer. Don't you have some handcuffs?"

Brett whipped around, stumbling into the wall. Lisa giggled, "Just teasing. No handcuffs."

Brett bent and swept her up in his arms. Using his foot, he kicked open his bedroom door. He laid Lisa on the middle of the bed and quickly stripped down to nothing. Lisa scrambled to undress, throwing her underwear across the room.

"No handcuffs and no talking," he grunted. He buried his face in her hair, which was fanned out on his pillow, and slowly slid down her toned body.

"How's your shoulder?"

"It's fine. No talking, remember?"

Obviously we are two consenting adults. Is this just sex or something else? He blinked. *Stop*, his brain ordered. This wasn't the time to analyze his feelings.

He continued the journey to the center of her heat. His pulse pounded. The kittenish noises she kept making ratcheted up his need. He kneaded her breasts as he used his knee to part her thighs. An inch at a time, he slid into her wet warmth. His eyes squeezed shut as pleasure tore through him. He shuddered. His hooded eyes watched her writhe beneath him.

Her sleepy eyes opened. Her hand caressed the side of his face. In a deep, throaty voice, she moaned, "Harder."

Brett's body convulsed. That one word nearly sent him over the edge. *Damn!* His hips ground into hers, pumping like a jackhammer. Her scream echoed in his ear as he roared, jetting into her body.

Minutes later, he rolled to her side. Their bodies were covered in a sheen of sweat. Propped up on his elbow, he stared down at her. His hand slid up her arm to her chin. He gently turned her head so he could see her face. Her cheeks were pink, her lips plump from his demanding kisses.

"Well, that's just what the doctor ordered," she purred.

Brett snorted. "Really? Did I hurt your shoulder?"

Lisa scooted closer and kissed his mouth. "No, I'm fine. For the record, I didn't come here to seduce you. I wanted to see if you wanted to go out for dinner, but once you opened the door, my hormones went crazy."

He wrapped her in an embrace. "For the record, I'm glad you stopped by."

"Good. Now I'm really hungry. Let's go get a pizza."

Twenty minutes later, after a quick shower, they left the house.

Al stood in the window and watched the car pull out of the driveway. He had appeared at Brett's just in time to see clothing flying across his bedroom. Their moans of pleasure haunted him. His past may have been fuzzy, but he remembered his wife. She was the center of his universe, and he missed her deeply. Brett and Lisa's romantic encounter only reminded him of his loss.

It wasn't often that he felt sorry for himself. Tonight was one of those nights. Plopping into the recliner, he pulled out his pipe. The familiar twang of tobacco soothed his nerves. He was glad that Anders was on their team. The man had ethics and moral fiber. Too many people today lacked that. He was shocked by the number of vampire and satanic movies and television shows. *My God! How did people think of these things?*

He chuckled aloud. Come to think of it, he did have a ghost thing going on. He didn't think he would have believed in ghosts when he was alive. Even though he was a ghost, he was good. He didn't suck blood from humans, like those creepy vampires he saw on TV.

Thunder erupted above the house, rattling the windows. Al glanced up, expecting to see an angel. Instead he got a lecture. "Got it. Not a ghost, but a spirit being." Tapping out the tobacco in his pipe into a metal wastebasket, he rose from the chair. He muttered under his breath, "Spirit, ghost, what's the difference. It ain't natural."

A crack of lightning lit up the front room. Al's body tingled from the electricity arcing through him. Smoke rippled out from underneath his shoes. Al sighed. When would he learn to shut up and pay attention to the rules? He already had received a couple of warnings from the big guy. He wanted to help Brett and find peace. Was that too much for a ghost to ask?

CHAPTER TWENTY-SIX

Anders kissed his wife, Caroline, good night and then reluctantly went back to his home office. The files on Mike O'Shea littered his desk. Scooting up to the desk, he sipped a steaming cup of coffee. His brow wrinkled in thought. The caffeine probably was a mistake.

A quick glance at the clock confirmed that he had two hours before meeting up with Brett. The O'Shea files were turning yellow with age. Staring at a photograph of Mike O'Shea, Anders pondered the picture. Brett looked a lot like his great-grandfather. Who in the devil was Al? Were Al and Brett connected somehow? Just thinking about it gave him a splitting headache.

Anders got the chills when he realized that he really was working with a ghost on a murder case. He couldn't tell his men. No one would believe him. One minute he was excited about this opportunity, and the next minute he wanted to run in the opposite direction.

Anders glanced at the doorway as a sudden breeze ruffled the papers on the desk. "Damn it!" Anders stood and kicked the chair out of his way. He began re-sorting the piles of paper. He paused and looked about the room. The door and window were closed. What could be making the breeze? Or who?

Anders lowered himself to the chair and froze. He was sitting on something or someone. Cursing under his breath, Anders realized that his gun was in the kitchen. Without turning around, he reached back and encountered a leg. He heard the chair being pushed across the floor.

Putting up his hands, Anders slowly turned to face the intruder. "All I have is a little bit of cash in my wallet. You can take it and leave."

Anders's heart pounded from fear. His wife was upstairs, alone and unprotected. He had to do something. A man stood before him, unmoving. The next second, Anders lunged at the man, his arms widespread. Anders fell to the floor with a thud. Stunned, he raised his head. He had missed the man. How had that happened? There was no way a man could move that fast.

"Here I thought we were friends," the man exclaimed.

Anders scrambled to his feet. The man calmly sat on the corner of his desk, watching Anders, as he smiled and stuck a pipe in his mouth.

"Who the hell are you?"

The man shook his head. "I'm sorry for scaring you. I forgot you hadn't seen or heard me speak until now. I'm Al. Brett's ghost."

Anders couldn't think. His eyes couldn't comprehend the sight before him. "You're Al?"

Al held up his fingers and waggled them at Anders. "Yep."

"How come I can see and hear you? What's changed?"

Al shrugged his shoulders. "Not quite sure, but now that you're on our team, I suppose my boss wants to make sure you know everything."

"Holy shit!" Anders grabbed the lukewarm cup of coffee and took a large gulp.

Al looked up at the ceiling. A frown marred his face. "I wouldn't be swearing like that if I were you. The boss doesn't like it."

Anders's laugh was drowned out by a brilliant flash of lightning.

"Told ya. Anyway, let's get started. Are you and Brett touring the city again tonight?"

"Yes. I'm supposed to meet him at eleven p.m.. Can you remove your hat, Al? I'd like to see who I'm talking to."

"What is it with cops? Brett has asked me that question a hundred times. But no, the hat stays on. I've got orders on the hat."

Grumbling, Anders began putting the papers back in the folders. "Hell! I don't know how we're supposed to work together if I can't even see your face." A loud crack of thunder shook the house.

In a reprimanding tone, Al said, "Like I told Brett, you've got to trust me." Glancing up, he added, "Our boss gets a little upset when you swear or don't listen."

"Okay! I get it. You're in charge."

"That's the spirit! Spirit, get it?" Al slapped his hand on his thigh. "I'll meet you at the station." A second later, Al faded from the room, his laughter trailing behind.

The room was empty. Anders's hand shook as he picked up his cup and drained it. What had just happened? He was a religious man. Ghosts weren't supposed to exist. But he had just witnessed the unexplainable disappearance of Al; what choice did he have but to believe in the supernatural?

CHAPTER TWENTY-SEVEN

B rett walked Lisa to her car.
"Promise you will call as soon as you're in the house."

She drew his head down, kissing him slowly. Her eyes sparkled. "I will. Talk to you later."

He quickly locked the door and hurried to his room. He had to meet Anders in thirty minutes. As he changed into his work clothes, thoughts of Lisa filled his mind. She could be addictive. He pulled into the station's parking lot with Anders right behind him.

He reached back, grabbed his gym bag, and hopped out. He threw the bag on the backseat of Anders's car. Sliding into the front passenger seat, he saw Al sitting in the backseat.

Brett saw Anders glance at him. His boss opened his mouth to say something, but nothing came out.

Suddenly Al announced, "Anders and I had a meeting earlier tonight."

Brett swung back to look at Al. "What do you mean, a meeting?"

Anders began backing out of the lot. "He visited my house tonight. For some reason, I can now hear and see him."

Brett's gaze darted from Al to Anders. "No shit! How did this happen?"

Anders met Brett's gaze. "According to Al, the *big guy* thinks I need to know."

"Wow! I can't believe this." Brett glanced at Al again. Finally, he shrugged. "Now I won't feel like an idiot talking to Al. Were you scared when you first saw him?"

"Yeah. It freaked me out. I go to church every week and read the Bible. I don't think it ever mentions that talking ghosts with hats will help the police solve crimes. But hey, maybe I missed something in the fine print."

Al smiled at their banter. "Ha, ha. Listen, let's head east tonight." Al's smile faded. "I've got a feeling about going that direction. We have to find the suspect's house for Miller and Lisa."

Anders turned to look at Brett, who groaned aloud.

"Anders, a bit of warning. When Al gets a feeling, it usually means something bad is coming."

Al's droll sense of humor was evident that night. "Oh ye of little faith."

It was near 1:00 a.m. when they turned toward Carney. Only the longtime residents of Des Moines, like Brett, even knew that this area of the city used to house a large Italian population who worked in the nearby coal mines. Once the mines closed, many of the residents moved away. The neighborhood was now a blend of rural and suburban. The houses sat on large lots, far from the street. Many homes were hidden by overgrown brush and towering trees.

Al leaned over the front seat, looking at the houses as they drove past. They slowed as they approached the next intersection. A dead-end street lay on their right. If they turned left, the road led back to the center of Des Moines.

"Take a right," ordered Al.

Anders hesitated. "I don't think there is much down there. Nothing that matches Lisa's description of the house."

"Go right," Al snapped.

Anders frowned as he turned the wheel. Brett smiled. He could tell that Anders looked annoyed. It was hard for a man like Anders to take orders from a complete stranger, no less a ghost.

As they came to the end of the road, Anders stopped the car and turned off the engine. Three houses sat on the left side of the street. The lone streetlight was broken. In the first house, a single light in the front room gave them a view of an elderly woman who stood and made her way into another room. The second house was completely dark. It was after midnight, so it was possible that the residents were sleeping. The last house was also dark.

Anders muttered, "I don't think any of these match Lisa's description. Shall we go?"

Brett turned to ask Al, but he was gone. "Shit!"

"What?" Anders asked.

"Al is gone," Brett hissed.

"What does that mean?"

Brett pulled his gun and grabbed extra ammunition. "Usually it's not good. His hunches are a sign that something bad is going to happen. Like the night that Captain Miller was murdered."

Brett opened the car door, crouched down low to the ground, and circled around to the other side of the car. He heard Anders's door open and close. Anders leaned toward Brett, "Let's split up. You cover house number two, and I'll take house three. We'll check the perimeter of the houses to see if we can find anything suspicious. We'll meet up back here. Be careful."

Brett nodded and started moving forward. Brett had to be careful not to alert the old woman in the house next door. He could hear her television blaring out by the street. He figured she must be nearly deaf.

He approached the first window. It was small. Probably a bedroom window. He quickly peeked inside. The curtains were drawn. He couldn't see a thing. He moved to the next window. It was higher and even smaller. Bathroom. Suddenly he tripped and pitched forward. He bit back a groan as he hit the ground. He reached out and felt a large aluminum watering can under his foot. It made a crunching sound when he stepped on it. He glanced up at the window; there were no lights. He rubbed his ankle. It had twisted when he fell. As he rose, the pain radiated up his leg. He limped toward the next window. From the fluffy look of the curtains in the window, he guessed it was a kitchen. He turned the corner of the house, and suddenly a light from next door lit up the yard. Brett dodged behind a large bush and watched. The woman watching TV next door had turned on her bathroom light. The blinds on the window were wide open. *Geez lady!* A minute later, the toilet flushed and light went off.

Taking a deep breath, Brett slid around the corner of the house to the backyard. He squinted, trying to make out the shadows before him. An overgrown garden and trees with overhanging branches filled the space. A one-car garage sat on the opposite side of the house. In the distance, he saw another shadowy figure edging along the structure. It looked like Anders.

His pulse pounding, Brett hurried past the back door and hid in the shadow of the garage. A side door to the garage was partially ajar. Could a motorcycle be hidden in this garage? He needed to check. With his foot, he edged the door open further. An older model Buick was covered in dust. Tools lined the wall. Whoever lived here was very organized. Brett's garage never looked this neat. Maneuvering in the dark Brett moved back to the door, slid outside, and closed the door behind him. He had one more side to check out. It, too, was a bust. He wondered where Anders and Al were.

Brett anxiously looked next door. They should all have been able to see each other by this point. Brett didn't want to go into the other yard and startle his boss. He'd end up getting shot.

Deciding to finish the perimeter, Brett walked back to the street. As he passed a window, he paused and sniffed. He started to choke. *Shit!* Someone or something was dead inside the house.

Looking around, Brett whispered, "Al. Al, where the hell are you?"

A tap on his shoulder kicked Brett's adrenaline into high gear. Whipping around, gun in hand, Brett jabbed the barrel into Al's stomach. Punching Al's shoulder, Brett snarled, "Where have you been?" Pointing to the window, he hissed, "Something's dead in there."

Al shook his head. "I know. I went in and checked it out. An elderly woman had her throat slashed. Poor lady. It looks like she's been dead for several days."

"Shit," Brett muttered. "Another murder."

"Where's Anders?" asked Al.

Frustrated, Brett pointed next door. "I don't know. I saw him a while ago."

Al looked to the sky as the full moon shone down on them. "I'll go see what I can find." A second later, Al was gone.

Brett finished his search and reached the car. Minutes ticked by.

He was growing more anxious with each second. "The hell with it." Brett traced Anders's path around the third house.

When he reached the corner of the house, the garage lay ahead, just like the house he had already checked. Brett shivered as the autumn wind picked up. The screech of a nearby owl broke the silence of the night. The screen door at the back of the house banged against its frame. The garage door was closed, but Brett pressed his ear against it and paused. He could hear muffled voices. Who could be in there? Anders? He slowly turned the knob on the side door. It was locked. His only other option was to raise the overhead door.

He shuddered as the wind increased in intensity. The light from the moon was suddenly blotted out by rolling clouds. Goosebumps broke out across his body. His gut was telling him to get the hell out of here and call for backup, yet he hesitated. What if Anders were in there with the killer?

As he bent down to grab the handle of the door, he saw something move out of the corner of his eye. Slowly standing, Brett looked about the yard. Litter swirled about the lawn, carried by the breeze. A pitchfork leaned against the side of the worn siding. Nothing out of the ordinary. He had to be imagining things. Feeling silly at his overactive imagination, he glanced at the pitchfork one more time. It was floating inches above the ground. Could that even happen? He rubbed his eyes, blinking several times. The tines turned until the fork pointed straight at him. This was not happening! With increasing speed, the pitchfork flew straight at him. *Shit!* He stepped away from the garage door, instantly assessing whether he could make it to the car. He ran toward the car as if the hounds of hell were on his heels. While running, he reached for his phone. He tried to punch in his security code. *Damn it!* He was fat-fingering all the numbers.

Thirty feet to go. Twenty feet to go. He was almost to the car. Then he made a mistake. He paused to turn and look behind him. The pitchfork was less than two feet from his back. Before he could take another step, his ankle gave out and he fell, landing on his back. Pain paralyzed his body.

Suddenly a heavy weight fell on top of him. Upon opening his eyes, he found himself staring at the back of Al's hat. Al stood with the pitchfork protruding out of his stomach.

Brett gaped at the sight above him. Moaning, he rolled over to vomit across the driveway. After wiping his mouth, he shakily rose to his feet. Al's face contorted with an unnamed emotion. Handily, Al drew the fork out of his body and tossed it aside.

"What the hell just happened? Are you okay?" Brett felt himself wavering from side to side.

Al nodded. "I think so. It's obvious that we are dealing with something evil. Whatever the spirits are, they sure don't like you, sonny. You almost got made into mincemeat."

Brett gave Al a crooked smile. "Thanks for saving my life. I thought my ass was done for."

A loud wail from the garage made them jump. "Anders!" Brett began running to the garage door, his gun in hand.

Brett started to reach for the overhead door handle, but as he did, the door burst open. Brett covered his eyes as a headlight from the motorcycle blinded him. The roar of the engine pierced his ears. He raised his gun, squinting into the dark garage. He couldn't see Anders. He couldn't shoot without seeing a target.

A gunshot rang out, and Brett was shoved aside by Al in time to hear the motorcycle rush past him. What had just happened? Was Anders alive?

CHAPTER TWENTY-EIGHT

Once again, Brett picked himself up off the ground. Every muscle in his body clamored for relief. He limped into the garage and saw Al bending over Anders's still body.

"Is he dead?" A sour taste rose in Brett's throat. He grabbed his phone and called for backup.

Al shook his head. "No, I think he fell and banged his head. He's got a bullet in the leg, though. While you're at it, call for an ambulance."

Brett's hand shook as he communicated with dispatch. Al removed Anders's belt and fashioned a tourniquet for his leg. He got down on his knees and cradled Anders's head in his lap.

Anders groaned, and his eyes jerked open. He immediately grabbed for his gun. Brett put a hand on Anders's shoulder to restrain him. "It's okay, sir. He's gone."

Gingerly touching his scalp, Anders muttered a curse. "Damn it. I walked right into his trap. Just like a stupid rookie." Obviously struggling to position his leg, Anders sat up. "I should be grateful that I'm not dead. I'm sure I owe you two my life. What the hell happened?"

The sound of sirens broke the quiet of the night. Brett stared at his superior. "I think we'd better get our story straight real quick. There's a dead body next door."

"I had that little pissant in the crosshairs. Lisa's description was smack on. Quick, get me up! I want to search the house and see what we can find."

Brett placed Anders's arm around his shoulders and slowly lifted. Anders sagged against Brett. "Hey, are you all right? You look like you're going to pass out. I don't think this is a good idea, sir."

His lips thinned, Anders snapped, "Get me in there."

Al came around to the other side of Anders. "Brett, let me get this. You get the door open for us." Almost effortlessly, Al was able to get Anders up the back steps and into the kitchen. The bleeding in Anders's leg had stopped by the time he hobbled to the kitchen table.

Brett flipped through the papers scattered across the counter. Empty pill bottles littered the room. Brett picked up one of them and glanced at the label. "Richard Brown. Never heard of the guy, but Richard is on some strong shit. Oxycodone, phenobarbital, Vicodin, Xanax, and who knows what else is here."

Flashing lights and the slamming of car doors drew their gazes to the front door. Heavy footsteps sounded outside before the door was kicked open. The first person on the scene burst into the house. Detective Donnellson slid to a stop upon seeing the men sitting at the kitchen table.

With gun in hand, Donnellson surveyed the room, his eyes darting to every corner. "Anders! O'Shea! What's going on?"

Brett nodded to his friend. "The house is secure. We found Captain Miller's murderer. Unfortunately, he shot Major Anders and escaped. Where's the ambulance?"

Donnellson holstered his gun. "It is only a couple of minutes behind me. I was near here when your call came in. Since I knew that you and Anders were together, I busted ass to get here first in case you needed me."

"There's a body next door. Will you go secure that house until the detectives arrive?"

Donnellson nodded. "Will do. Glad to see you two are okay."

Brett smiled at his friend before turning toward Anders. He was speaking to someone on his cell.

After pocketing the phone, Anders turned to Brett. "I called my men who are on duty tonight. They'll be here in ten minutes. I want this house and the one next door turned upside down. We're going to find the bastard. He's got nowhere to hide now."

"I'll stay here and wait for them. You need to go to the hospital." Brett checked the bleeding on Anders's leg.

Anders grimaced. "My wife will have a fit. I've never gotten shot before. I should call her. Otherwise, she will shoot me in the other leg."

The ambulance arrived and quickly loaded Anders. Several detectives had arrived and were now going through the house. Brett was ordered to be at the station the next day to file a report.

Brett couldn't do anything else for the night, so he headed for Anders's car. He needed to go get his car and head home. He let out a deep breath. It felt like the first time he had breathed all night. His mind kept rewinding the events of the night. *It had to be a horrible dream. Pitchforks don't levitate and fly at people. Especially at my body!*

As Brett drove back to the station, Al appeared in the seat next to him. He was quiet for a change.

Brett gripped the steering wheel, his fingers turning white. "Can you explain what we saw tonight?"

"Never seen anything like this before. Luckily I got to you before the pitchfork skewered you like a piece of shrimp." Al shook his head, appearing to be completely at a loss. "I'd say we're dealing with something evil. This is out of my league. If I had to guess, I'd say we're up against something satanic."

Brett's breath caught in his chest. He could barely swallow. "The devil! Shit! Are you pulling my leg?"

Al whipped his head toward Brett. "You're naive if you believe he ain't real. God is real, and so is Satan. We're fighting something unworldly, Brett."

"You think! Flying pitchforks was a big clue for me." Brett's voice rose to a hysterical level. He could feel his pulse speeding up to match his stress level.

"Calm down. We're on the right side of this fight. Besides, we're getting close to solving the murders."

Brett gripped the wheel tighter. "Calm down! How would you feel if Satan was trying to skewer you?"

"I guess I'm the lucky one." Al chuckled. "You've got to trust that things will work out right. I don't believe it was an accident for me to be sent to work with you." He reached out and patted Brett's shoulder. "You know, we don't always know the bigger plan for our lives."

Brett snorted. "Yeah, I just hope the plan isn't for me to die by some damn hocus pocus shit."

"I'll do everything possible to make sure that doesn't happen," Al assured him.

Brett parked the car and transferred his belongings to his own car. Once home, he dropped his clothes and turned on the shower. Hot steam filled the bathroom. He grimaced as his muscles contracted against the hot water. Gradually, the tension left his body. Only when the water turned cool did he turn it off.

He crawled into bed, pulling the pillow over his head. Within seconds, he fell asleep.

Al sat in the recliner, gazing out the window. He was worried for Brett's safety. He was more than pissed off that he hadn't been given any advance notice that all of this was coming down. They were up against something much bigger than he expected. He knew the big guy was making new plans in lieu of the current events and attack. Heads were going to roll; he wanted to make sure his wasn't one of them!

CHAPTER TWENTY-NINE

Terry Anders gritted his teeth as he rolled to the side of the hospital bed. Luckily it was a clean shot. The bullet had passed through his thigh without damaging any bone or muscle. Putting both feet on the floor was an effort. He bit his lip as fire shot through his leg.

A nurse bustled through the door, and a look of shock came over her face. "Mr. Anders! What are you doing? You know that you're supposed to call for help if you need to use the bathroom."

"I don't need to use the bathroom. I'm just trying to get to the chair," he growled.

A knock on the door drew his attention. Brett walked in but stopped when he saw the nurse. "I can come back later."

Anders waved him in. "No, come on in. She's helping me to the chair."

A few minutes later, Anders wiped the sweat from his brow. He felt as weak as a baby. Brett fidgeted in his chair. Finally the nurse left the room.

"How are you feeling, sir?"

Anders grimaced as he slowly straightened his leg. "Better than I deserve. I can't believe that scrawny SOB got me. How are you doing? We didn't get to talk much last night."

Brett leaned forward. "We'll I'm glad it wasn't any worse. You could have been killed. You do remember that there was a body found next door to the suspect's house?"

Anders nodded. "I heard from my guys that it was an elderly woman, Mae Carter. She had been dead several days. Can you believe all the meds we found in Brown's kitchen?"

"Yeah. It seems our guy has a lot of mental problems." Brett shook his head from side to side.

Anders shifted in the chair, trying to get comfortable. "Speaking of Brown, any word of his whereabouts?"

Brett looked at the closed door and lowered his voice. "Not yet. We've got men stationed at the bus terminal. Since we know the pharmacy he uses, we're watching that also. Every cop has his picture and license number, so it's just a matter of time before we get him." Brett clenched his hands. "There's something I want to mention to you before I fill out any reports." Anders studied the younger cop. Brett looked spooked.

"This whole case is weird," said Anders. "Speaking to a ghost is weird. At this point, I don't think you can surprise me. What happened now?"

"After I heard you scream, I started running toward the garage, but something came after me."

"You mean *someone* came after you?"

"No, something. To be exact, a pitchfork leaning against the garage flew through the air and tried to gut me."

Anders's smile faded as he began to fully comprehend the words Brett had uttered. "What do you mean, a pitchfork?" he growled.

"A sharp pitchfork," Brett said. "If it hadn't been for Al, I wouldn't be here today."

"Oh shit! I have to accept the fact that ghosts exist. Now you want me to believe that an inanimate object is able to fly through the air and try to kill you? C'mon O'Shea, quit bullshitting me."

"Sir, it's the honest truth. According to Al, the pitchfork was possessed by some evil spirit. This murder case is not a normal case."

Anders stared at Brett, waiting for him to start laughing. He felt it had to be a joke. "Okay, you got me. Don't tell me, but *the devil made you say it*."

Brett gripped his arm. His eyes widened. "Sir, it is not a joke. Al believes that we may be dealing with demons or Satan."

Anders sat frozen in the chair, realizing his mouth was hanging open. "Demons? Satan? Oh shit, we're screwed if you're right. How are we supposed to handle this? I mean, how can a few cops like us even think we can go up against Satan, the devil, or whatever he is called?"

Brett's fist pounded a nearby table. "This is why we needed to talk before I meet with the detectives. They're going to think I'm crazy."

"Do not mention the pitchfork incident to anyone, do you hear me?"

"Yes."

Both men turned toward the doorway when they heard footsteps in the hallway. Anders's wife, Caroline, breezed into the room. She walked over and pressed a kiss to Terry's forehead. "Hi, sweetie. Are you feeling better?"

"Much better. I'm waiting for the doctor to release me. It will be good to get home in my own bed. I'm sorry, Caroline; this is Officer O'Shea. We're working the Miller murder case together."

Caroline smiled at Brett. "I'm so glad you were with my husband last night. He told me that you will make a great detective."

Blushing, Brett stood and shook her hand. "Thank you. I'm going to get out of here and leave you two alone. It was nice to meet you, Mrs. Anders."

Terry gave his wife a squeeze. "Dear, you're not supposed to repeat what I tell you about my men. O'Shea, I'll call you later."

CHAPTER THIRTY

Richard hid in the wooded area behind his house. He lay flat on his stomach, his elbows digging into the damp soil beneath him. The chill from the earth permeated his clothing. His stomach rumbled, reminding him that he hadn't eaten since the previous morning. He cupped his hands and blew on his fingers, trying to get the blood flowing to the tips.

Police were still rummaging through his house and the neighbor's house. Would they ever get done and leave? He wanted to get back in the house to collect his clothing and medicine. After that, he didn't know where he would go. He had no place to stay. The night before, he had ditched his motorcycle. There were too many cops looking for it. After killing the old biddy next door and taking her car keys, he took one of her cars and hid it in the woods. At least he would have transportation, if nothing else.

He hoped he had killed the officer in the garage the previous night. At first he thought it was O'Shea. Then, as he burst through the garage door, he almost ran over the young officer. Richard wasn't sure whom he had shot, but O'Shea was like a damn cat with nine lives. Why couldn't that guy just die? It was like he was protected by someone.

Crawling on his stomach, he reached the car. With only a few dollars in his pocket, McDonalds would have to do. Afterward, he would make a new plan. For the first time in days, Richard felt hopeful. He had shot one officer. The next time it would be O'Shea. It had to be!

Al chose to remain unseen in Anders's hospital room. Thoughtfully, he rubbed his chin. It seemed the major would need some evidence to convince him that they were up against supernatural forces.

After seeing the level of evil they were up against, Al had tried talking to the *big guy*, requesting help or something to give them an advantage. Al was scared shitless! Sure, he was a spirit and communicated with beings in heaven, but he had no knowledge of how to fight this nasty shit from hell. It was out of his league. When the pitchfork attacked Brett, Al was terrified. His instinct had saved Brett, but what was going to be their next obstacle?

Al ranted and raved, trying to get someone from up above to tell him what was going on. All Al kept getting in return was a Bible quote, Psalm 23:4: "Even though I walk through the valley of the shadow of death, I fear no evil; for Thou art with me; Thy rod and Thy staff, they comfort me."

Al understood the message, but when he was facing evil, he preferred to have a plan. At this point, he was out of ideas. They had to be strong and be ready to fight the next battle, for it was coming whether they were ready or not.

CHAPTER THIRTY-ONE

Brett released a deep breath as the door closed behind him. He was relieved that the interrogation was over. He could only hope there were not any discrepancies between his statement and Major Anders's.

He exited the stairway and entered the lobby of the police station, where he skidded to a halt. Lisa stood at the main desk, visiting with Anders. Anders leaned on a cane. The whiteness around his mouth indicated he was in pain.

Anders motioned to him. "O'Shea, over here."

Lisa flashed a smile at Brett. She looked very sophisticated in a black pin-striped suit. "Is everything all right?" she asked, glancing at the closed door.

"I'm glad it's over. Taylor was in there asking all kinds of questions."

Anders retorted, "What a prick. He was there when I was getting grilled."

"He wanted to know why we didn't call for backup earlier. I told him what I was doing when all hell broke loose."

Anders gave him an odd look. "You didn't mention what we talked about, did you?"

"No."

Lisa glanced at the two men, looking quizzical. "What are you guys hiding?"

They both spoke at once. "Nothing!"

Lisa folded her arms across her chest. Her head tilted. "Right. You know I will find out later, don't you?"

Anders grunted. "You're just like my wife. Keep digging until you get what you want. Be careful, Brett."

"Don't worry about me, sir. Did you still want to meet at my house?"

Anders clapped Brett on the shoulder. "I'll be there around five tonight. I've got physical therapy this afternoon. Caroline will kill me if I miss that appointment."

Brett was worried about the older officer. "Sir, why don't we take another day off?"

"Do you want to catch the bastard or what," he hissed.

Brett shrugged, raising his hands. "Of course! I was thinking of your injury."

With red cheeks, Anders mumbled, "Well, you just take care of you. I don't need two wives harping at me."

After helping Anders to his car, Brett turned toward his own car. Lisa walked beside him.

She cleared her throat and said, "I wanted to let you know that I'm getting pressure from my boss about this case. Because we're seeing each other, he thinks I'm going to get inside information. I wanted you to know. Whatever you want to tell me is fine. I will not betray your trust."

Brett wrapped his arm about her waist and pulled her closer. He pressed a light kiss to her cheek. "Thank you. Knowing that means a lot to me. I would love to tell you everything, but I don't want to put you in danger."

Lisa leaned her head against his chest. "I'm not going to get hurt. Besides, I've been chased and kidnapped, and I'm fine."

"Well, you were lucky. Lisa, you have no idea what we're up against. I'd rather not push our luck."

Lisa leaned her head back, gazing into his eyes. "Then tell me what we're up against."

He hesitated, glancing around the parking lot. He pleaded, "I can't. I wish I could, but we're dealing with more than a normal murder."

Lisa crinkled her nose. "Normal murder? I won't even ask what that means." After checking her phone, she muttered, "Hey, I've got to go to work. I'll call you later tonight."

Brett kissed her good-bye and drove home. After dropping his keys on the kitchen table, he grabbed a beer from the fridge. He went to living room and sat in his recliner, his thinking chair. Taking a large gulp, he found himself relaxing. He stared out the front picture window. The late afternoon sun gave the room a golden glow.

He was tired. Mentally and physically exhausted. *If only this case would end.* Doubt crept into his thoughts. Maybe they would never catch the cyclist. Maybe he would always be a street cop. Maybe Al would haunt him for the rest of his life. There were so many maybes that it made his brain hurt.

He turned and saw Al lying on the sofa. His hat was pulled down, covering his entire face. In a muffled voice, Al prodded, "Well, go ahead and say it."

Brett frowned. "Say what?"

"You don't think we have a chance in hell of solving this case, do you?"

"I don't know what I think anymore."

Al rose to a sitting position and adjusted his hat to the normal position, which hid the upper part of his face. "Sure you do, sonny."

A half smile broke across Brett's face as he took another swallow of beer. "I thought we were done with the name-calling."

"Nah. I like to keep you on your toes. Shit! I feel bad that you got drawn into this mess."

Brett drained the bottle and set it on the floor. "It's not your fault. Besides, I wanted the opportunity to actually solve a case. Who knew it would morph into something out of a horror flick."

"I wanted to let you know that I tried to get the low-down on what's going on. I got a pep talk instead."

"What kind of ghost are you? You can't even communicate with angels or God."

Al broke out into laughter. "That's the O'Shea I know."

Their raucous laughter and taunts came to a halt when a knock sounded on the door. It was Anders. After they were all seated, Anders gave them an update. His detectives had reported that a suspicious man drove by the pharmacy several times but finally left. Camera footage from the pharmacy showed the plates, which confirmed that the car was owned by Mae Carter, the murdered woman that lived next door to the suspect. Police now knew the suspect was driving a white 1999 Buick.

Anders leaned back on the sofa and elevated his leg on the coffee table. "Chief Ellison called me today. He thought I needed to take some time off for my leg wound. He wants to put Taylor in charge of the case."

Brett shot to his feet. "Oh, hell no! Why would he do that? Taylor isn't a detective."

"You're not telling me anything new. I told Ellison that my doctor has released me for work, so I asked if he was upset with my performance on the case. He backtracked a bit, but he said he thought I should take a vacation."

"A vacation? Be gone during the biggest case of the year! What the hell is he smoking?"

Al leaned forward. "Wait a minute. Taylor has been in Ellison's pocket for years, according to rumors. Taylor has it out for Brett. Why?"

The three men all looked at each other. Finally Brett spoke. "He's always bitching about me having a college education and telling me that I need to put in my dues and time like everyone else."

"I know that Taylor's pissed because I had you reassigned to my team. Ellison has close ties to some shady thugs. It's rumored that he is tied to the Eastern Europe crime ring in Chicago. But the mayor and city council won't hear anything bad about the guy. They think he's some damn superhero."

Al scratched his square chin. "Well that makes me wonder what he has on them. Sounds like there's a rotten apple or two in the basket."

Anders nodded in agreement. "Let me check on Ellison. I never understood why he and Taylor are so close. They have nothing in common. It's like Taylor has something on Ellison."

Brett waved his hands in front of them. "Hey guys! We have enough on our plates without going after Ellison and Taylor."

Al shook his head. "No, I agree with Anders. We need to make sure our house is clean."

"Just make sure word doesn't get out about what we're doing. We don't need any extra heat." Brett thought they were taking on more than they could chew. But at this point, he was outvoted.

Al zapped himself out of the room to go start his investigation. Anders wanted to drive past the suspect's house again. Even though his right leg was uninjured, he asked Brett to drive. After deciding they were hungry, the men pulled up to a drive-up window. They chowed down in the car as Brett drove toward the east-side home. There were several hours of daylight left in the day, and he hoped it was enough.

CHAPTER THIRTY-TWO

They pulled up to the dead-end road. Yellow crime tape was draped across the front doors of the two houses.

Anders got out of the car and slowly made his way into the suspect's house. Brett followed, anxiously looking around. Funny, he hadn't noticed the wooded area behind the houses the other night. The starkness of the tall trees set his nerves on edge. He looked around the yard for the pitchfork. Where the hell was it?

Once inside, he found Anders wandering from room to room. He returned to the kitchen and sat down, gazing about.

Brett kicked out a chair and sat down. "Not much left after the detectives packed up everything."

"They're combing through the evidence. Did you notice the bathroom mirror?"

"Yeah. Looks like a fist went through it."

Looking at Brett, Anders shook his head. "What makes people do shit like this?"

Brett shook his head as well. "I think our suspect, Richard, is a very sick dude."

As sunlight faded, Brett got up to switch on the light. He glanced out the kitchen window. Had something moved in the yard? He could swear he had seen a flash of white. He flicked off the light and returned to the window. He slid his gun from its holster.

"I think there's someone out in the woods behind the house."

Anders jumped up and peered out from the side of the window. "Yeah. I just saw something move." Glancing at his leg, he sighed. "Whoever is out there will run as soon as they hear the sirens. Are you up for checking it out?"

"Let me take the lead since you're hurt."

The men went out the front door and crept toward the backyard. With guns drawn, the men separated, but they remained close enough that they could still see each other. A loud thrashing sound drew their attention. A man jumped up from behind a bush and began running away from them.

"Police! Stop or we'll shoot," Anders ordered.

Without thinking, Brett called out, "I'll get him." Brett holstered his gun and took off running through the thick brush. Wild rose thorns tore at this skin. He was closing in on the man. Was it their suspect? It was almost completely dark now. The man's light-colored shirt fluttered out behind him as he ran. Brett could hear the harsh breathing of the runner. The man looked to be tiring. His strides were growing shorter.

Brett could almost reach out and touch the man. Two more steps and Brett lunged and grabbed the man's shirt, taking both of them to the ground with a sudden thud.

The man swung his fists at Brett's body. Brett quickly grabbed one wrist, captured the second arm, and snapped on the cuffs. Brett sat on the man's back as he wiggled beneath him.

"I can't breathe. Get off of me," the man pleaded.

Brett smacked the back of the man's head. "Shut the fuck up!"

In the distance, Anders called his name. "Over here," Brett yelled.

Within minutes, Anders broke through the trees. "You got him! Good job, O'Shea. Let's get him up and head back to the car. We can figure out who this guy is."

Brett yanked the man to his feet. He gave him a pat down, checking for hidden weapons and an ID. Brett pulled out a wallet and tossed it to Anders. As they walked back to the house, the man whimpered, "You're hurting me. Take off the cuffs. I can't feel my hands anymore."

Brett read the man his rights as they tramped through the woods.

Brett was relieved when the house came into view. He remembered his last trip here. It was so dark he could barely see a few feet in front of him. He wished he knew where the damn pitchfork was.

Upon reaching the car, Brett shoved the suspect into the backseat before shutting the car door. Anders grabbed a flashlight off the front seat and shone it in the man's face.

A large smile lit up Anders's face. "Well, well. We got our man, O'Shea. Richard Brown, you are under arrest for murder, unlawful discharge of a weapon in the city, burglary, and assault. I'm sure we'll come up with additional charges." Anders pulled out his phone to call for backup.

Brett studied the trembling man through the open window. The pupils of his eyes were dilated and filled with a wild look. Richard looked totally disoriented. His cheekbones suddenly took on a sunken look, giving his face an odd shape.

The prisoner's whimpering and whining started to get on Brett's nerves. "Shut up, Richard."

Richard's eyes darted around the yard. Lowering his voice, he leaned toward Brett. "Help me."

Brett was startled. What did the prisoner expect? He wasn't about to let him go. "Richard, you need to calm down. They'll take you to the hospital and get you fixed up with your meds."

The man's hysterical laughter gave Brett shivers. Anders glanced at them. "What are you doing, O'Shea?"

"Mr. Brown wants me to help him."

"Don't talk to him. He's the guy that killed Miller. I find it hard to have any sympathy for the guy."

Richard's head twisted from left to right several times. His high-pitched moan filled the night. Brett tensed. He nervously glanced over his shoulders toward the wooded area.

"Hey, Anders. Let's get out of here and take him to the station ourselves."

Anders looked up from his texting, staring at Brett. "What's wrong?"

"I don't know. After the pitchfork incident, this place makes me jumpy."

Anders chuckled. "Hell, this entire case is weird. Don't worry; the paddy wagon will be here any minute. Then we'll get out of here."

Brett swore under his breath. Nothing good was going to come from waiting here. He glanced at their prisoner, who continued to make inhuman sounds. Brett gently patted Richard's cheek. The guy looked as if he were going to faint.

"Hey Richard! You okay? Anders! This guy looks bad."

Anders sighed and put his phone away. He opened the car door, pulling Richard out. With their prisoner leaning against the car, Anders tipped Richard's face upward. Richard's eyes rolled back in his head.

"Shit! O'Shea, call an ambulance," Anders ordered.

Richard's head lolled toward them. His mouth fell open. A deep voice came from his body, which sounded nothing like the high-pitched voice used earlier. "Stupid cops."

Richard's free hand whipped from behind his back and grabbed Anders's throat. The scrawny fingers tightened around Anders's neck, causing him to choke and gasp for air. Anders's hands flew up as he tried to pry the hand from him.

Realizing that Anders needed help, Brett jumped into the fray and tried to pull Richard's hand off Anders. Using both of his hands, Brett couldn't break the hold that Richard had on Anders. *What the hell! How can he overpower us using only one hand? How did he get the cuffs off?* Anders looked scared as he struggled to breathe.

Smashing his fists into Richard's body, Brett shouted, "C'mon, c'mon. Let go!" Brett looked at Richard's face and stopped. The prisoner stood smiling at him, looking as if this struggle were effortless. As Anders's body began to crumple from lack of oxygen, Brett felt a surge of adrenaline course through his body. He drew back a fist and slammed it into Richard's face using all the force he could muster. The sound of breaking bone gave him a sense of satisfaction.

Richard's hand dropped from Anders's neck. Brett dragged his boss away from the car. Bent over at the waist, Anders coughed and wheezed, trying to catch his breath. Relieved that Anders was still alive, Brett cringed as he looked at Richard. Blood ran from his nose.

The man's eyes narrowed and revealed an unnatural hatred. Brett shuddered and automatically took a step backward.

Richard took a step toward him, dangling the broken cuffs in his hand. With a tilt to his head, Richard smiled as he dropped the handcuffs to the pavement. He stiffly walked toward Brett.

Oh shit! The man didn't even look human any longer. One of Richard's arms reached out, and long talons shot out where his hand and fingers should have been. Brett continued to back up until his back bumped up against the car. There was nowhere else to go.

Richard whipped his other arm forward, his talons cutting into Brett's shirt. Each tear was dotted with blood—his blood. Brett knew he couldn't take his gaze off of Richard—or whatever it was that stood before him.

"You O'Sheas have plagued me long enough. You have thwarted my plans for the last time," Richard's unnatural voice boomed.

What the fuck is this guy talking about? Brett hoped to stall for time. He knew the wagon should be there any minute. Anders lay on the ground with his eyes closed.

"Dude, I don't have a clue what you're talking about."

Richard's face erupted into red boils. Hot, foul breath hit Brett in the face as the entity leaned closer. "You have a smart mouth just like your great-grandfather. I killed him, and now I'm going to kill you," the creature hissed. "You're the last O'Shea on the force. I will tear your heart from your body and feast upon it."

Brett tightened his legs before they buckled and forced a smile. "I bet you studied drama in high school, didn't you? I have to admit that you're looking kind of scary."

The creature roared, startling the sleeping birds from the trees. The sounds of rushing wings filled the air. Bats swarmed above them. This was a fucking horror movie, and he was going to be the victim. He locked his muscles, refusing to cower before the monster.

"Man, you'd better do something about the boils on your face. They look infected. Just some advice, man to man: women don't care for pus-filled sores. I'm sure a doctor can prescribe something for it."

The creature trembled in rage and took another swipe at Brett's chest. Tears filled Brett's eyes. His hand automatically covered the wounds, trying to halt the blood flow. He could feel blood running down his body. He had to do something. He grabbed his gun from the holster and pressed the Glock into the creature's stomach. The monster glanced down at the gun pressing into his body.

"Surprise!" Brett pulled the trigger twice.

The creature jerked in response and screamed in pain. His long talons curled inward. Yellowish liquid oozed from the open sores on its face. When its angry gaze turned back toward Brett, he responded by emptying the entire magazine into Richard's legs and feet. The smell of gunpowder filled Brett's nostrils. Richard collapsed on the ground, writhing in pain. A blue-colored fluid leaked from the wounds in Richard's body. *Crap! What is that?*

Brett quickly reloaded his gun, not taking his eyes off of the body on the ground. Richard's facial features began returning to normal. The creature retreated. Brett breathed a sigh of relief. The ambulance sirens grew louder. Anders staggered to his feet and walked to Brett's side.

"Did I just see what I think I saw?"

Brett nodded, too exhausted to speak. They watched the creature morph back into Richard Brown before their very eyes. The bullet wounds were healing at amazing speed. Brett snorted. If only his wounds could heal themselves like that.

The paddy wagon and ambulance pulled up to the curb. The new arrivals jumped out of the car with guns drawn and aimed at the man lying on the ground. The medics ran to Richard's side, ripping apart his clothing. A large amount of dark liquid had pooled on the ground next to him. Brett knew they expected to see a multitude of injuries.

The medics ceased their movements. Their mouths dropped open. They shot Brett and Anders puzzled looks. There were no wounds on Richard's body. Only a few scratches remained. When they saw Brett bleeding, one of the medics quickly came over to clean his wounds.

Just when Brett thought it couldn't get any worse, a squad car pulled up. Sergeant Taylor got out and walked across the lawn. He was shaking his head as he assessed the situation.

"Anders, I thought you knew better than to hook up with O'Shea. It looks like you two have a mess on your hands again."

Anders folded his arms across his chest. "Fuck off, Taylor. Did you happen to notice that we caught the suspect in Miller's murder?"

"Humph," Taylor groused. "What the hell happened to you, O'Shea? Did a bear attack you?" Taylor chuckled, failing to notice that no one else was joining in.

Richard moaned and started to rise. Anders nudged the medic out of the way and quickly slapped on another pair of cuffs.

Brett cursed when the medic pressed on his open wound. "Better watch him, Anders. He's dangerous."

As soon as the words were out of his mouth, Brett cringed. Taylor looked puzzled. "How did he get the jump on you?"

Anders cut in. "He had a knife hidden in his boot."

"Didn't you two search him first?" Taylor planted his fists on his hips.

Brett grumbled, "We had just chased him through the woods and were walking toward the car when it happened. It's kind of dark out there, you know."

Taylor's brow rose in anger or disbelief, Brett didn't know which.

The medic helped Brett to the ambulance. "We need to get you to the ER and get those wounds looked at. You may need stitches."

As Brett was helped into the ambulance, Anders stood by the door, pulling up his collar to cover the red marks on his neck. "I'll meet you at the hospital. You'll need a ride home. I'll go to the jail and make sure the suspect gets booked and locked up."

Brett nodded and lay back on the stretcher. His head was swirling with thoughts. He had almost died. Again. This was becoming a too-common occurrence. Twice in a week was a little much. Maybe he needed to start wearing a cross or carrying a Bible. How come all this weird stuff was happening to him? It's not like they were in New Orleans with voodoo and rumors of vampires. Where was Al, anyway?

Upon Brett's arrival at the hospital, his wounds were quickly cleaned and dressed. Police got high priority in the ER. It was almost 3:00 a.m. by the time he was ready to go home. Anders waited out front. Brett walked to the door and gingerly got into the car.

"Sore?" asked Anders.

"Every time I move my arms, it feels like little darts are shooting through my chest." Brett winced as he fastened the seat belt. "Thanks for the ride."

"No problem." Anders turned off the radio and turned to Brett. "Well, I guess we now know that we are really dealing with the supernatural. Shit! Did you see that guy? He looked like something from *Poltergeist*."

"Ya think? I was standing inches from it. I don't mind telling you that I was scared shitless."

Anders sighed. "I am not sure how I'm going to tell my wife what we're dealing with. Once she sees the marks on my neck, she'll have a fit."

"Are you sure you want to tell her? She'll want you to retire."

Anders snorted. "She knows me better than that. I'm in this mess now, and we're going to finish it."

Once home, Brett waved Anders on as he made his way into the house. He tossed his keys on the table, grabbed a bottle of vodka out of the freezer, and poured a big shot. He sat in the dark, alone with his thoughts. He wanted to turn off those thoughts, but it wasn't happening. Snorting, he tossed back the drink. He was becoming a seasoned hocus-pocus warrior, if there even was such a thing. First flying pitchforks and now a demon. He was beginning to feel like Dorothy in *The Wizard of Oz*. Lions, tigers, and bears, oh my! What could possibly attack him next? He was thankful he hadn't seen any flying monkeys yet.

CHAPTER THIRTY-THREE

Brett rolled over, pulling the bedcovers over his head. He knew it had to be midday, judging by the way the sun lit the room. He raised his arms to stretch and then jerked them back down. He groaned, holding his sides. "Shit, shit, shit!"

He shuffled into the bathroom and turned on the shower. He felt as if he'd been run over by a truck. The hot water felt wonderful on his bruised, battered body. After dressing and brushing his teeth, he felt alive once again.

He checked his cell phone. Lisa and Anders had called. Hungry, he threw a frozen sausage biscuit into the microwave. He flicked on the TV and wolfed down breakfast while watching the news. After he dumped the dishes in the sink, he turned toward the living room. Al stood in the doorway, watching him.

Brett jumped, his nerves shot after the previous night. "I hate when you pop in unannounced."

"Chill, sonny."

Brett glared at Al as he walked to the sofa. Wincing, he sat down.

"What happened? Are you injured?"

Brett lay down, stuffing a pillow behind his head. "I'm lucky to be alive. We caught the guy we think killed Miller."

"The motorcyclist?"

"Yeah. The suspect is Richard Brown. You wouldn't believe what I saw last night."

Al sat down near Brett and propped his feet on a coffee table. "What happened?"

"Just a couple of things. First, Richard's fingers turned into claws and ripped my skin to shreds. Second, big blister things that oozed goop popped up all over his face. Man, anyone like that isn't human. When I unloaded my gun into his body, some strange blue liquid came oozing out."

Al's feet fell to the floor. He sat and stared at Brett.

Brett slowly rose. "What do you think? It's like the guy is possessed or something. Definitely not normal."

Al grabbed his hat and yanked it down lower. "This is worse than I ever thought."

Brett paced the room. "Oh, it gets better. Richard, the demon, or whatever he is, said that he killed my great-grandfather and he was going to kill me because I was the last O'Shea cop. I don't know what Mike O'Shea did to piss off this evil thing, but it must have been serious."

Al moaned, holding his head.

"Hey, what's wrong? You look like you're going to pass out."

Al tugged his hat over his nose. "Damn it all. My head is killing me. I think part of my past memories are returning. I will check with the boss man and see what else we can find out about Mike."

Brett leaned over, trying to see Al's eyes. "Are you sure you're okay?"

Al jumped to his feet and began pacing back and forth in front of the sofa. Before Brett could ask any additional questions, Al's figure shimmered into the air. Brett bit back a curse. Al knew something that he wasn't sharing. Before Brett could decide how to get the information from Al, the doorbell rang. Changing direction, he opened the door. Lisa brushed past him carrying a pizza box. The aroma of pepperoni made his stomach growl.

"Have you eaten yet?"

"Just a sandwich. God that smells good. Let me get the plates."

Lisa set down the box and turned to hug him. He groaned as she squeezed him.

"What happened? Is that blood on your shirt?"

Brett glanced at his aching stomach muscles. "Yeah, I ran into a little trouble last night."

Lisa went to the sink and began washing her hands. "Take off your shirt," she demanded.

Using one arm, he slowly removed the shirt. Lisa gasped. "A little trouble! What happened?"

He shrugged. "I got cut."

Tossing her golden waves over her shoulder, she muttered, "Duh! I can see that. Who cut you?"

Brett bit back a smile, imagining what her reaction would be if he told her the truth. Before he could think of a logical explanation, Lisa grabbed his face in her hands.

"Don't you think of lying to me, Officer O'Shea," she snapped. "You're probably going to tell me some outrageous story about monsters just to make me laugh and forget your injuries."

Brett couldn't help it. He burst out laughing. Gasping from the pain, he bent over. "Ow."

Lisa stood with her hands on her hips, staring at him. "Are you making fun of me?"

"No, it's what you said."

Blinking in confusion, Lisa tilted her head and studied him. "Out with it."

"You said something about monsters. It was just a little too close to the truth." Not meeting her look, Brett grabbed a piece of pizza and bit into it. "Mmm, this hits the spot."

Before he could take another bite, Lisa grabbed the slice from his hand and slapped it back into the box.

"Hey! I'm hungry," Brett complained.

"O'Shea, you're in deep shit. You've got ten seconds to tell me what the hell is going on."

As if to emphasize her point, her foot tapped angrily on the tile floor. He wanted to confide in her, but he couldn't put her in danger again. He glanced at her determined stance and sighed. Could he trust her?

Taking her hand, he led her to the living room. Once they were seated, his brow furrowed. He absently rubbed the palm of Lisa's hand.

Lisa gripped his hand and pressed a kiss to his cheek. "You might as well quit stalling."

"You're right. I suppose you heard that we captured Captain Miller's killer last night." Lisa nodded as he tried to continue. "This is harder than I thought."

"Brett, you can trust me. I promise."

"That's not the issue, believe me. Okay, here goes. Anders and I caught the suspect and handcuffed him. The guy started making weird noises and looking crazy. Somehow, he broke the cuffs and—"

Lisa jerked backward. "Wait a minute. Broke the cuffs?"

"Yes, broke the cuffs. The guy started choking Anders. I punched the guy in the face and finally got him to stop."

Lisa shook her head. "But how could a man break the cuffs. I don't know anyone who could."

Brett met the puzzled gaze in her eyes. "This is where it gets really weird. After I punched the suspect, he got pissed off at me." Brett shivered and glanced out the window; his eyes glazing over. "One minute there was a man standing before me, and the next it was a monster."

CHAPTER THIRTY-FOUR

Lisa waited for Brett to start laughing. He was screwing with her. Why wasn't he smiling? She was used to interviewing people and knowing when they were lying or hiding something important. What did he mean by "monster"?

"Monster? You mean like a crazy man? Or someone with mental issues?"

Brett shook his head. "No. A monster, like something not human."

A brittle laugh escaped her. "Damn it, Brett. Be serious."

When he didn't react, Lisa felt faint. "You're serious, aren't you?"

Staring stoically at her, he subtly nodded.

"Not human? What did he look like?"

"One minute his face was normal, and the next it was covered with some kind of boils. His voice changed." Brett paused, his face flushed. "Then his fingers changed into long claws and raked across my chest. Lisa, I was scared. For a second my life flashed before my eyes. I thought I was done for."

Lisa fell back on the sofa and closed her eyes. Her heart pounded. Could Brett be mistaken? Maybe she should talk to Anders. If both men had seen the same thing, then what? Monsters existed? No, she wasn't ready to accept that. She opened her eyes and found Brett watching her.

"Do you believe me?"

Lisa softly replied, "I'm sure you thought you saw the *thing*. Something did happen, and you were attacked."

Brett's frown grew more pronounced. She sensed his frustration. "Hey, I'm a reporter. I deal with facts. I am trained to do my research and then double-check my facts before doing a story."

"Oh right. I'm just a dumb cop who doesn't know fact from make-believe. After all, monsters and ghosts don't exist, so what I'm saying is a big, fat lie."

Lisa jumped to her feet. "Well, don't get pissed off at me! I didn't say that. You have to admit that your tale is a little far-fetched."

Brett stomped over next to her. "What I told you is the truth. Either you believe it or you don't. I really don't care at the moment."

Realizing he was really angry at her, she softened her tone. "Brett, it's not that I don't believe you. I just need proof. That's me. It's the way I am."

Brett opened his mouth to reply but stopped. His eyes focused on something behind her. She turned and saw a man standing there.

"Oh, hello." She reached out to shake his hand, but the man faded away. She quivered and turned back to face Brett, who suddenly looked very nervous. "Who was that man?"

"Man?" he squeaked. "You could see him?"

"Yes, where did he go?" Her gaze whipped around the room.

"Uh, I'm not sure."

Lisa froze as she felt a hand on her shoulder. Slowly turning, she stiffened with fear. It was the same man. She tilted her face, trying to see under the brim of his hat. All she saw were shadows. That was strange. Maybe his hat was pulled down too far? Even though she couldn't see his eyes, she sensed his amusement. She felt off kilter.

"Hi again. I'm Lisa. And you are ...?"

The man stepped to her side. This allowed Lisa to get a better look at him. His clothes looked really outdated. Her nose wrinkled as she took a breath and choked back a cough. Who smoked pipes anymore?

"Call me Al. I've heard all about you."

She glanced at Brett, who was shooting angry glances at Al. "Really? Brett hasn't told me a thing about you."

Al chortled while Brett mumbled under his breath. Lisa glanced from man to man. What was wrong?

Al took her hand and led her to a chair. "Have a seat, miss. Brett has quite a crush on you."

"Al, don't you have somewhere else to be?" Brett snapped.

"No, I heard you two getting into an argument about monsters and ghosts and whether they are real or not. So I decided to pay you a little visit."

Brett groaned. The muscle in his jaw twitched. "Well, I can handle my own personal affairs, so get the hell out of here."

Lisa glanced from man to man. What was going on? How could Al know about their conversation? He hadn't been here.

Al patted Brett on the shoulder. "Calm down, sonny. You know by now that you can't control me. Your guest needs a little reality check."

Lisa jumped to her feet. *Reality check? Who needs a reality check?* She reached into her pocket and pulled out her car keys. "It seems like you guys have something to discuss, so I'll leave. I've got work to do. Catch you later, Brett."

She turned and almost raced to the front door. She let out a gasp and nearly fell to the floor as she suddenly collided with Al. How could he have moved so fast and gotten around her? She hadn't even seen him budge.

Unbidden tremors coursed through her. Something was really wrong here! She blinked her eyes to keep the room from rolling. Brett hurried to her side.

"Are you okay? Don't pay any attention to Al. He gets carried away with his jokes."

Breathe in and out, she said to herself. *Air in, air out*. She could hear them arguing. About what, she didn't know. She wasn't really trying to eavesdrop, but in such a small room, what did they expect?

"She needs to know."

"No, she doesn't."

"She didn't believe you when you told her what happened last night. She'll be better prepared if she knows."

"No she won't. Quit meddling in my personal business."

"I'm telling her that I'm a ghost."

"No you're n—"

Both men stared at her. She fell into the chair, drawing her legs up to her chest. Her lower lip trembled as she fought back the hysteria. "Ghost?"

Brett punched at Al's face but somehow missed. "Look what you've done now?"

Al vaporized and reappeared next to Lisa. She instinctively recoiled and covered her face. "Get away from me!"

Brett hurried to her side, pulled her hands away from her face, and tipped her chin to meet his gaze. A crooked smile graced his ashen face. "Lisa, it's okay. No one will hurt you."

Pointing her finger at Al, she cried, "Who is he?"

"His name is Al. He has been helping me and Anders on the murder case."

"But he's a ghost. I've seen him go poof and then reappear." She could no longer stop her body from violently shaking.

Al broke out laughing. "Poof! I like that. Watch this." And just like that he disappeared again. His figure shimmered and came into focus on the other side of Brett.

Lisa screamed. She felt that she had to get out of there. She tried to stand, but her vision darkened as she slid to the floor with a thud.

CHAPTER THIRTY-FIVE

Al regarded Lisa sprawled out on the floor. Brett was ready to explode. Sometimes Al could be a real pain.

"I'll catch you later," Al chirped.

Before he could disappear, Brett grabbed his arm. "Oh no, you don't. You created this mess, and you're going to help me fix it."

Bending over, Brett shifted Lisa's body and picked her up in his arms. He strode down the hall and carefully laid her on his bed. He brushed the strands of hair out of her face. He felt a fissure of doubt tear through him. Could Lisa comprehend what was really happening? How could Lisa see Al? More importantly, why now?

When he returned to the kitchen, he found Al pacing the room. Brett jerked out a chair and sat down. "Explain what the hell is going on."

Al sighed and leaned against the granite counter. "I owe you and Lisa an apology. I shouldn't have scared her like that. I was upset that she didn't believe you."

Brett's anger drained from him as he ran his fingers through his hair. "Thanks for trying to help. I know you didn't do it out of spite. But why can she see you now and not before?"

"I don't know, but if I were to guess, I would think things are coming to a head. The guy upstairs has a plan. Perhaps Lisa is a part of that plan."

Brett kicked out his feet, shaking his head. "Damn it! Can this get any more complicated?"

Both men jumped as Brett's cell phone rang. "O'Shea. Oh shit! Yeah, he's here … Okay, we'll see you shortly."

Laying the phone on the table, he glanced at Al. "Richard Brown escaped the county jail. Anders is on his way over."

Al grunted, "Well, well. That's a surprise. Not!" Brett glared at him. Shrugging, Al muttered, "What?"

"You've been here too long. You're talking like some high school girl."

"At least I'm not texting all the time, like some people I could name."

"Quit screwing around. We've got bigger things to talk about."

A sound down the hallway drew their attention. Brett jumped up and saw Lisa walking toward them. She looked horrible. Her face was as white as a sheet.

He hurried forward and took her arm. "Here, lean on me. You shouldn't be up yet."

"Well, I heard you two talking, and since I'm now part of the *plan*, I'm going to join you guys to see what I need to do." Sliding into a chair, she whispered, "Do you have any coffee?"

Brett grabbed a coffee pod and turned on his Keurig. Minutes later, he set a cup of coffee in front of Lisa, who gripped the cup with both hands as if to warm herself.

Hearing voices, Brett turned to see Al open the door for Anders. The men joined them in the kitchen. Anders paused when he saw Lisa.

"Don't worry about Lisa. She can see Al and knows what's going on."

Lisa smiled up at Anders. "I know what's going on, but I don't quite believe what's going on."

Anders chuckled as he sat next to her. "I was a real mental case when I first met Al. You'll be fine, trust me."

As they all sat down, Al brusquely demanded, "Spill the beans on Dick boy."

"I got the call early this morning. The cells are all monitored by cameras. After reviewing the video tapes, we could tell that he was in the cell at two a.m. At five a.m., his cell was empty. The door was still locked. According to the jailers, none of the other prisoners heard a thing." Anders got up and fixed a cup of coffee.

Brett swore and stood up. "How can we fight something that's not human?"

Every head swiveled in Al's direction. Al threw his hands up in the air. "I don't know! I'm still trying to figure out why I'm here."

"Would a priest be able to help?" Lisa asked.

"It couldn't hurt. After all, me and sonny are good Irish boys."

"O'Shea, we need to hit the streets and find this guy before something horrific happens."

Brett nodded to his boss. He glanced at Lisa, who suddenly looked like a little girl ready to cry. "What's wrong?"

"I'm afraid. I don't want you to get hurt."

Al's chest puffed up. "He ain't going to get hurt. I'll be with them. I'm counting on some support from above."

"Above?"

"Don't ask," said Brett. "C'mon guys, we gotta get going."

Brett hung back after Anders and Al went outside. He took Lisa's hand and drew her to him. "You're welcome to stay here if you want."

Pulling him closer, she pressed a kiss on his lips. "Thanks, but I'll head home. I've got to work tomorrow. You'd better call me so I know that you're okay."

He ran a finger across her full lips and framed her face with his hands. Leaning closer, he melded his mouth with hers. He felt her thread her fingers into his hair. His pulse increased as their tongues wove together. Her soft moan increased his arousal. Outside, the sound of a honking horn drew his attention. Five more minutes and he would have laid her on his bed.

As they stared at each other, he was filled with regret. "Hey, I gotta go. Lock up when you leave."

After kissing her again, he hurried out to the car. They had one goal tonight: find creepy Dick.

Lisa watched the men drive out of sight. After turning off most of the lights, she picked up her purse and coat. As she reached the door, she hesitated. Turning, she dropped her stuff on the floor. What was she doing? Brett was heading into a life-and-death situation. Was she supposed to go home and wait until she heard from him? Hell no! She was a research reporter. She'd even won two national awards for her detailed work and stories. She was going to figure out how to help Brett, starting right now. She marched into his office and started working.

Surprised at the number of hits that came up when she began her Internet research on the occult and ancient spells, she added more paper to Brett's printer. It was going to be a long night.

CHAPTER THIRTY-SIX

"G et in here and shut the door," Chief Ellison ordered.

Sergeant Taylor quickly closed the door. He had never seen Ellison look so disheveled.

"What are you doing about O'Shea? I thought you told me you could keep him under control?"

Taylor glanced at his feet before answering. Ellison had lots of secrets—secrets that he didn't want to know about. "It's Anders. He has taken O'Shea under his wing. You approved the transfer. I assumed you wanted Miller's murder case solved?"

Ellison slammed his fist on the desk. His brow furrowed and his face took on a reddish hue. "I do, you freaking idiot! But Anders and O'Shea won't look the other way like you and some of the others. If Anders continues to make all the headlines, he'll get promoted. If he's promoted, then he will start nosing into our project. If that happens, then my job is in jeopardy. If I go down, then so do you. Get it?"

Taylor cleared his throat, trying to control his trembling hands. Ellison was out of control. The man couldn't seem to focus. "So does this mean that we'll quit selling info?"

Ellison pursed his lips and leaned over the desk. His face scrunched into an unidentifiable fury. "Think carefully about what you say next. Just do what I tell you. Got it?" he hissed.

Taylor nodded, avoiding the chief's angry glare. He couldn't afford to lose his job. The money that Ellison gave him was not enough to go to jail for. One look at the chief's face told him that now wasn't the time to ask about getting out of the deal. Right or wrong, good or bad, he was in too deep.

"Right. Roll call is about to start. If you don't mind, I need to go."

"Keep O'Shea and Anders away from our business. Do you hear me, Taylor?"

Taylor gave a curt nod and escaped the chief's office. He felt the blood drain from his head. What the fuck had he gotten into? Angry about the verbal beating, Taylor marched downstairs. He was the last one to enter the room.

A chuckle from the back of the room drew his attention. There stood O'Shea and few of the other detectives in the corner, smiling and joking with one another. Were they joking about him? Bristling with animosity, he snarled, "Obviously, O'Shea and other detectives don't share our commitment to catch the crazed killer on the loose in our city. They prefer to joke and laugh as if nothing is wrong."

Silence filled the room. Men turned in their seats to stare at the group of detectives. After carefully setting down his coffee, Brett walked toward the front of the room and stood by an empty chair.

"Yeah, you're right. Oh, wait a second. Anders and I were the ones who caught the guy the first time."

"O'Shea, sit your ass down and shut up. I can still fire your ass even if you work with Anders."

Brett's face flushed with anger. Biting the inside of his cheeks helped keep him from saying something he'd regret. Brett slid into the chair and smirked at the sergeant. With blood pounding in his head, he found it hard to concentrate on what Taylor was saying to the group. He stood as the officers filed out of the room. As he made his way outside, his phone started buzzing.

"Hi, Lisa. What's up?" He waved at Anders, who was standing near the car. "No, Al doesn't have any ideas. You're researching spells! Did you find anything significant? Great, why don't you print the articles and we'll take a look at them tomorrow. Maybe Al will know more then. See you later."

Getting into the car, he nodded to Anders. Al greeted Brett from the backseat.

"Lisa just called," said Brett. "Being a reporter and all, she is into research. She is hoping to find a book or something that will help us control this thing we're up against. She's looking into ancient spells."

Al sat forward, leaning over the front seat. "A spell? Hell, I guess it can't hurt. Though I don't put much stock in hocus pocus." Peering upward, Al grumbled, "Unless the guy upstairs starts communicating better, I'll take what we can get."

Brett and Anders looked at each other and burst out laughing. "What did I say?" muttered Al.

"You don't think much of hocus pocus, but you're a ghost." Brett started laughing again.

Folding his arms across his broad chest, Al pouted. His lower lip stuck out. "Oh, go ahead and laugh. Ha ha. It's not like I had a choice in the matter. My mother would yank my ear if she could see what I've become."

Their laughter faded as they made their way down York Street. There was a citywide manhunt for Richard Brown. Anders had suggested they start looking at the Miller house.

Silence filled the car. Flashes of light from passing headlights created shadows. A somber glare reflected in each of their eyes. Brett tensed when Anders stopped in front of Captain Miller's house. The house had an abandoned air about it. After his friend and superior was murdered, his widow moved to another state to live with a daughter. A "for sale" sign stood in the front yard. They'd be lucky to sell the house, especially with it being the site of a horrific murder.

"C'mon," ordered Anders. "Let's take a look around the outside before we go in."

Brett forced himself out of the car. His chest tightened as he glanced at the empty house. Memories and images flooded his thoughts. He couldn't remember the number of times he had been here for dinner with his grandmother and the captain. He had never understood when his mom or grandmother said that time flew by. Yet in this moment, staring at the dark house, he finally got it. It seemed just like yesterday that he was a kid running around the yard, playing tag or baseball with the captain. Absently, he wiped moisture from his cheek.

As an arm draped over his shoulder, Brett turned to meet Anders's gaze.

"Are you okay?"

Nodding, Brett turned back to face the empty house. "I guess I can't get over the fact that Miller is gone. I knew him my entire life."

"I wish I could say something to make it better."

Brett looked at Anders. "We can make it better by solving his murder and getting this guy locked up permanently."

Anders gripped Brett's hand and shook it. "Okay then. Let's nail the son of a bitch."

CHAPTER THIRTY-SEVEN

Lisa threw up her hands in frustration. Who knew that there was so much information on the Internet about demonic spirits and possession? Pile after pile of papers littered the desk. She was tempted to sneak in a quick nap. But it was after midnight; there wasn't time for that. She needed more coffee.

As she headed to the kitchen, she came to a sudden stop. A shadowy figure sat hunched over the table. She turned to run.

"Calm down, Miss Winslow. It's me, Al."

Putting a hand over her thundering heart, Lisa turned and looked closer at the man in Brett's kitchen. She flipped on the lights and staggered to the coffee pot.

"Geez! You know how to scare a person to death. I thought you were with Brett and his boss?"

"I was. I decided to come see you." Al smiled at her. "I hear you're giving us a hand by doing some research. I don't understand how that flat thing called a laptop works. All the little lights and the noises it makes are very disarming. Did you find anything to help us yet?"

Lisa poured a cup of steaming coffee and took a quick sip. "I think I found something. I'll be right back." She ran down the hall to Brett's office, snatched the papers off the desk, and returned to the kitchen.

Al took the papers and began reading. Lisa had highlighted key facts. She watched as he rubbed the back of his neck. After filling up her cup again, Lisa sat down at the table.

"Well, you seem to think we're dealing with demonic possession."

Lisa reached for another page lying nearby. "Yes, according to this article, people who are possessed may experience drastic changes in vocal intonation."

"Check," Al snapped.

"Changes in facial structure ..."

"Check."

"Superhuman strength." Lisa's smile grew with every acknowledgment Al made.

"Check."

"And sudden appearances of cuts and lesions.

"Double check." Al shuddered, probably thinking about the pus-filled sores that Brett had described.

"I believe that Richard doesn't really have any control over his body. This spirit or demon controls Richard. Until the spirit is forced to leave Richard's body, the murder and mayhem will continue."

"Just how do we get rid of this nasty creature?"

Lisa hesitated, staring at Al. "Well, I was hoping that you would know what to do, being a ghost and all."

Al's mouth twisted in a smirk. "Me? I am a mere ghost. There are much higher beings in heaven than me. The angels have not been very forthcoming with tidbits of wisdom to help us. You would think that as a spiritual being myself, I would get some reinforcements."

The kitchen lights flickered a few times before dooming the room to darkness. Lisa gasped and jumped to her feet. "I think Brett has some candles in a drawer. I'll try to f—"

The lights suddenly came back on. She stared at all the papers scattered about the kitchen floor. "Damn it, Al. You didn't have to throw the papers on the floor," she snapped. She bent down and began to sort them into piles.

"I didn't touch the papers."

"Right!"

Al rose and stood over her. "I am not lying to you. I think an angel was a little put out when we criticized their support."

Lisa bit her lower lip. "A pissed-off angel threw the papers to the floor?"

With a hint of arrogance, Al nodded. "That's what I said."

A giggle escaped her. "Oh, Al. You have a weird sense of humor. Forget it. Just don't toss my papers on the floor again. You don't want to see a pissed-off reporter."

Al snorted. "Be careful, woman. Don't brush aside things because you can't understand them."

She set the papers on the table and filled her cup for the third time. Lisa bristled. *How dare he lecture me!* "Did you just call me *woman*?"

Al nodded, sitting down in a chair. He was really getting on her nerves. Surely it wasn't the caffeine making her so edgy. "You really are prehistoric, aren't you?" Not waiting for a response, she continued. "I've accepted that you are a ghost and that I can see and talk to you. But don't you try scamming me with angels and other things. There is no way that angels are hanging out in a kitchen in the middle of Iowa, tossing papers to the floor."

Al nervously glanced around the room. "You shouldn't have said that."

A second later, the jumbled pile of papers lifted from the table and floated through the air. Lisa's mouth gaped open as the papers hovered above her head. Without warning, the pile tumbled down on her body, scattering throughout the room.

"Told you so." With that, Al disappeared, leaving her chilled.

Lisa stood in the middle of the room, not moving. She was afraid to move or do anything that would cause another strange occurrence. Frustration coursed through her. *How could I be so stupid? If ghosts exist, then why not angels?*

Looking up at the ceiling, she softly whispered, "Sorry. My bad."

She wouldn't take anything for granted from here on out.

As Brett and Anders sat in the Miller kitchen talking about the case, Brett felt a breeze. Al suddenly materialized in the empty chair next to them.

"Jesus! You scared me to death," Anders yelled.

Brett smiled at seeing his boss caught off guard. "Where have you been?"

"I checked in on your girlfriend."

"Why?"

Stretching out his legs, Al rubbed his chin. "Just wanted to see how her research was coming along."

Brett relaxed. "Hmm. Did she find anything interesting yet?"

"Based on what she discovered on the computer and our earlier observations, it's pretty certain that we're fighting a demonic spirit. This Richard guy appears to be possessed. Now we have to find a way to force the spirit to leave."

Anders moaned, running a hand through his graying hair. "Great. Now we're talking about exorcism on top of everything else."

Brett muttered, "Bring on the flying monkeys." Anders choked out a laugh. Brett cast his glance at Al. "Sorry, you probably never heard of the *Wizard of Oz.*"

"Of course I have. It was originally called *The Wonderful Wizard of Oz.* I think it was published around nineteen hundred. Very popular book. I even bought a copy for my daughter. Though I don't remember the flying monkey part."

"They were in the movie, but we digress. We need to get a hold of Richard and try forcing the demon from his body."

Anders nodded. "Why don't we do it here? No one is living here. Since Brett knows the family, why don't you call Mrs. Miller and talk to her about using the house as our base. Plus, your family already has the spare key to the house."

Al nervously drummed his fingers on the table. Brett glanced over at him. "Al, is there a problem?"

"I'm not sure. The question is whether you have a problem. This is where your great-grandfather was murdered."

Brett felt a chill crawl up his spine. He knew this was the same house where Mike O'Shea had died. Even though the house had been remodeled over the years, Brett had never ventured down into the basement. He didn't want to see the place where his great-grandfather died.

"Yeah, I know. It's not a problem. I want to catch this guy. Miller's death needs to be avenged."

Al shuddered. The invisible veil that had hung over his mind all these years was suddenly lifted. He knew! He understood the connection between his death and Miller's death. He knew why he had been brought back to help Brett. It all made perfect sense. He jumped to his feet and danced a jig around the room.

Suddenly coming to a halt, he stared at Brett. He was going to tell him.

A loud voice in his head halted his thoughts. *You cannot tell Brett about your relationship.*

Al puffed out his chest and stared upward. *Why not?* he asked nonverbally.

A shot of electricity flowed through Al, making his body jump and twist several times. *Because I have said so.*

Al's shoulders slumped. He couldn't argue with the big guy and expect to win. It was time to zip it.

Anders and Brett stared at him as if he had suddenly sprouted a second head. Al could barely contain the joy in his heart.

"Al, what the hell is going on with you?" Brett asked.

Al grabbed both of Brett's cheeks and planted a swift kiss on his cheek. Brett jerked back, wiping his lips with the back of his hand.

"Gross! What was that for?"

Al couldn't keep from smiling. "Sorry, sonny. I need to go check on some things. I'll catch up with you later."

He disappeared before the two men could argue with him or ask any questions. He couldn't believe that his prayers had finally been answered. He remembered his past. He knew who he was. He choked back a sob. He was Mike O'Shea. Why had it taken so long for this to be revealed to him? He shook away his concerns. There wasn't time to feel sorry for himself. If he was lucky, he would soon join the love of his life and have peace.

CHAPTER THIRTY-EIGHT

Richard shivered as the damp, cold wind swirled through cracks in the walls. He had no money, no place to go. His back was against the wall. Literally. He was scared and felt that he would probably freeze to death in this garage. The attached house was abandoned. Another foreclosure. He'd prefer to be in the house, but all the windows in it were gone. Since the garage's windows were all intact, it had become his temporary sanctuary.

Before the police had carted him off to jail, they took him to the ER. He faintly remembered fighting with a nurse and orderlies when they tried to inject him with some drug. As the drugs took hold, his fears—and more importantly, the voice—evaporated. Richard smiled as he remembered the relaxing feeling that had stirred his body. At that moment, he no longer had any fears. None. In fact, he felt so carefree that he tried to joke with the jailers as they booked him. They rudely ignored his attempts to make conversation, which he brushed aside. Handcuffed, he was led down a long hallway to an empty cell far from the guards and other prisoners. He felt a sense of relief as the metal door locked behind him. Closed spaces calmed him. As a child, he was terrified of being locked in the closet. But over the years, he welcomed the sanctuary. Being in a closet prevented beatings and torture. Jail offered him a warm bed and hot meals. For the first time in months, he felt a few moments of peace.

Now those warm feelings were a memory. Everything after that moment was a blank. He couldn't even imagine how he had escaped from jail. With the numerous guards and cameras positioned inside the jail, how had he just walked out of the building? It didn't make sense.

He picked at a sore on his cheek and wiped the blood on his jeans. His fingers clenched together and dug into his thighs. He needed more medicine. Richard was so confused. One minute he hated the voice. It made him do bad things. He didn't want to be bad. And the next, he reveled in it. He was stronger with the voice.

He was afraid to light a fire, for fear of drawing unwanted attention. His knees pressed up against his chest. Resting his head on his knees, his eyes squeezed shut. He was so cold. He rocked back and forth as a familiar voice whispered taunts that would make a priest recoil in horror. Tremors gripped his body. His life sucked, and he saw no way out.

Hunger pains made his stomach hurt. Tears coursed down his sunken cheeks.

"Quit whining, you stupid idiot!"

Shaking his head, Richard put his hands over his ears. He had to block the sound! He jumped to his feet, pacing the small building. With his hands still in place, he began to hum. After several minutes, he cautiously lowered his hands. He grinned. The voice was gone. He was getting better. Maybe he didn't need the medicine after all.

He walked to the small window and glanced outside. As he started to turn away, something caught his attention. A reflection in the glass stared back at him. He tilted his head from side to side to better see who was looking at him. Piercing red eyes captured his attention. Evil glittered in those eyes. Richard took a step back, clutching his rolling stomach. The face in the window was starting to change. The man's nose was disappearing, leaving bare nostrils exposed. Teeth elongated. Blood ran down the man's chin as his incisors cut into his lips. What kind of creature leered at him?

Richard felt something wet on his chin. Absently, he wiped his face and looked down. Blood coated his hand. His blood! Filled with horror, he stumbled closer to the window. He stared at the distorted reflection that watched him. The only thing that now looked familiar was his hair. Richard slid down to the dusty, cold cement beneath his feet. "No! No, no, no, no," he crooned. He couldn't accept what he saw. Why was this happening to him? *No more!* He couldn't take it.

The creature in the window was him! That was the last cognizant thought he could form.

CHAPTER THIRTY-NINE

B rett felt a brush of air caress his face. His senses on alert, he peered through half-opened lids. Lisa slipped out of bed. What time was it? The room had a grayish cast. Rolling over, he grabbed a pillow. He molded it around his head and went back to sleep.

When he woke a second time, the room was much brighter. The smell of bacon drifting throughout the house was incentive to roll out of bed. He grabbed a pair of sweatpants from a drawer and sauntered down the hall.

"Hey there, sleepyhead." Lisa stood by the stove, flipping steaming pancakes onto a platter. "Breakfast is ready. Juice or coffee?"

He kissed her cheek, snatched up a piece of bacon, and popped it into his mouth. "Both, thanks." He moaned aloud, savoring the thick cut, hickory bacon. "Crispy, just the way I like it."

After eating his way through four pancakes, a pile of bacon, and three eggs, Brett groaned and pushed the empty plate across the table. "You surprise me. You can really cook."

Lisa smiled back at him. "Duh! Did you think because I am a blonde that I can't cook?"

Brett rose and stood by her chair. Bending down, he nuzzled her neck. "No, I'm just saying that you're a good cook."

Lisa's brows rose as she studied him. "Uh huh. I'm here to serve. Now, you can clear the dishes while I go take a shower."

He chuckled as she flashed him a saucy look. He quickly loaded the dishwasher and wiped off the stove and table. By the time he returned to the bedroom, Lisa was blow-drying her hair. On his way past her, Brett patted her on the bottom.

As Brett dried off after his shower, he heard voices coming from the front room. He hurried and finished dressing, anxious to see who was here.

"Hey, sonny! Lisa has been keeping me company."

Brett shook his head at the sight of Lisa curled up on the sofa with Al massaging her shoulders. "I see that. Is something going on?"

Al patted Lisa's back before sitting next to her. "Now that we're working out of the Miller house, I wanted to see what else Lisa came up with. You know, about getting rid of demonic spirits."

"Miller house?" Lisa asked.

"I haven't had a chance to tell you yet," said Brett.

Lisa narrowed her eyes. Laughing, Al broke in. "Okay, Missy, calm down. We're going to use the Miller house as the site for the intervention. We still need to figure out a plan for getting Demon Boy there."

Brett groaned. Al was a wild card in their whole plan. "Demon Boy? You mean Richard?"

"That's what I said, didn't I? Now, Lisa, what do you have for us?"

Lisa plunked down stapled packets in front of each of them. The title page read "The Best Ways to Get Rid of an Evil Spirit."

Al roared with amusement, slapping his knee. "I like your style, Missy."

Lisa glared at Al. "Quit calling me derogatory names. My name is Lisa. Say it: Li-sa."

Hoping to get control of the situation, Brett gave a sharp whistle. "Guys! Let's focus. Lisa, tell us what you found."

"I'm not an expert, but it appears that there are several possible methods for getting rid of spirits. One of the oldest beliefs, of course, is holy water. Water is one of the natural elements. Once the water is blessed, you dip your fingers in it and spread it on doorways and windows. This creates a barrier to keep out evil spirits."

Brett sighed. "I hate to be a downer, but our problem is that the evil spirit will be in the house with us. We want to keep it in the house."

When Lisa frowned, Brett hurried on. "I don't know how the holy water will help us, but we should get some. It may come in handy. What else do you have?"

Lisa flashed him a brittle smile. "Next page. Another option is a banishing ritual. The effectiveness of this spell varies from person to person. Supposedly the person with the problem is to write down the problem on a piece of paper. Then you focus on the problem that is written on the paper. After that, you burn the paper. Some people use a white candle or place the burning paper in a white bowl."

"Well, I don't like that one," Al muttered. "If the spell varies from person to person, that's a problem. I can't imagine crazy Richard being able to focus on much of anything."

Lisa grunted as she flipped through the pile of papers before her. "Jeez, guys. I guess it depends on how well you identify the problem and focus on the problem before burning the paper."

"As I just said, Richard is going to be a problem. How can we get him to focus when the demon inside of him is trying to kill us?"

Lisa's look of annoyance grew. Bret snapped, "Knock it off Al. She's trying to help us."

"You're right. Sorry. Have you got anything else?"

Lisa smiled back at Al. "I have just one more thought. Salt."

"Salt? What does salt have to do with demons and hocus pocus?"

Lisa sighed. "It is supposed to have purifying qualities, like water. Salt on the floor or window ledge will keep a spirit from entering a room."

Brett set the packet aside. "How much salt will we need?"

Lisa shrugged. "I'm not sure."

Al shoved his hat forward even farther down over his nose. "With everyone worrying about their health, maybe we should use sea salt. I hear it is healthier." A wide grin graced his face.

"Actually, sea salt is preferred," Lisa said.

Brett stood and went to the window. All the possibilities that Lisa had shared raced through his brain. He was so out of his league. They had never covered demons and shit like this at the police academy. He stiffened for a second as familiar arms wrapped around his waist. He turned and kissed the top of Lisa's head.

"Well, this is my cue to skedaddle out of here," said Al. "See you lovebirds later."

Suddenly, they were alone. Brett inched toward the recliner and pulled Lisa onto his lap.

"Thanks for your help. I really appreciate all the work you did."

Pressing her forehead against his, she smiled. "Anytime. I'm not sure that Al thinks anything will work. With him being a ghost, I thought he might have some knowledge about this kind of stuff."

"Yeah, me too. I guess we're on our own. All I know is that we have to find Richard before there is another murder."

CHAPTER FORTY

Sergeant Taylor had been staking out the chief's house for the past week. He was not surprised when Ellison left his house each night to head to the one of the nearby casinos. The man was dropping a ton of money. Sooner or later, it would all come to an end. He needed to distance himself from the chief. It was each man for himself at this point in the game.

When he had pulled into the station lot earlier in the night, Ellison slipped him an envelope. It was his payment for the week.

As Taylor walked down the hallway, he heard footsteps approaching. *Damn it! O'Shea.* He quickly shoved the money into his pocket.

Brett slowed his steps before resuming his stride toward Taylor. Taylor felt his lip curl in disgust before he forced himself to relax.

"O'Shea. I see you're in early tonight. I've been listening to the radio chatter on the guy that murdered Miller. Did they ever figure out how that guy broke out of jail?"

Brett stopped before him, seemingly to study his face. "No, but I bet someone's head is going to roll. We're following up on a couple of things. Who knows if it will amount to anything. Is there anything else? I'm running a little late. I'm supposed to meet Anders before we hit the street tonight."

Taylor forced a smile. "No, nothing else. I just wanted to see how things were going. Keep your head down, and watch your back."

Brett nodded and proceeded down the hall.

A muscle in Taylor's temple throbbed. He had disliked O'Shea since he started with the department. The man was so damn smug. So confident. Taylor had scraped his way to make sergeant, but he couldn't advance any further. O'Shea had it all: family, connections at the station, and education. Taylor was jealous.

That is why he looked for other ways to make it. By helping out the chief, he could make extra money to compensate for not making a higher rank. Now the world was changing once again, and he was determined not to go down with Ellison on a sinking ship. The chief was out of control. Therefore, Taylor's life was out of control, and he didn't like it. Not at all.

Taylor had been sleeping with the chief's secretary, Maureen, for the past three years, so he knew most of Ellison's secrets. Maureen had let it slip that the chief was receiving a number of calls from some Russians in Chicago. After the Chicago calls, the chief would seclude himself in the office for the remainder of the day, often cancelling appointments. When Maureen had told him that the chief seemed to be hiding something, that was like waving a red flag in front of Taylor's face. A red flag of opportunity.

Two days after she gave him this news, Taylor was called into Ellison's office. He met the chief's formidable glare as he shut the door of the office.

"Sit down," Ellison ordered. "Why were you in the parking lot the other night when you were on scheduled comp time?"

Not flinching, Taylor shrugged. "I couldn't sleep and decided to come in and finish up paper work. I wasn't going to put in for the time."

Ellison grunted and studied him. Ellison's fingers drummed on the top of the immaculate desk. Not one piece of paper littered its surface. Motionless, Taylor sat and waited for the chief to make the next move. It didn't take long.

"I've known you since you started on the force, Taylor. I hear you run a tight ship. I might be able to use a guy like you, if you're interested."

Taylor bit the inside of his cheeks to keep from smiling. Satisfaction coursed through him. He let the silence fill the room. He didn't want to seem too eager.

"Well, what do you have to say?"

"I'm not sure what you're asking, sir."

Ellison growled, obviously frustrated. "Taylor, I am working on a big project and need some help. There will be extra pay in it for you."

"A cash job?"

Ellison grinned. "Of course. I will warn you that I will require your complete silence on this subject. You will tell no one, not even your wife, Evelyn. Do you understand?

"Completely. What do I need to do?"

Ellison stood and came from behind the desk. "Just make a few deliveries when I tell you. You'll take a packet and drop it off. Nothing else. It's nothing illegal, mind you. Just some personal business I'm conducting with an out-of-state corporation. They wish to remain anonymous; that's why it's a secret. It could mean a big payoff to you if you can follow my instructions."

For a second, Taylor felt uneasy. But just for a second. "It's nothing dangerous, right?"

Ellison chuckled, clapping Taylor on the back. "As long as you follow directions, it will be fine. You'll make some extra cash, and I will have some help. It's a win-win, Taylor. Are you in?"

"Why not! You can count on me."

The men shook hands. Taylor felt as though he had conquered the world when he left the chief's office that day.

That was three years before. Taylor had since learned that Ellison had a huge gambling problem and owed the Eastern Europeans in Chicago a ton of money. Taylor wasn't sure what other schemes Ellison had in play, but he had his suspicions that it was some dangerous shit. The previous week, Taylor spotted a black town car sitting next to the chief's car when he arrived at work for the second shift. Ellison got out of the backseat, looking ashen and beaten down.

Even though Taylor was getting several grand a month in cash payments, he was growing worried. All it would take was one reporter following the chief to the casino and the roof would start caving in on their heads. He had to keep his name out of the damned newspaper.

CHAPTER FORTY-ONE

Brett jumped out of his seat as soon as roll call was over. He was supposed to meet up with Anders again. As he turned a corner, he spotted Anders at the end of the hallway.

"I hope you're not carrying your smelly gym clothes in that bag," Anders growled. "I don't want my car stinking like your underwear."

Brett scoffed. "You wish it was my underwear. Seriously, I've got a few things that may help us." Brett tossed the bag in the backseat before climbing into the front seat.

Anders's brow rose as he stared at Brett. "Well, are you going to tell me or keep me in suspense?"

"I've got some holy water and sea salt. Remember I told you that Lisa was doing some research for us? Well, once we get Richard in the York Street house, we'll spread this stuff by all the exits. It's supposed to keep demonic spirits out. I'm betting that it will also keep them in."

Gripping the steering wheel, Anders turned to stare at Brett. "Are you sure we shouldn't call a priest?"

"I'm not sure of anything at this point. Based on Lisa's research, this is the best we've got."

Anders grunted. "Well, have you figured out how we can kill this thing once we corral it?"

Brett pursed his lips. "Not yet. Maybe Al will have some ideas."

"Ideas about what?" asked Al from the backseat.

Both Anders and Brett jumped and jerked toward the backseat.

"Holy shit! Will I ever get used to him just popping in?" growled Anders.

"I guess I need to ring a bell when I arrive." Al's laughter lightened the mood.

"We were talking about using the holy water and sea salt to seal Richard in the house, if we can find him."

Al groaned. "I was afraid that you would decide to use Lisa's ideas. I just don't feel right about it."

"Well, Mr. Ghost, do you have a better idea? Has the big guy given you a better plan?" argued Brett.

Al leaned forward over the front seat and thumped Brett's forehead with his finger.

"Ow! What was that for?"

"You know what it was for. You know I would tell you if I got a plan from the big guy. Other than a few bolts of lightning aimed at my feet, I'm not sure what He's thinking." Pushing himself back against the seat, Al continued mumbling to himself.

Anders turned the ignition and began driving. "Well, now that we have that out of the way, we still need to figure out how to get rid of this demon. I almost feel sorry for this Richard dude. Can you imagine being possessed?"

Brett shook his head, lost in thought.

Twenty minutes later, Brett saw they were back in the neighborhood where Richard had held Lisa when he kidnapped her. He glanced at the backseat to confirm that Al hadn't disappeared again. It looked as if he were sleeping. Brett opened the car door and followed Anders.

The men stood in the front yard, staring at the darkened house where Lisa had been held. A few shredded pieces of yellow police tape fluttered from the nearby barren trees. The light breeze ruffled Brett's hair.

"What are we doing?" Brett stiffened as he met the steely gaze of the senior detective.

"When I think about this case, I keep coming back to two locations. This house and the Miller house on York Street. Don't ask me why. It's just a gut feeling. Let's go look around."

Brett stood, unmoving. Words from his grandmother and from

Al suddenly stirred long-forgotten memories. The nightly stories that his grandmother recited at his bedside explained that Mike O'Shea solved case after case by using his "gut instinct." Even Al had talked about how the good cops have an inborn sense of knowing. Did he have this needed quality to be a good detective? Would he even make a good detective? Shutting his eyes, he raked his fingers through his hair, pushing it off his brow. He had always sworn that he wasn't going to be like his great-grandfather, but now things looked different. Had he acquired a new perspective from working this case with Anders and Al?

Brett jerked as he felt a slight nudge against his shoulder. His hand automatically flew to his gun.

"Relax. It's me," Al responded.

Brett exhaled and slipped the gun back into its holster. "I must have been daydreaming. I need to catch up with Anders. He's checking out the house and yard."

He hadn't taken more than two steps when Al suddenly grabbed his arm.

"You have the right stuff to become a good detective. I know for a fact that you're going to be the best damned detective this force has ever seen."

Brett shivered as a cold wind brushed against his face. Al's lips curled slightly in the corner.

"Yeah right," Brett laughed. "I'm glad someone thinks so."

Al stepped back and straightened his jacket. "Don't ever second-guess yourself, Brett. Never!"

"But why would you—"

Al walked off, trailing after Anders. "Don't worry about it. Just remember my words. Got it?"

Brett smiled to himself. Al had called him Brett, not sonny. He figured he must be rubbing off on the old ghost or Al was getting sentimental.

His good mood dissipated as a loud wail shattered the night. Brett took off running, drawing his gun. Whatever the sound was, it was not human.

CHAPTER FORTY-TWO

Brett ran toward the back of the house just in time to see the entire garage explode. He slammed to the ground as shards of glass and fragments of wood flew toward him.

When the debris cleared, Brett slowly stood to his feet. "Anders! Where are you?" A quick glance at the garage confirmed that the structure was completely obliterated.

The pile of debris shifted as Anders threw off a large piece of plywood that covered most of his upper body. Dusting himself off, he walked back toward Brett. "O'Shea, are you okay?"

Brett reached out to steady Anders, who brushed the dust off his face. "Yeah, but what the hell happened?"

"After that bloodcurdling scream from the garage, I looked in the side window. I cou …" Anders shook his head, glancing down at his feet. "I've never seen anything like it before. There was a body huddled on the floor. A second later, a creature stood in the window, looking at me. The next thing I remember is lying on the ground."

"Creature? Was it the demon thing we saw before?"

Anders shrugged. "Hell, I don't know. The only thing I remember is a god-awful face with red eyes and huge, open nostrils. Damn, it was the ugliest thing I ever saw."

Before Brett could ask any more questions, Al popped up next to them, staring at the pile of wood. "Are you two okay?"

"We're good. Where did you go?" Brett asked.

"Just before the explosion, I saw demon boy in there and figured there'd be trouble. The demon is growing more powerful. It was waiting for us. I guess it was trying to kill us by blowing up the garage."

Anders's eyes grew wide and darted around the yard. Then Al regarded the sky for several minutes. Brett's nerves ratcheted up to a new level.

Al reached into his jacket and took out an empty pipe. Jamming it into his mouth, he mumbled, "We're close."

Brett's body tensed. "Close to what?"

"Close to the end. The grand finale! I don't know. I'm not getting much help from the guys above. I don't know what they expect me to do. I've followed their orders up to this point, and we're not getting anywhere. I'm fed up with their crap. I think I'll start doing things my way."

A sudden flapping sound above their heads made them jump. In unison, they jerked their gazes up to the majestic maple tree in front of them. A large horned owl perched on a limb tilted its head and peered down at the men.

Anders thrust his hands into his pockets. "What are we doing wrong? We're the good guys. The white hats!"

"That's my question." Glancing at the owl, who continued to screech, Al shook his fist. "Do you hear that? I'm not the only one who has questions."

The owl hopped back and forth on the branch. Its yellow eyes narrowed as if it were daring them to keep antagonizing the heavens above. Without warning, its wings shot out. It dived out of the tree and flew directly at their heads.

"Duck!" screamed Brett. He and Anders hit the ground. Al stood with his pipe hanging out of his mouth. The dangerous bird seemed to be zeroing in on Al's head. "Al, disappear!"

The shrill screeching made Brett's ears ache. With his arms folded over his head, he peeked out. He was surprised to see Al still standing, but shrouded in a veil of light. A golden glow draped itself around Al's body, shimmering in the darkness. Al's mouth was moving as if he were talking to someone. *Could that be what I think it is? Nah! Stuff like this doesn't happen.*

Brett slowly turned his head, ready to stand up, but his body seized in fear. The owl was on the ground, inches from his face. The brown and white feathers on its large breast fluttered in the breeze. The unnerving yellow eyes pinned Brett to the ground. The bird's head swiveled from side to side as if studying him. Brett slowly slid his outstretched arm closer to his body. The bird hopped closer, pecking the ground near his arm. From this viewpoint, the bird seemed to be huge; maybe the size of an eagle.

Not wanting to disturb Al's concentration, Brett kept his eyes downcast, whispering, "Calm down, I won't move my arm anymore. Nice birdy. Everything is fine. I'm staying right here."

Anders's shoulders began shaking. Worried that his boss was afraid, Brett hissed, "Anders! Don't worry about the owl. It's just standing here watching me."

Anders's shoulders shook harder. Turning his head, Anders met Brett's gaze. His eyes crinkled together, as if he were in pain. Slowly wiping away his tears, Anders flashed a grin. "Nice birdy?"

Brett felt his face infuse with heat. "Asshole! I'm just trying to keep the bird from pecking out my eyeballs. But hey, you might think that is funny too."

"Birdy ..." choked out Anders. With his head buried in his folded arms, Anders shook with laughter.

Brett's anger faded as the owl hopped closer to Anders. The bird's beak was only inches from the man's head. "Anders," Brett whispered, "cool it. The bird is right by your head."

Just uttering the word "bird" seemed to set off Anders. His legs visibly twitched up and down as he laughed himself silly. The guy was obviously having a meltdown. When Anders finally raised his head, Brett had to bite his lip.

Anders's eyes widened and his body stilled. Anders watched the owl staring at him as if he were a mouse, ready to eat. The owl hooted and proceeded to hop on Anders's back. The owl walked up and down Anders's back, stopping every couple of seconds to peck the back of Anders's jacket.

"Well, do something! Get it off of me or I'll shoot it!" Anders appeared to be ready to jump to his feet.

"Calm down! You can't shoot it. It might be some special bird. Didn't you think it was strange how it sat in that tree watching us? Besides, he's got some big claws. Just lie there and be quiet." The owl had turned to watch Brett as he spoke to Anders. He could have sworn the bird was smiling.

Al's voice boomed over their heads. "What the hell are you two doing on the ground?"

When Brett looked back at Anders, there was no sign of the owl.

Anders rolled over on his back and groaned. "Shit. That thing scared me to death."

Laughing, Brett helped Anders to his feet. "Serves you right for making fun of me." He turned back to look at Al. The golden veil was gone. "What was going on with you? You were glowing as if you were radioactive. It looked like you were talking to someone. Were you?"

"I was. Not to the big guy himself, but an archangel. Evil has been let loose. Our job is to catch this thing before it harms any other people."

Before Anders could ask any questions, his phone rang. Anders's facial muscles tensed as he barked quick commands into the phone. After pocketing his phone, he began walking back to the car.

"There's been a murder about a mile from here. We need to go check it out."

Brett caught up with his boss. "Is it connected to our case?"

Anders nodded. "I think so. The victim's heart was pulled out of his chest."

Al stood among the trees as the detectives scoured the crime scene. The victim appeared to be a middle-aged male. His ripped-open body lay on the ground. The man's eyes were frozen in horror.

Sighing, Al leaned against a tree, lighting his pipe. He hated the idea of going into the house on York Street, but no matter how he looked at it, all options led there.

A TV crew pulled up nearby. A cameraman quickly hopped out,

trying to get as close as he could to the scene. Al smiled as Lisa exited the van. She gave him a slight smile and kept walking.

Soon she stood next to Brett and Anders while preparing for an interview. Al swore as he saw Sergeant Taylor getting out of his car. He couldn't put his finger on why he didn't like the man. He was too slick. Al knew Brett didn't trust him, and neither did he. A private investigation was in order.

Al emptied his pipe and put it away in his jacket. He followed Taylor as he meandered toward Brett and Anders.

Brett glanced up and nudged Anders as Taylor approached.

"What do we have, Anders?" Taylor surveyed the scene. His eyes widened as his body wavered. It was obvious that Taylor hadn't seen very many dead bodies.

"Other than the one victim, we're not sure. Evidence is being gathered."

"I heard some muttering on the radio about a man's chest being ripped open. Is that true?"

Anders crouched down to look at something on the ground. He motioned for a member of his unit to take a picture of the foot imprint in the soft soil. After several minutes, he rose and looked at Taylor. "The chief will receive my report as soon as I'm done."

Watching Anders walk away, Taylor turned toward Brett. "Is he always such a dick?"

Brett opened his mouth to say something but hesitated. "It's been a rough night. I'd better go and see what he wants me to do." Brett quickly followed Anders.

Taylor glared at the two men as they climbed into their car. They were staring at him. He really wished he could hear what they were saying. Realizing that there wasn't much else he could do here, Taylor returned to his car. He glanced down at his phone as it rang. Ellison. He knew he had better take it.

"Chief, what's going on?"

"What did you find out?"

"It's pretty gory. Anders and O'Shea are here. Of course they're not telling me anything. It's a guess, but considering how the body has a huge hole in the chest, it may be the captain's killer."

"Fine. Just stay on top of things. I need you to make a pickup tonight."

Taylor gritted his teeth. "Where?"

"Regular place. What's wrong? I don't like the sound of your voice."

Taylor rushed on. "I have reservations, that's all."

Ellison's voice was crisp. Not a good sign. "What do you mean by 'reservations'?"

"It doesn't feel right. I don't know what you're doing, and I don't want to know. But you have to know that this can't continue. Whatever you're paying me to do, I want out. I'm done." Leaning back in the seat, Taylor let out a deep breath. His fingers squeezed the cell phone until they turned white.

Ellison's laughter startled Taylor. "You're delusional if you think it's that easy to walk away. I've paid you tens of thousands of dollars and you are just going to walk?"

"Sir, you know that I'm not going to say anything. I feel like someone is watching us. When this goes down, I don't want to be involved."

"You listen here, Taylor," growled Ellison, "if I had a choice, I'd say good riddance. It's not up to me. It hasn't been for some time. The guys in Chicago—"

"Stop! I don't want to know the details, Ellison. The less I know, the better off I am. I'll make the run tonight, but it's the last time, damn it! You hear me? The last time! You need to find someone else." Taylor pressed the disconnect button and tossed the phone in the backseat.

Al ducked as Taylor's phone breezed by his head. Instinct kicked in even though the phone would have flown through him.

Taylor gripped the steering wheel as he stared sightlessly out the window. Al didn't envy the poor sap. It was obvious the man was trying to decide what to do.

Taylor reached back, grabbed his phone from the backseat, and quickly dialed a number. "Evelyn. It's me. I'm leaving for the cabin after work. No, I can't stop and pick up the milk." With a sigh, Taylor interrupted his wife's chattering. "Listen, Evelyn. I won't be able to call you. There is no reception up there. I'll try to call you when I get supplies. Okay, love you too." Taylor started the car while mumbling, "Thank God she couldn't find the cabin if she tried. Stupid bitch."

Al frowned at Taylor's comments. The man was just plain nasty. With nothing else to do at the moment, Al decided to mess with Taylor's head for a while.

Taylor stilled as a breeze ruffled papers on the front seat. Al laughed as Taylor jerked this way and that, trying to see if anyone else was in the car.

When Taylor's phone buzzed, Al peeked over the sergeant's shoulder. Ellison again. How long could Taylor continue to ignore Ellison? Would the gang that Ellison was working with allow Taylor to walk away? Al was willing to bet that wasn't going to happen. As Taylor moaned, Al jerked his gaze to Taylor's face. Suddenly, Taylor leaned out the door and retched onto the street. *Ewww!* Al leaned back so he couldn't see the sergeant puking his guts out. Taylor was in as much trouble as they were.

After tailing Taylor all evening, Al had a pretty good idea of what was going on. Greed was alive and well in the twenty-first century. Ellison's gambling problem had mushroomed into money laundering. The gang from Chicago weren't likely to let Ellison or Taylor walk away.

It was evident now why Taylor always seemed so nervous. Taylor had worked his entire career and was stuck being a sergeant. He wanted to advance, to be recognized and looked up to. When he couldn't get reach that goal, he found a way to work a scheme with the chief. Sure, the money had probably been a windfall to Taylor. Now it seemed that the scheme had been too good to be true. Cause and effect. Criminals never seemed to understand that basic law of nature. Al had seen enough. He needed to get back and help out Brett. They had another murder to deal with.

CHAPTER FORTY-THREE

The murder scene was deserted. The man's body had been taken to the morgue. The reporters were gone. The detectives had gathered the evidence and taken numerous photos. Tattered pieces of yellow crime scene tape were left hanging on the nearby trees.

Michael's former police training had returned. The name Al quickly faded from his memory as he remembered everything about his life as Detective Michael O'Shea. He stooped down to look at the bloodstain on the sidewalk. Was this it? A man's life was snuffed out way too early. And all that remained was a splotch on the sidewalk. Disgusted, he rose and looked around the neighborhood. They were only a mile west of York Street, close to Lutheran Hospital. It was the same blue-collar area as York Street. The two-bedroom bungalows weren't fancy, but they were nicely kept. It was 3:00 a.m., so Al expected the homes to be dark. His gaze zeroed in on a home at the end of the block. The lights in the house pierced the night like a beacon.

Michael's brow scrunched in puzzlement. He felt drawn to the house. Why? He'd never been here before. Never seen the house before. Slowly, he made his way down the dark street, keeping away from the trees. He paused at the end of the driveway, looking up at house. A bay window faced the street. Al tensed as the edge of the curtain dropped back into place. Someone was watching. Were they waiting for him or just looking out the window in the middle of the night?

Since he had no intention of ringing the doorbell, Michael made his way to the back door. He blinked and found himself in the kitchen. Harvest-gold appliances dated the room. An oval table with padded vinyl chairs stood in the center of the room. Chipped black-and-white-checked linoleum covered the floor. A lone light hung above the kitchen sink. The house was quiet; dead quiet.

Soundlessly, Michael drifted through the dining room. He pushed his hat back off his brow, trying to discover what was unusual about this place. Pictures of family members lined the walls. Michael paused to glance at each picture. None of them looked familiar. A crackling sound drifted in from the front room, which was warmed by a yellow glow. Michael peered around the corner and saw a log burning in the fireplace. Red-hot coals cast shadows about the room. A dark leather wing-back chair faced the fireplace.

"Come in and sit down, Al. I mean Michael. Have you forgotten your real name after all these years? I've been waiting for you."

Michael shook his head and walked in to the room. It seemed he could be surprised after all. Guarded, he sat on the worn sofa, never taking his gaze off the man. His nemesis. The physical body was different this time, but the spirit within was the same.

"You and I finally meet again. Are you surprised?"

Michael glared at the slender man sitting before him. "Why are you here? What do you really want?"

Richard's body looked relaxed. He even had an amused grin plastered to his face.

"Michael, Michael, slow down. You have always been so impatient. So quick to rush in to save the day. It didn't work out so well for you back when you were alive, did it?"

"I need to know why I was killed. What did I ever do? I was and still am a God-fearing man."

Richard sighed, shaking his head. "And that's the problem. You were always such a do-gooder. You probably didn't even realize how many officers looked up to you. I was trying to win souls over to our side, and there you were, always in my way. I wanted to get a hold in law enforcement to truly upset the balance of good over evil. Do you know how easy it is to convert a good police officer with the lure of money? You would be surprised at the number of police officers who can be bought to look the other way with just a few hundred here and there. Just look at the current police chief. Now that's a man I can count on. That's how it's always been, Michael. Until you got in my way."

Michael growled. Richard smiled, revealing pointed teeth. "You were so easy to kill. I knew you would rush down those basement stairs, trying to save the poor woman. She did struggle, but it was so fun to slash her throat. I must admit I was surprised to see you here in this century. Someone up above must still be looking out for you. Dare I ask why you are here now?"

Michael leaned forward, ready to lunge at any second. "To put an end to you, of course."

Richard's face grew red. His voice deepened, "You and who else? You are nothing but a mere ghost. You have no special abilities. Shall I show you some of my abilities?"

Michael straightened, forcing himself not to react. Evil wanted to make others suffer, to torture people. The maniacal laughter brought back every minute of that night long, long ago—the night of his death.

Michael leaned back and smiled. "You picked a sorry-looking body to be your host. Poor Dick Boy. He wasn't much of a challenge for you. I bet you always pick the easy ones."

The demon roared to his feet, quickly shedding its frail human body. Seconds later, the figure towered over Michael. Roaring with displeasure, the demon swiped its claws at the sofa next to Michael.

Michael calmly brushed the pieces of foam from his tweed jacket. With a smirk, he ducked under the limbs imprisoning him. "Please. Can't you do better than that? Am I supposed to beg you for my life? Oh, wait! You already killed me. It seems like I might owe you one."

With a roar of his own, Michael swung at the demon's head and sent him flying across the room. Stunned, Michael looked down at his fist. He could do that? When had he gotten that kind of power?

Michael relished giving a good ol' ass kicking. He hadn't felt this wired since he was twenty years old. "Come on you son of a bitch! I've got eighty-plus years of pissed off saved up just for you!"

Michael ducked his head and rammed into the demon's stomach.

The demon didn't budge this time. It smiled down at him and grabbed him by the back of the neck before tossing him to the other side of the room.

Michael sailed through the wall and rolled to a stop on the dining room floor. Shaking his head to clear the sudden dizziness, he smiled as he rolled up his sleeves. Oh, this was going to be good. He relished this battle.

With his arms widespread, Michael jumped through the wall, landing in the center of the room. "I'm back! It's not so easy, is it, when you're dealing with a spirit instead of a human."

Michael gaped as the creature smiled and altered its physical shape into something he hadn't seen before. "Great heavens above," said Michael. The demon continued to alter its form. Large, scaly black wings thrust out from the backs of the creature's shoulders, knocking table lamps on the floor. A large tail swished toward Michael's head. Michael instinctively ducked as the horned tail narrowly missed his face. He scratched his chin and studied the dragonish thing in front of him. It was going to be a tough battle, but Michael intended to win at any cost. He grabbed the fireplace poker from the floor, took a deep breath, and charged the cocky demon.

As if his thoughts had been heard, a brilliant ray of light filled the room. Michael averted his gaze, unable to look at the figure cloaked in light. He jumped as the sound of fluttering wings came near. After several minutes of quiet, Michael lifted his head. The demon was gone. Michael stomped his foot, bellowing, "I'll be damned. Where did it go?"

Shifting his body, he found an angel hovering in the center of the room. The angel warned. "You *could* be damned if you're not careful."

The angelic tone of the voice rattled him. It was as if thunder were rumbling and echoing in the room. Michael silently sent up a quick prayer of forgiveness. Surely God wouldn't be upset with a swear word now and then. Would he?

"Michael O'Shea! You are as compulsive as I've been led to believe."

"Me? Who told you that?" He picked up his hat off the floor, punching it back into shape.

With a snap, the angel's wings retreated into his shoulder blades.

The angel studied Michael. "You constantly fail to listen to orders. You are not supposed to be here tonight. Yet, for some unknown reason, here you are."

He tried not to flinch. "Well, I couldn't help it. I had to come and check out this house. You do know that there was a murder just down the street."

The angel, floating several inches off the ground, circled Michael several times, staring at him as if he were a germ under a microscope. Michael shifted from foot to foot nervously.

Finally, the angel stopped to face him. "Perhaps I should have given you more information."

Raising his chin, he said gruffly, "That would help. So far I haven't had much help, you know."

The angel's eyes glittered with an emotion that looked like anger. "Although I may only be a guardian angel, don't make me call in reinforcements. You've were sent here to help Brett solve a murder case that happened to be linked to your death. You, a mere ghost, are not equipped to take on demons at this time and place. I was forced to intervene to save your ass—again, I might add."

"Hey! I didn't think angels could swear."

"There is much you do not know, Michael."

"I thought the big guy was going to help us with the case and get rid of this thing that is killing innocent people."

The angel shuddered, his wings unleashing at a speed that nearly blew Michael across the room. "'The big guy'? Have you no reverence?" Before Michael could respond, the angel continued. "Yes, of course you will be directed. From now on, pay attention to your orders. For your sake and Brett's, you must follow the path."

Michael grunted and folded his arms across his chest. "Forgive me for being ignorant, but I've been in limbo land for over eighty years, and I sure don't understand what path you're referring to. I want my future to be resolved. I'd like to see my wife and children again." His anger withered as he mentioned his family. He used his thumb to wipe tears from his eyes.

The angel's solemn voice seemed to convey his regret. "It is noted that you have been patient. Please realize that I know only certain things. Be assured that God is aware of your long-suffering. Neither you nor I knows what his final plan is."

Michael took a deep breath. "I guess I've lasted this long. What's another few weeks or months? As long as it's not years. When can I tell Brett who I am?"

Surprisingly, the angel smiled. "When you are told. Now that everything is settled, cease being a pain in my arse. Trust me, you do not want me to intervene again."

A second later, the brilliant light again filled the room, causing Michael to shield his eyes. Adjusting his hat, Michael returned outside in time to spot Brett and Anders walking down the street. Luckily they hadn't witnessed the brief skirmish. He didn't want to think about them getting hurt.

It was good to know that he was going to get another opportunity to even the scoreboard with the devil's spawn. He definitely had a score to settle.

CHAPTER FORTY-FOUR

B rett spotted Al walking down the street toward them. He and Anders had returned to the scene of the most recent murder. They continued to walk slowly around the area, stooping every so often to check something on the ground. It would have been much quicker if the spirit of the dead man could have come forth and told them what happened.

Al stood on the curb, staring down the street. Brett paused to watch Al. "What's down the street that has captured your attention?"

Al shrugged and dug his hands into his pockets. "It's a long story. Have you found any leads yet?"

Brett walked over to Al's side. Al turned as if hiding something. "Yes, but answer my question first. You act like you're hiding something. So spill your guts."

Al sighed, rubbing the back of his neck. "I had a little run-in with our demon boy."

Anders stopped taking notes and jerked his head toward them. Brett gripped Al's shoulder. "What! Why didn't you tell us?"

"That's what I'm doing. See that house with the chain-link fence across the street? I saw someone looking out the window, so I went to check it out. I can't say I was surprised to see Demon Boy there."

Anders edged Brett aside and faced Al. "What the hell happened?"

"Well, he tried to intimidate me by turning into a dragon."

"A dragon?" raged Brett.

"Horny tail and all. I was so pissed off, we got in a tussle."

Brett and Anders started running to the house only to pull up short when Al popped up in front of them. "No one is in the house now. He's gone."

Gritting his teeth, Brett snapped, "Where is he?"

"After I got thrown into a wall, our fight was broken up."

"For God's sake, Al, quit drawing this out. What happened?"

Splaying his hands in front of his chest, Al muttered, "Okay. Like I was going to say, the fight was broken up by an angel. Apparently I don't pay attention to directions."

Anders squeezed his eyes closed. Brett stepped forward until his nose touched Al's. "Do you want us to kill you?"

The edge of Al's mouth turned upward. "Calm down, sonny. I'm getting to the good part."

His eyes narrowing, Brett ordered, "Spit it out."

"The angel indicated that I'm supposed to follow the plan. If I pay attention, we will know the plan. The angel was sent to break up our little fight. I did learn some details about your great-grandfather's death. The demon we've been dealing with is trying to destroy you like he destroyed your grandfather."

"Why?" Brett gasped.

"For the same reason that has existed since time began. Good versus evil. You have morals and standards. So did you great-grandfather. You and Anders probably don't even realize the influence you have on other people. Evil never likes good interfering with their plans."

"When do we get this thing and prevent any more people from dying?"

Al shook his head. "That I don't know. When it happens, we'll know it."

Brett and Anders stared at each other. Brett felt as confused as Anders looked. Unsure of what to do next, Brett began walking back to their car. He stopped when Al hollered at him.

"Oh, before I forget, I've got a scoop on Sergeant Taylor and your chief."

Brett turned back to Al. "In ten words or less, give it to me. I've got a splitting headache, and I'm going home to make friends with my bed."

"Ellison is up to his neck with gambling debt and has gotten into money laundering with the help of men in Chicago. Taylor wants out, but you and I know that the guys from Chicago aren't going to let either one of them walk away." Clapping his hands together, Al smiled. "That's it for now. See you guys later."

Before Brett could blink, Al disappeared. Anders glanced at him. "Do you believe that?"

"I don't think Al would lie to us." Brett covered his mouth to stifle a yawn. "It's late, and we're both beat. What do you say we deal with this tomorrow? I can't even think at this point."

Anders nodded. "I'm like you. Too tired to think. C'mon, I'll drop you off at home. My wife will be shocked to have me home before sunrise."

CHAPTER FORTY-FIVE

B rett leaned against the wall after locking the back door. He didn't know how long he stood there. Finally he pushed himself away from the entry and shuffled toward his bedroom. After shedding his clothes, he fell onto the bed.

Hours later, his cell phone buzzed on the nightstand. Without opening his eyes, he grabbed it. "Hello."

Lisa's voice brought a smile to his face. "Good morning, sunshine."

"Hi yourself. Are you working?"

"Not yet. The station manager told me to come in late. With the murder last night and all, I probably got home later than you." Lisa's next words were muffled. "Did you learn anything last night?"

Sitting on the edge of the bed, Brett rubbed the sleep from his eyes. "You know that anything I tell you is confidential, right?"

"Of course. I haven't said anything yet. We got a couple of shots of the body. It looked pretty gruesome."

"It was. The guy's heart was gone."

Lisa gasped. "You mean his actual heart?"

"Yeah. Anders and I are sure that Richard Brown is behind it."

"Oh my God! We've got to get this guy before any more innocent people die."

With phone in hand, Brett made it to the kitchen to start the coffee. "I agree. We're going out again tonight. Also, Al and Richard, a.k.a. Demon Boy, got into a fight last night. Al learned why this guy is trying to kill me."

Lisa's voice cracked. "Why?"

Brett regretted mentioning the topic. "Don't worry. I don't plan on dying anytime soon. Al said it had to do with me being a good cop. Supposedly that is why my great-grandfather died."

The irritation in her voice was evident. "Well crap. If that's true, most of the cops in the country should be dead."

Brett walked around the kitchen, continuing to make breakfast. He jerked the phone away from his ear as the sound of a loud crash blared through the receiver.

"Lisa! Are you okay?"

He heard the sound of glass breaking, followed by a loud thud. Lisa's shrill scream sent chills up his spine. Gripping the phone, he yelled, "Lisa! Lisa!"

She didn't answer. He quickly glanced down to see if the connection had been lost. It hadn't. Trying once more, Brett roared, "Lisa, answer me!"

A deep, raspy voice responded. "Office O'Shea. It seems we're always running into each other."

Brett's blood pounded in his head. He couldn't think. "Who are you?" But he knew who it was. There was no way he could ever forget the sound of that voice. It was the creature that controlled Richard's body. The demon. "Where's Lisa? Put her on the phone right now."

Gruff laughter echoed in the phone. "If you want to see her alive, you need to follow my instructions. Meet me tonight at the Miller house on York Street. Come alone—or else."

"When?"

"Shall we say midnight? After all, that is the witching hour." Richard cackled. "Remember, O'Shea, you come alone or you'll never see your girlfriend again."

Brett stared at the phone in his trembling hand. Finally, he laid it on the table and opened the closet door. He lifted up a large box filled with ammunition, and set it on the kitchen table. As he loaded his guns, Al appeared next to him.

Al's smiled faded as he watched Brett. "What's going on? You seem really upset. Let me tell you that my day hasn't been a bowl of cherries either."

Brett blinked at Al, trying to drive away the fog that had been clouding his brain since his conversation with Richard. "What the hell are you blathering about?"

Al leaned in closer, studying the multiple guns laid out on the table. "It looks like you're preparing for Armageddon."

Brett shoved a handful of magazines into his pocket. "I am."

Al shuddered. "Don't screw with me. What the hell is going on?"

Brett grabbed the remaining gun on the table to load it. "He's got Lisa," he muttered softly.

Al's fists slammed into the table, sending the loose cartridges scattering to the floor. "When do we go?"

"Midnight. I'm supposed to go alone to the York Street house."

"Alone? There is no way that I am letting you go there alone. It's a trap."

Brett sighed. "I know it's a trap, but what choice do I have? If I don't show up, she's dead. I can't have that on my conscience."

"Dead people don't have a conscience. That's why I need to go with you."

"Al, this is serious. For once, quit being a smart-ass."

Brett tried to push his way past Al. Annoyed when Al refused to budge, Brett growled, "Get out of my way."

Al folded his arms across his chest, glaring back at Brett. "I can't let you go."

Brett bent and dropped his bag on the floor. It was obvious that this was going to get physical. "Get out of my way." As he straightened, Al's fist plowed into his face. Clutching his nose, Brett pinched his nostrils together in an effort to stop the bleeding. As the pain abated, he said, "Damn it! What is your problem?"

Al's lips curled in determination. "I will help you, and we're doing it my way. Understand? Now go sit down so we can talk."

Brett hung his head, putting out his hand to brace himself against the wall. His face pounded, and he was overcome with desire to kill Al. It was too bad that he was already dead. Fed up with Al's antics, Brett marched toward his room. He decided he would climb out his bedroom window. He wasn't going to allow Lisa to die. He slammed to a stop as Al appeared in the bedroom doorway.

"Wait. I need to tell you something."

Brett paused at the tone of Al's voice. There was a catch in his words that Brett had not heard before.

"Brett, you'd better sit down. I want to share something with you."

Throwing himself on a chair, Brett glanced at his watch. "Okay, now what?"

With his head bowed, Al reached up and slowly slid his hat off. Running a hand through his sandy brown hair, Al raised his head to meet Brett's gaze.

CHAPTER FORTY-SIX

Brett's anger faded as he stared into the face he had only seen before in pictures. The same face that lined the hallway at his grandmother's house. His eyes crossed, causing his vision to blur. His sight wavered.

"Lean over and lower your head. We need to get the blood flowing in that brain of yours." Al massaged Brett's back. No, it wasn't Al. It was his great-grandfather.

"Oh God, oh God," Brett moaned. He glanced up, somewhat surprised by the concerned look in his great-grandfather's eyes. He felt the contents of his stomach begin to rise up in his throat. He swallowed hard, forcing it back down. He could not get sick now. He had to think; to figure out what was going on. Was this some kind of mind trick that Al or Michael was using on him? Maybe it was a diversion so he wouldn't go rescue Lisa. *Shit!* As his stomach rolled, his vision grew blurrier. He gasped as he felt his eyes roll back in his head.

Michael caught Brett before he hit the floor. He carried him to the bed, lifting his legs off the floor. Glancing down at his descendent, Michael felt relief as color began returning to his face. Brett moaned, drawing his attention. When Brett tried to rise, Michael held him down.

"Take it easy. You passed out. It will take a while before you're steady again. Let me get you a glass of water."

Minutes later, he returned to Brett's side. Brett had not moved. His eyes remained closed with his arm resting on his forehead.

"Here, take a drink of cold water. It will help get the blood pumping again."

Brett struggled to sit. He took the glass and slowly sipped the water while glaring at Michael. Michael felt like public enemy number one. He was glad that he was already dead when he saw the visual daggers Brett shot at him. They sat in silence as Brett drank the water. Finally, Michael took the glass and set it aside. No use avoiding the inevitable.

Michael positioned a chair in front of Brett and sat down. The way Brett continued to glare at him was not a good sign of how this conversation was going to go. "How are you feeling?"

"How do you think I'm feeling, Al? No, I forgot! You're not Al, you're my dead great-grandfather, Michael O'Shea."

"Ha ha. Just let me explain."

"I can't believe anything you say. You've lied to me from day one."

Michael balled up his fists. "Listen, I didn't know. All my memories were gone."

"Hmmph! I doubt that."

"Let me tell you a story. A long time ago, there was a young detective—about your age, by the way."

Brett snorted, not acknowledging Michael's attempt at a bit of humor. "As I was saying, there was this detective who was headstrong. He occasionally ignored orders and was impatient with people and cases. He wanted to make things right; to do good. One night, he made a major mistake. He got sent on a burglary call. You need to remember that this was before car radios, cell phones, and the tablet things you use today. Calling for backup was a headache. You had to go down the street and find a call box. Then you waited for help to arrive."

Obviously still pissed, Brett snapped, "Caveman age, right?"

"Sonny, you're more like me than you know. Now where was I? The detective approached the large house. It was a mansion back then.

Rather than call for backup or wait like any sensible cop would, the detective ventured into the house. He found the first body. Body parts were strewn around the room. If this detective had been smart, he would have run screaming out of that house, but it was the Depression. Times were tough; much tougher than you can imagine. The detective had to work extra shifts, as he had a family of three with a new baby on the way. So when he heard a woman's scream come from the basement, he ran to help her. He didn't even think twice. He knew he had to save her. But he ran right into a trap—a wire stretched across the bottom stairs. He broke a leg when he fell. Before he could get his gun, while lying on the floor, the killer surprised him. An—"

By now Brett was sitting on the edge of the bed, frowning as he met Michael's gaze. "What happened to the woman?"

"She was dead by the time he ran downstairs. She didn't have a chance."

"What happened next?" Brett paused before whispering, "Who killed the detective?"

Michael cleared his throat as he resisted the urge to break down and sob for all the lost years, the lost time with his family, and the years of not knowing when he would be reunited with his wife. Reliving the events of that night was agony.

"The killer was possessed, just like our demon boy, but no one knew it at the time. The detective's body was mutilated beyond recognition. His body was dismembered. Of course, the detective struggled to survive, to return to his family."

Brett stared at him, heedless of the tears streaming down his cheeks. "I'm so sorry. I never knew any of this."

Michael shrugged. "It doesn't really matter now. My point is that I died because I was full of pride and cocky. I have had time to regret many of my actions that night. I never got to say good-bye to my wife or children. Can you imagine that type of pain?"

Michael stiffened when Brett suddenly rose and embraced him in a tight hug. Tears were running down both their faces. When the men broke apart, Brett cracked a lopsided smile.

"Now I know why you kept that damn hat on all the time. Without it I would have recognized you from all the pictures Grandma, your daughter, showed me. I grew up thinking you were a god, better than Thor and Superman combined."

"I had strict orders that the hat had to stay on and low. You don't know how many times I wanted to yank off the dang thing. Believe me when I say I didn't know you. I didn't know about my life." He grabbed Brett for another hug. "I love you, Brett. I am so proud of the man you've become."

Brett squeezed him in return. Pulling back, he looked at Michael. "What am I supposed to call you? 'Grandpa' may raise some questions."

Michael chortled. "Well, we can't have two O'Sheas running around. No one would believe us. How about calling me Mike?"

Brett reached out and shook his hand. "I like that. Can I tell Mom?"

Michael nodded. "Yes, but let's wait until all of this is over. Since Lisa is our priority, let's pretend that I'm Al for the time being. I'm keeping the hat so Anders doesn't wonder what's going on. We need to come up with a foolproof strategy for when we enter that house. It's time to get rid of Demon Boy once and for all."

CHAPTER FORTY-SEVEN

An hour later, Brett and Michael picked up Anders at the station. Frown lines marred his face.

"What's wrong?" Brett asked as he pulled out onto the street. "Or should I ask?"

Anders muttered, "I'm worried sick for Lisa." He turned toward the backseat. "Hi, Al. Any advice for tonight?"

Brett watched his relative adjust his hat in the rearview mirror and bit back a smile.

"No. I think Brett has everything ready for tonight." Michael winked.

"Hey, guys, we're almost there," Brett softly interjected. "You ready?"

Brett stopped the car several hundred feet away from the target. As they got out of the car, Michael looked up at the house.

Brett nudged Michael. "Are you okay?"

"Yeah. Just thinking."

Brett leaned into the trunk, pulling out several magazines for his gun and a flamethrower. "This is the night we even the score. Just remember to follow the plan. Lisa's in there."

Nodding at the flamethrower, Michael asked, "What is that thing?"

"Extra insurance."

Michael pointed up to the sky. "My extra insurance is up there. I just hope they're paying attention."

Strapping on a protective vest, Anders snapped at them. "Enough talk. O'Shea, get your vest on."

Brett patted his chest. "Got it. Let's go nail the son of a bitch."

Michael quickly made the sign of the cross and reluctantly filed in behind them.

Michael watched as Brett and Anders split off in opposite directions. He gazed up at the front of the house. The sweeping porch looked nothing like it did in 1933. There was a sense of despair that cloaked the house. His feet felt like lead weights as he slowly walked up the wooden steps.

He faced the front door, just as he had done decades before. The glass panels on either side of the door were still there. A cool night breeze scattered the dead leaves at his feet. He closed his eyes and breathed deeply, strengthening himself for the coming chaos. Oh yes, he knew exactly what he was walking into. There were no more second chances. This evening would determine his final fate.

Glancing at the door, he saw the curtain drop back into place. *Hell no!* It was as if he were reliving the same events of that hateful night.

A loud cackling sound broke his reverie. There was no use in delaying the inevitable any longer. The guys should be in place by now. He quickly passed through the closed doorway and paused to get his bearings.

The house was quiet. Movement at the end of the hallway caught his attention. Richard stood waiting for him. Taunting him. As Michael moved in that direction, Richard disappeared. Upon entering the library, he saw that the walls were still lined with the mahogany bookcases. Other than a few modern furniture pieces placed around the room, it looked as it had all those years ago. He sighed, relieved not to find a dismembered body lying on the floor.

Michael left the library and wandered through each of the other rooms on the main floor. The kitchen was the last room to check on this floor. The sink was filled with dirty dishes and plates of half-eaten food. Two glasses sat on the counter, giving him hope that Lisa was alive. He glanced out the kitchen window and saw Brett placing sea salt on the windowsill. Quietly, he made to his way to the back door and turned the lock so Brett could carry out his plan. He then silently drifted back down the hall to the stairway.

The banister gleamed as moonlight filtered through the windows. It swept upward into the dark hallows of the house. Halfway up the stairs, a small round window graced the landing. Michael paused to look outside. The wind had increased in intensity, causing the barren oak branches to wave frantically in the air. It was as if their jerky movements were trying to get his attention, telling him to flee this godforsaken house.

He climbed the remaining stairs, occasionally glancing behind him. Passing through the bedroom walls, he rapidly completed his search of the upstairs rooms. When finished, he groaned with disappointment. The top two floors were clear, which meant he had to go down to the basement. The place where he was murdered. The one place he never wanted to see again.

Keeping to the shadows of the wall, Michael made his way downstairs. He and Brett made eye contact before Brett opened the door to the basement. A chill coursed through Michael as he stared toward the bottom of the stairs. Hissing, he motioned for Brett to return. Brett shook his head and shut the basement door behind him.

Damn it! He should have gone down the stairs before Brett. He was already dead. He couldn't let anything happen to Brett.

Anders came out of the kitchen, his gun drawn. Michael shimmered and appeared next to Anders.

"Where's Brett? He was supposed to wait here," Anders whispered.

"He just went downstairs."

"Damn it. I'd better go down."

Michael grabbed his arm. "No, I'll go down. Make sure all the doors and windows are marked with salt. I'm not sure if it will work, but it's worth a try."

Without waiting for an answer, Michael opened the basement door. He stared down into a sea of darkness. Fear crept through him. He couldn't move. Until he heard Lisa's scream.

CHAPTER FORTY-EIGHT

A second later, Michael found himself running down the stairs, reeling from déjà vu. He paused at the bottom of the stairs, trying to get his bearings. The basement looked nothing like it did all those years ago. The entire lower level had been renovated since he had last been here. Gone were the dull red brick walls, as well as uneven cement floor. The lower level was now segmented off into several rooms. A series of doors lined the darkened hallway in front of him.

Shit! Where are Brett and Lisa? Above his head, the ceiling light flickered. Luckily he could see in the dark this time around, but Brett would be at a disadvantage. The door at the top of the stairs creaked. Whirling around, he saw Anders motioning to him. Michael waved him forward.

Once the two were side by side, Michael whispered to the detective, "I'll head left and take the long hallway. You check out the area behind us."

Anders nodded and stealthy moved around the corner. Reluctantly, Michael inched toward the first door. Should he kick the door in or dissipate and show up in the room? Perhaps it would more prudent to sneak in. With a sigh, he blinked and found himself in a dark area. Quickly getting his bearings, he found he was in a bedroom. The pillow on the bed was indented, as if someone had recently rested there. He picked up the pillow and breathed in. *Lisa!* She had been in this room. *Where did she go?*

He searched the closet and any place someone could hide. He whisked back to the hallway. Door number two was next. Tension gripped the back of his neck, squeezing like a pair of hands choking the air out of him.

This time he kicked in the door, shattering the frame. Pieces of wood flew through the air and littered the floor. Cautiously, he entered the room. Another bedroom. Moonlight from a window cast shadows about. After checking potential hiding places, Michael turned to leave. As he did so, a soft thud grabbed his attention.

Where did that come from? The sound claimed his attention again. He lifted the foot of the bed and gasped as a figure rolled toward him.

He quickly bent to remove the tape covering her mouth. Her teeth chattered nonstop. "Lisa, are you okay?"

She nodded, motioning for him to untie her wrists. "Where's Brett?" Staring up into his face, tears welled up in her eyes.

Michael ripped off the ropes and looped his arm about her shoulders. "It's okay now. Don't worry; I'll get you out of here."

Lisa bowed her head, resting it against his chest. After several minutes, she raised her head and wiped away the remnants of the tears. She took a deep breath and tipped her chin, looking determined. "We've got to help Brett."

"I need to get you out of here."

She grabbed his forearm. "No. I'm not leaving until I know Brett is safe."

Michael pulled Lisa to her feet and steadied her. He pretended not to hear her opposition. He opened a window, removed the screen, and tossed it outside on the lawn. "Give me your foot. I'm going to boost you up through the window."

With her hands on her hips, Lisa shook her head. "Al. Listen to me. I'm not leaving."

Michael sent up a silent prayer for patience. "Listen, we don't have time to chitchat. Brett will clobber me if I don't get you out of here."

Lisa seemed to ignore the note of urgency in his voice. The color returned to her cheeks. She straightened her shoulder, tossing her hair. "I'm going with you, so get over it. Lead the way."

Michael narrowed his eyes before gripping her shoulders. "Are you aware of what we're up against? You or Brett could get killed."

Tilting her head to meet his gaze, she said, "Of course I know! I've been kidnapped twice by this nut job. Now, what are we doing?"

Jabbing a finger at her chest, he warned, "Stay close and be quiet. I need to find Brett."

He pointed to the hallway before vaporizing outside the room. Standing before the next door, he pressed his ear against the barrier. As he pulled away from the door, he bumped into Lisa.

He wiggled his fingers at her, trying to convey that she should move out of his away.

"Is the killer in there?" she whispered.

He shook his head. With a smirk, he disappeared through the walls to enter room number three. The cold air crept through his jacket. None of the other rooms had made him feel this uneasy. He didn't fully materialize, choosing to remain less visual than normal. He immediately felt a vise close about his throat. He reached up and rubbed his neck while looking around the room. He then flipped on the light switch, hoping to discover the source of his unease.

The room was in shambles. It was obvious that this was some kind of craft room. A bloody hammer lay near Michael's feet. A nail gun rested on the workbench. Cut ropes were piled up in the corner of the room. Michael carefully made his way across the room, picked up the ropes, and examined them. Brett had been here. *Did he escape?* The door clicked behind him. Swiftly turning, he saw Lisa entering the room. *Damn it!* Couldn't the woman listen?

She quickly clasped her arms around her waist. "It's cold in here."

"Shh!" Michael arched an eyebrow in disapproval. Although he was thankful she was okay, she was starting to get on his nerves.

They both jerked toward the hallway, hearing the thud of footsteps running up the basement stairs. They rushed out, but they missed whoever had run upstairs.

"Brett? Are you up there?" Lisa murmured, peeking around the corner.

"For god's sake, woman! Can you please be quiet?" Michael threw up his hands in frustration. "I'm going upstairs. It's clear there is nothing down here now."

Lisa gripped the back of his jacket, hobbling behind him. "I'm not staying down here alone."

Although Michael could hear the fear in her trembling voice, he pried her hand off of him. "You must let go. How can I vaporize with you hanging on?"

With a stomp of her foot, Lisa glared at him. "Fine. Leave. I'll meet you upstairs."

"You should have left when I asked you to. Now it's too late." Halfway up the stairs, he paused and turned to see her forlorn figure watching him. A sense of pity filled him. "Damnation. Come on, then."

He could sense her fear. Not that he blamed her. People didn't expect to fight supernatural beings.

He tiptoed up the stairs, holding Lisa's hand. At the top, he poked the door with his foot, pushing it open enough to look around the kitchen. Standing in a corner, he nodded toward the outside door.

"Please go! Brett will be angry if I don't get you out of here."

She smirked at him. The girl had guts. He pressed a kiss to her cheek. "Don't say I didn't warn you. Stay close."

Husky laughter echoed through the house. Moments later, there was a loud crash in the front room. Silently, but swiftly, Michael hurried toward the sound. He skidded to a halt. Lisa, who was gripping his jacket, ran into his back.

Anders was barely conscious on the floor. A trickle of blood dotted his forehead. Michael breathed a sigh of relief to see Anders's chest continue to rise and fall.

Richard stood over Anders. Richard's facial features were distorted beyond recognition. His eyes had become red orbs that watched every move Michael made as he entered the formal living room. Richard's fingers had been replaced by the deadly pointed claws that he vividly remembered from their last confrontation.

Where the hell is Brett? Michael thought. Leaning toward Lisa, he whispered, "Get ready. I need you to get Anders out of here."

Michael stepped to the fireplace. He sighed as he relaxed against the mantle. "Tsk, tsk. I see you have reverted to tormenting those weaker than you."

The claws appeared to lengthen as Richard snarled. The creature seemed to study Michael for several minutes. *What is going on?* Michael wondered.

"Key. You are the key." The demon came toward him.

"Key? What the hell are you talking about?"

"You are the link between now and nineteen thirty-three. Your family is the root of my problems. Your great-grandson is just like you. You and he must die." The demon swiped those deadly claws, catching on Michael's tweed jacket. The material gave way, revealing one arm.

"Hey! This is my favorite jacket, asshole!"

The demon lunged forward. Michael dodged to the side, narrowly escaping.

"Please, don't tell me you are really going to fight me. If my memory serves me, an angel saved your ass last time by letting you escape. But hey, if you want a repeat match, then let's go, Demon Boy!"

Richard took a step forward, his arms outstretched. Saliva dripped from the corner of his crooked mouth. Michael tensed. A fight it was going to be, and he was more than ready to end this thing.

Out of the corner of his eye, Michael spotted Brett in the doorway behind Richard. From the look on Brett's face, Michael knew he had seen Lisa and Anders. Richard paused, slightly turning to follow Michael's gaze.

A look of glee lit Richard's face. He whipped around, instantly morphing into the unsightly creature with webbed wings and sharp, protruding teeth. The demon lunged for Brett.

Brett bent low and ran toward Michael, evading the outstretched claws. Scrambling to his feet, Brett pulled out his Glock and emptied the magazine into the chest of the creature facing them.

"Well, that made a statement," chirped Michael.

The demon threw back his head and roared. Brett hoped that his erratic breathing was the only outward sign of his terror. Michael was grinning as if they had already won.

Brett leaned toward Michael and asked, "Any ideas?"

Before Michael could answer, Anders's eyes popped open. The demon strutted toward Michael and Brett as Anders and Lisa scurried along the outside wall, making their way to the connecting room.

"If we go at him from different directions, we might have a chance. On the count of three, let's rush him," Michael suggested.

Brett nodded. "One ... two ..."

Before Brett could reach three, Michael lunged forward, jumping on the demon's back. Michael wrapped both arms around its neck and held on. The creature jumped so high that its head broke through the ceiling. Chunks of drywall rained on the floor. When the demon fell to its feet, it rolled on its back. Michael disappeared.

The creature quickly jumped to its feet and stalked toward Brett. Brett slowly stepped back until he could go no further. His back was up against the wall, literally.

"Shit! Why do you have such a hard-on for us O'Sheas?"

The creature leaned close to Brett's face and dug his claws into the wall on either side of Brett's head, effectively imprisoning him. Instinctively, Brett pressed his head against the wall.

"I detest your righteous attitude. How's that for a starter?" growled the demon.

Thick spittle with a noxious smell landed on his face. Suppressing his gag reflex, Brett casually reached up and wiped his face with the back of his hand.

"Personally, I think you're being rather judgmental, but maybe it's just me."

Brett's eyes widened as Lisa crept up behind the demon. She held a fireplace poker in one hand. What was she doing? She was going to get killed!

As Lisa jabbed the poker into the demon's back, Brett rammed his knee between the creature's legs. He scrambled out of reach, taking Lisa with him. They fell to the floor, with Brett quickly rolling on top. He could feel Lisa shaking with terror. Both of them jolted as the demon's shrill scream reverberated around the room. Brett had to draw its attention. He had to give her a chance to escape. He jumped to his feet, grabbed a vase, and threw it at the demon's head. Shards of glass flew through the air. Brett covered his head as some of the pieces cut into his arms. Streams of blood dripped from the demon's head. Blue splatters dotted the floor.

He saw Lisa roll to her feet. Panic was etched on her face. She ran into the library. When the demon crept toward him, Brett took off running. The size of the demon in his dragon form hindered its movement through the narrow hallway. Luckily, several rooms branched off the hall, so the demon would have to search many of them, giving Brett precious moments to get his demon toaster, the flamethrower.

Brett nearly tripped over Michael when he popped up in the middle of the hallway. "Move!" Without stopping, Brett tore off down the hall.

Michael turned and took off after Brett. "I'm right behind you." As a shadow loomed over him, Michael shuddered. "Shit!" He quickly blinked himself to the kitchen.

Brett looked up as Michael entered the room. He bent over, yanking out the flamethrower he had stored in the cupboard when they entered the house. Michael eyed the weapon as if it were a chocolate bar.

"Can I use that?"

"No. You don't know how to use it."

Michael shrugged. "What could go wrong?"

"Please. You could burn down the house or kill us."

"Fine," Michael sniffed. "Be selfish."

Anders's scream brought them to a stop. "I thought he got out." Brett and Michael quickly returned to help Anders. Anders lay on the carpet, his abdomen split open, with Lisa crouched next to him. It wasn't hard to speculate what had caused the wound.

Brett knelt and ripped off his shirt to press it against the injury. Anders was conscious, cursing like a drunken sailor.

"Hold this on the wound. We've got to slow that bleeding."

Anders's face was pale, but his eyes were alert. "Damn thing. It got me with those claws." Nodding toward the adjoining room, Anders warned, "He went that way. He's probably watching us now. Watch your back, guys. Don't worry about me. I'm not going anywhere."

Adjusting the shoulder harness of the flamethrower, Brett opened the valve for the propane and lit the ignition. "Enough of this bullshit. We're not losing another man to this thing."

He stormed out of the room. He was so pissed off that he didn't even worry about the noise. He turned the corner and slammed into a slimy wall. The creature turned to see who or what had hit its back. For one long moment, neither moved. They just stared at one another.

Brett's fingers suddenly seemed stiff and uncooperative. The flamethrower wand clattered to the wood floor. The noise jerked Brett out of his reverie. He had only seconds to get a stream of fire going or he was as good as dead.

CHAPTER FORTY-NINE

The only sound Brett could hear was his own harsh breathing. Grabbing the wand securely in his hand, he squeezed the trigger. It was enough to shoot a five-foot stream of hot flame right into the belly of the demon.

Brett jumped back to escape the heat of burning flesh. The stench of burning skin filled the air. A cloud of black smoke engulfed the narrow hall, making it impossible for Brett to see farther than the end of his arm. The demon's roar shook the rafters of the house, rattling the windows. He shot another blast of heat in the direction of the smoldering demon.

Brett ran back to the kitchen to escape the demon's fury, skidding to a stop when he saw Michael.

Michael was beaming. "That was a sight for my eyes. It gave me pleasure seeing that thing burn."

Brett slipped off the flamethrower harness and collapsed into a chair. He rubbed his forehead, pushing his hair to a standing position. He stared at his hand, which continued to tremble.

"Breathe. It is just nerves."

"I need to go back and nail it again. If we keep blasting it, it will turn to toast."

Michael arched his brows. "If we're lucky, it will, but we haven't been lucky yet. You stay here. I'll go check on the thing."

Brett closed his eyes, concentrating on his breathing. When he opened his eyes, several minutes had elapsed. Utter quiet filled the house. Where was everyone? Jumping to his feet, Brett glanced to where he had dropped the flamethrower. It was gone. *Who took it? Son of a bitch!*

The floor trembled as if something large were moving through the house. Brett quickly reloaded his gun. Although the Glock couldn't kill the demon, it sure in the hell would slow it up.

Brett soundlessly inched his way to the front room. Peeking around the corner, he fixed his gaze on the spectacle before him. Michael and the demon ran at each other from opposite sides of the living room. A strange light cast a shimmering hue upon the room. *Holy shit! What is going on?* Wounds on both parties were significant. They fell and rolled across the room, slamming into walls, which shattered on impact. The house was literally being torn to pieces. Sections of sheetrock littered the floor.

Anders and Lisa huddled together in the far corner, watching the action. Brett rushed to their side and stood in front of them.

Anders groaned as Lisa pressed on the wound. Anders's raspy voice rose above the chaos taking place before them. "Shouldn't you be helping Al?"

Brett's gaze darted about the room. "I'm about to. Where's the flamethrower?"

Anders looked shocked. "Damn it! How can you lose a flamethrower?"

They both looked up as Michael roared and charged into the creature. Smoke lingered in the room from the charred flesh on the demon.

The demon hit the floor with a loud thud. Every window in the house rattled. Michael frantically motioned for Brett to pick up a knife that had dropped during the fight. Crawling on his knees, he gathered up the weapon and sank it into the demon's leg. Bluish fluid oozed from the wound. The creature whipped around, pinning Brett to the floor. As he struggled to free himself, claws pressed deeper into his side. His body split open like a zipper being torn apart.

Michael jumped onto the creature's back, wrapping his arms about its neck, trying to draw the creature's attention.

Brett screamed in agony. Unbidden tears blurred his vision. His body writhed in desperation to escape the relentless pain. He was dying. His head fell to the side in time to see Michael run into the other room and quickly return with the flamethrower. The air rushed from Brett's chest. There was no way that Michael could operate it.

"Give it to Anders."

Michael glanced at Anders and shook his head. "I can do this. I watched you do it."

The demon lowered his mouth to within inches of Brett's face, continuing to press the claws deeper into his body. Brett felt his heart stutter. He shuddered in relief as it continued to beat. He didn't want to die yet.

Brett's eyes widened as Michael grabbed the flamethrower wand and pressed the trigger. A whoosh of fire lit up the dining room, which was behind Michael. Looking perplexed, Michael turned and gasped.

Through a haze of pain, Brett watched flames dance up the wall. *Oh shit.* Michael really was going to burn the house down. Brett could swear that the demon was grinning at Michael's antics.

The demon's foul odor took Brett's breath away. "Who's going to save you now, Officer O'Shea?"

Brett's thoughts ran through his mind in slow motion. He saw Anders and Lisa staring at him, horror written on their faces. Anders's eyes were filled with tears. He knew he must look bad off if Anders was crying. Anders restrained Lisa, who was hysterical and looked as though she wanted to rush to his side. Oddly, he wasn't really worried about dying. Even the pain seemed to lessen. He was mentally prepared to die.

Michael roared his frustration. *What an idiot!* The walls in the next room were on fire because of his mistake. He had to get Brett, Lisa, and Anders out of here. There was no one else to save them but him.

Jerking the hose and wand into the correct position, Michael aimed at the demon's feet. With a roar, the demon growled and continued to press his fingers deeper into Brett's side. Blood continued to pump out on the floor.

Michael paused. Just like before, he wasn't thinking. He was reacting. He glanced toward the heavens, sending a silent prayer for help. Was this the lesson he should have known all those years ago? It had taken years for him to admit that he was like a bull in a china shop. He was cocky and brash, but he was a good man. Now it was just him against the demon. He had to save the people he loved. He needed help from the big guy. He couldn't do this by himself. He suddenly realized that he had never been alone. No matter how good of a detective he thought he was, he was nothing without the help from above.

Something wet trailed down his cheek. He absently reached up and wiped his face. A drop of liquid covered the end of his finger. A tear? Ghosts couldn't cry. How could this happen? Michael staggered to his knees, realizing his request for help had been granted. He glanced upward. A big smile graced his face. Pure power now flowed through his veins. Michael was empowered! He tossed his hat to the floor. Lisa gasped. He smiled at the thought that she might recognize him.

There would be no more hiding. Michael O'Shea was in the house!

Tightening his grip on the flamethrower, Michael aimed the nozzle at the creature's tail. Within seconds, the smell of burnt monster filled the room. The creature straightened, removing his claws from Brett's body. He had to defeat the demon now. Brett was dying before his eyes. He was whiter than a sheet.

Holding the flamethrower in one hand, Michael marched up to the creature. As it reared up to strike at him, Michael drew back his fist and plowed it into the demon's chest.

Michael jerked with satisfaction as his fist sank into the chest cavity. The demon stiffened with surprise, trying to twist away from his reach. Michael felt the pumping heart against the palm of his hand. His fingers surrounded the organ, squeezing and twisting.

The demon roared its outrage. Its arms flailed wildly, trying without success to grasp Michael. Michael had an invisible shield protecting him. He laughed as a wild light filled the demon's eyes. Its struggles weakened and it dropped to the floor.

Hatred poured from the red eyes. "You will not defeat me! You are nothing. Nothing but a mere detective. Nothing but a damn ghost."

Michael met the gaze of the demon, still holding its heart in his hand. "Au contraire, I may have been a mere detective, but I have a higher power on my side. Unfortunately you picked the wrong team."

Without hesitation, Michael yanked the heart from the demon's body. Blood pulsed out on the floor. As the demon lay defeated and dying on the floor, Michael readied the flamethrower. Unleashing the flame, he torched the demon until a pile of ashes was all that remained. He wanted to make sure the beast didn't rise like some sort of phoenix.

A flash of light appeared in front of Michael. He instinctively shielded his face. When he opened his eyes, the angel stood before him. As before, the light was so bright that Michael couldn't make out the facial features of the angel.

The angel turned to gaze about the room. With a sound of dismay and a wave of the hand, the angel reduced the fire in the dining room to a smoldering memory. The angel then leaned over Brett, shaking his head.

"Please save him?" Michael whispered.

A shimmer of light coursed through Brett's motionless body. The angel straightened, hovering nearby. Michael watched Brett for any sign of life. He gasped as Brett's chest rose and fell. Then Brett's fingers and arms began to move. Michael looked at the angel. "Thank you," he whispered.

Silently, the angel nodded. Brett moaned, drawing Michael's attention.

Michael dropped the flamethrower, anxious to help Brett. Swearing, Michael quickly bent to retrieve the flamethrower. Somehow the trigger was stuck in the on position. A stream of fire shot out, encompassing the angel.

"Damn it!" Michael cursed. His fingers didn't work, and he fumbled with the weapon, trying to shut it off. Finally the flames dwindled and disappeared.

Feeling chagrined, Michael profusely apologized, "Sorry. I don't know how that happened. You didn't get burned, did you? Oh my, your feathers." Michael rushed over and brushed the angel's wings.

With folded arms, the angel glared at Michael. Several feathers on his wings were charred black. "Michael O'Shea. It seems that accidents and strange events follow you in life and death. You need to thank the big guy, as you call him, for sending me to watch over you and your friends."

"Brett will be okay, won't he?"

"Yes. See for yourself."

Michael looked down at Brett. Blood no longer flowed from the wound. Color slowly returned to Brett's face.

Brett opened his eyes and gripped Michael's hand. "I said you'd burn down the house if you touched the flamethrower," Brett weakly uttered.

Michael dropped to the floor, wrapped his arms around Brett, and kissed him on the forehead. "Thank God you are alive. How are you feeling?"

Brett pushed Michael's arms away. "You're smothering me. Other than that, I feel like a truck ran over me. Where's Richard ... I mean the demon thing?"

Michael pointed across the room. "See that pile of ashes? That's all that's left. We did it!"

Brett slowly raised his head. "Where's Lisa and Anders?"

Anders rose from the floor, leaning on Lisa. The detective had a huge grin on his face as he inspected his abdomen. Minutes ago it had been a gaping wound. Now it was completely healed.

Lisa, on the other hand, looked shell-shocked and bedraggled. Her clothes were torn and covered with Anders's blood. Once Anders stood, Lisa rushed to Brett's side. Tears ran down her cheeks as she leaned down and pressed a kiss to his lips. She buried her face in his shoulder, quietly sobbing.

"Oh my God. Can you believe that?" Michael chuckled and slapped his thigh.

"Yes, I believe I can," the angel remarked in a dry tone.

Michael nodded to the pile of ashes. "What do we do with the remains?"

The angel pointed downward. "He is getting a personal escort back to Hades."

The angel blinked, and a hole in the floor opened up, revealing a deep pit. Michael peered down into it. Several hundred feet below, a reddish glow met his eyes. A rotten-egg smell drifted up into the house. The people in the room started coughing and quickly covered their noses.

The angel twirled his hand, causing the ashes to rise up. In a single strand, the ashes flew down the hole and vanished. Before Michael could blink, the floor returned to normal.

The angel shimmered, ascending upward. He paused to flash a benevolent gaze at Michael. "You do know that we've been watching you for years. You were a good detective, O'Shea, and a good husband and father. It has been difficult for some of us to remain aloof. I wanted you to know that this adventure of yours turned out the way it was planned. All good soldiers are rewarded."

Hope flared in his heart. "Does this mean that I can be with my wife and my children again?"

The angel bowed his head. Michael swore he could see a smile. Iridescent light shone from the angelic being. "Prayers are always answered, Michael. You know that by now."

Michael's heart filled with joy. Excitement flourished in him. He wanted to dance an Irish jig.

A flash of light blinded Michael. Once again it was just the four of them in the room. Michael couldn't wait to see his family again. The ability to hold his wife in his arms was a thrill he had expected never to enjoy again.

As Brett prepared to stand, the angel's voice once again commanded Michael's attention.

"Michael, I should mention one more thing. God does answer prayers. He knows your heart better than you."

A spark of trepidation rushed through Michael. "What does that mean, exactly?"

Soft laughter filled the room. "Just that. He knows you better than you know yourself. Good luck, Michael O'Shea, detective extraordinaire.

EPILOGUE

The four of them stood silently facing one another before bursting out in laughter. Relief echoed in each of their faces. Brett wrapped his arms around Lisa. He couldn't believe it was actually over. No more hocus pocus!

As Brett glanced at Michael, he realized Michael was not wearing his hat. He reached out to ruffle the ghost's sandy brown hair.

Michael grinned. "Do you like my new look?"

"Yeah, I do. You look just like the pictures I remember. Why did you ditch the hat?"

"Well, I figured it was time." Michael reached up and pushed his hair off his forehead. "I don't know if you heard or not, but I don't think I will be here much longer. I get to see my family."

Brett's good mood faded. *Michael gone? Will I ever see him again?* Brett was used to Michael popping up unexpectedly. In fact, he kind of liked having Michael around.

Lisa pulled away from Brett to face Michael. "Are you who I think you are?"

Brett grabbed her hand. Michael winked at Lisa.

"Who do you think I am?"

"Well, you look like Mike O'Shea. But really, are you him?" Spots of color stained her cheeks.

Anders stepped closer to glare at Michael. "Al? I mean, Mike O'Shea? The infamous Mike O'Shea?"

Brett groaned. Michael grinned like a boy with a new toy. "Yep, that's me.

Anders slapped Michael on the back. "Shit! Have I got a few questions for you. I need to know whether some of the stories are true. But now, let's get out of here."

They gathered the weapons. The angel had restored the house to its original condition. No burnt walls. No holes in the drywall. Everything was fixed.

Anders and Michael headed to the car as Brett walked Lisa to her vehicle.

"Are you okay?" he asked.

She ran her fingers through her hair, sighing. "I think so. What a night, though."

He pulled her into his arms and pressed his lips against hers. His tongue wound around hers. A horn honked nearby. Brett pulled away in time to see Michael lean out the window and flash a stupid grin.

"Hey, I'd better go. I'll call you later. Maybe we can get together tonight and celebrate."

Lisa kissed him and waved as she drove away. Brett hopped into the front seat of the waiting car. Relief flooded him. It was over.

Michael rode home with Brett. He had come so close to losing his grandson only hours before that his protective instinct was in overdrive. After the harrowing events of the past weeks, Brett dropped onto his bed and slept the day away. Michael perched on the nearby chair, watching the young cop sleep.

Michael mulled over angel's words from early that morning. He hated cryptic messages. He was going to see his family again. His assignment had been to help Brett solve a murder case. He'd done that. Mission accomplished! So when was the payoff? He was anxious to see his wife and parents again, but he was torn with his thoughts of Brett. The two of them had grown close during the past couple of months. His eyes grew misty as he thought of never seeing Brett again.

At that moment, he knew that when he reached heaven he would put in a special request so he could communicate with or visit Brett in the future. By now they knew him well enough to know that he would be persistent until he got his way.

The next morning, the sound of a ringing phone woke Brett from a deep sleep. He blindly reached for his cell.

"Yeah."

"O'Shea, are you awake? It's ten a.m.. Get your ass out of bed and get down to the station ASAP."

Brett sat up. The excitement in Anders's voice was evident. "I'll be there in an hour. Can't you tell me what's going on?"

"No. Now hurry."

Sluggish from sleeping around the clock, he went to the kitchen for a cup of coffee. On the table was a folded piece of paper. His hand shook as he picked it up. He stared at the note. It was from Michael. It read as follows:

> Hi, sonny. It's time for me to leave. You are sleeping, and I don't want to wake you. It's easier for me to write this than to try to say the words to you. First, I want to say it has been an honor to get to know you. I love you like a son. Mark my words, you will be a great detective. Without you, I wouldn't have discovered who I am. We had quite a time together. I'm going to miss hanging out with you and using your ~~iiod~~ iPod. Just remember that I'm always with you and I have your back.
> Love always,
> Michael O'Shea
> P.S. I'm putting in a request to the big guy to see if we can stay in touch. I'll be

a pain in their ass until it happens, just so you know.

Brett stared at the note. Emotion tightened his throat. Using the back of his hand, he wiped away the tears. Tears of loss, yet tears of joy. He visualized the havoc Michael would create. They'd probably toss his butt out of heaven. He had learned a lot in the past few months. Rules were good, but sometimes they had to be bent to get the job done. He was happy that Michael would be with his wife and family at last.

His phone rang again. It was Anders again. *Crap!* He rushed through his shower and hopped into the car. His stomach growled and made him wish he had stopped for a cup of coffee and a danish. Damn, it was going to be a long time until lunch.

The first thing Brett noticed was that the officer parking lot was overflowing. Where had all the cars come from? As Brett climbed the front steps of the building, he found Anders waiting for him.

"What were you doing? Watching cars pull into the lot?"

Anders nudged him in the shoulder. "Funny." He led Brett into an empty office and shut the door. Brett's smile faded. Something serious was going on.

"Chief Ellison and a few other officers were arrested last night by the FBI."

Brett studied Anders's face. Surely, the man was joking. "Seriously? What about Taylor?"

"Michael had it right. Ellison was into gambling. Taylor tipped off the FBI. Somehow he got immunity. Ellison got hooked up with the Eastern Europeans out of Chicago. They were forcing him to give them confidential data on our staff, and they were involved in money laundering."

"Shit! You mean Social Security numbers and names?"

Anders nodded. "And more."

"Damn it. I had to replace two credit cards this year due to fraudulent transactions. I bet it was all connected."

"I think you can count on it." Pacing the floor, Anders looked uneasy. "I need to tell you something else."

Brett braced himself. Now what?

"The mayor's office and commission met early this morning. They are naming me as interim chief effective immediately."

Brett clasped Anders's hand and shook it. "Man, that's great! Congratulations. They couldn't have picked a better person. I'm glad they didn't bring in some jackass from the outside."

Anders beamed, but Brett could tell that he was still apprehensive. "My wife is more excited than I am. She is glad that I'll be off the street. This has been a tough couple of months with you, O'Shea."

"I can't tell you how much I have appreciated your help and support with our case." Brett smiled broadly. "But I will never forget the look on your face when you saw Michael for the first time."

Anders's cell phone buzzed. He glanced at it quickly and pocketed it. "I've got to go. I'm being sworn in right away. I want to say something before I go. My first official act is to move you to the Detective Bureau, if you still want the job?"

"Hell yes I want the job." Overwhelmed, Brett grabbed the new chief and hugged him. Brett didn't know which of them had a bigger smile.

Anders paused at the doorway and turned toward Brett. "Oh, one more thing. Sergeant Taylor will be testifying against Ellison. Taylor will be reprimanded and probably demoted, but he'll be back."

"Too bad you can't just fire the asshole."

"One battle at a time, O'Shea." Anders's phone buzzed again. This time he didn't even look at his phone. With a sigh, he turned and left the room.

Brett stood, soaking in all that had just transpired in the past few minutes. He couldn't contain himself any longer.

"Urgh!" he roared. He pumped his fists in the air several times and bounced up and down. He felt like he had just won the best prize in the world.

When he felt in control of his emotions, he opened the door. A crowd of people stood outside of the room, staring back at him. In the center of the crowd were Lisa and his mother, as well as most of the detectives. His mom rushed to his side and gave his a tight hug.

"Mom, why are you here?"

"Detective Anders called me this morning. It was so nice of him to take the time to invite me down today for the party.

Brett pulled back with a frown. "Party?"

Lisa's eyes twinkled as she grabbed his arm. "Yes, Detective O'Shea. A party! The other detectives got together and ordered a cake for the celebration."

Brett looked at his friends and family. "You mean you all knew about this before I did?"

His mom smiled and patted his back. "Yes, we did. Now let's go check out your new office. I'm so proud of you."

After the party ended, Brett was given the official tour of the unit by Jake Foster. Brett had already met most of the other detectives, so introductions were brief.

"I suppose you heard that I'll be filling in for Anders until they can permanently replace him," Foster announced.

Brett cast a sideways glance at the detective. "No, I hadn't heard. Congratulations. I bet you're excited."

Jake shrugged. "I'm not sure how I feel. Being management means a lot more paperwork, but I like learning new things. You know, Anders was really impressed with you. He hasn't said much, but this last case you two worked must have been a bitch. He had more war wounds than I've ever seen."

Brett bit back a smile. "Yeah, it was a tough case. I'm glad it's over."

It was nearing the end of the shift. Many of the other detectives had already packed up for the day. Brett lingered in his new office. He even had two windows. He still couldn't believe that he was a detective. Not that he wanted to be exactly like his great-grandfather, Michael, but there were a few qualities that he would like to emulate.

Brett sat down, testing out his new chair. It was obvious that no one had used this office for years. A fine layer of dust covered the desk and phone. He picked up the phone to call Lisa.

She picked up on the first ring. "Hello."

"Hey. It's me."

"So this is your new work number? I'll add it to my phone."

Brett leaned back and put his feet up on the desk. "What time do you get off?"

"Anytime I want, Detective."

Brett could hear the laugher in her voice. "How about celebrating tonight. I'll stop and pick up something to grill."

"Great. See you in an hour."

Brett reflected on his life. He was surprisingly satisfied with how things had turned out. He and Lisa were great together. He wanted to continue to develop his relationship with her and see where it went. He had never thought about marriage before, but it wasn't something he was going to avoid. He had his dream job. He was going to concentrate on becoming a great detective. Maybe not as infamous as Mike, but just as good.

Tomorrow would be the first day in his new life. He was through with all the paranormal shit. With Michael and the demon gone, everything would be normal again. No hocus pocus was going to screw with his brain ever again.